PERVERTS IN PARADISE

"There were delights everywhere and
the land appeared as none other than
an image of earthly paradise."

Fr Manoel Calado do Salvador (1636)

"Where is Brazil?
What does this place matter
if every place
is somewhere to see and not to be?"

Carlos Drummond de Andrade (1977)

PERVERTS IN PARADISE

JOÃO S TREVISAN

Translated by
Martin Foreman

First published in April 1986 by GMP Publishers Ltd,
PO Box 247, London N15 6RW

British Library Cataloguing in Publication Data

Trevisan, João Silvério
Perverts in paradise.
1. Homosexuality – Brazil – History
2. Homosexuality – Brazil – Social aspects
I. Title II. Devassos no paraiso. *English*
306.7′66′0981 HQ76.3.B6

ISBN 0–907040–78–0

Cover art by Sue Dray
Photosetting by Wilmaset, Birkenhead
Printed and bound by The Guernsey Press Co. Ltd, CI.

Contents

Warning

In writing this book, the main object of my research has been the male homosexual experience. For a more specific approach to lesbianism, it would have been necessary to carry out equally specific research, starting from very different premises – eg. that it is a question not simply of a female version of homosexuality but of a very different experience of life. Obviously, it was my decision to make the male focus a priority; I also took into consideration that the material initially available was more relevant to men than to women. Nevertheless, wherever possible I have tried to make parallel references to lesbian love in Brazil.

Acknowledgements

To Antonio Cadengue, who helped by reading and discussing the chapters, researching and offering abundant material, making suggestions and assisting with the typing of the manuscript – but above all for believing in me and encouraging me with his unstinting friendship. To Gabriel Bechara for generosity in granting me precious research material. To Márcia Myriam Gomes for reading the text and for her constant affection. To Nestor Perlongher and Alcir Lenharo for reading and discussing the original text. To Claúdio José Trevisan for innumerable free books and firm affection. To Jomard Muniz de Britto, Mário Miranda (Maria Aparecida), Sérgio Domingues and Nívio Ramos Sales for their willingness to give information. To Allen Young, Conrado Silva, Carlos Eugênio Marcondes de Moura, Glauco Mattoso and Antonio Carlos Tosta for information and rare material. To Marcelo Dantas and Didi Chiarelli for transcribing tapes. To Sílvio Pinto for some of the typing. To Carlos Vezzá for trying to be my secretary. To David Fernbach for his British patience. And to innumerable others who have kindly helped me with small items of information or rare material but whose names I have forgotten to note down.

João Silvério Trevisan
São Paulo, Easter 1984

Introduction

"Brazil is not my country: it is my abyss
my poison
our cancer."

Jomard Muniz de Britto (1982)

Within the framework of this book, the reader will be confronted with the enigma of two identities: Brazilian and homosexual. If, for methodological reasons, we suppose that it is possible to speak about "identity", we then face two uncomfortable and, in this case, complementary questions. Is there something which can be called "the Brazilian character"? Is it appropriate to talk of a "homosexual identity"? Complex issues are involved in both cases, in their parallel implications as much as in their definition.

To Be or Not To Be Homosexual

Whether is is appropriate or worthwhile to define homosexuality and grant it a specific character and distinct nature is often discussed nowadays. This debate stems from the idea that we are not dealing with a condition (such as the female condition) or an innate form of existence. In the past homosexuality has been considered a *circumstance*, for throughout history – including the history of individual lives – sexual desire has been influenced by changing cultural trends rather than remaining a law of nature. This means that there are neither absolute sexual objects nor watertight divisions of desire. Desire fluctuates in a movement that is essentially volatile and beyond ideologies; indeed it is ideologies which seek to establish patterns and norms. In this sense "coming out", ie. the assertion of a gay identity, might end up by creating a new means of categorising desire, precisely by granting it a different nature and legitimacy and establishing new parameters of normality – exactly as the medico-psychiatric establishment does in its attempt to repress desires considered deviant. Thus defining someone as homosexual would serve the purposes of "normalisation" more than a real liberation of sexuality, and it would also encourage the politics of the ghetto, separatism and sexual racism in inverse discrimination. Such objections have become more forceful in certain sectors of the gay movement itself and produced intransigent opponents of a gay identification. In Brazil, as in other countries, many former activists have preferred to move more cautiously in accepting a definition of homosexual, whatever it may be. Their attitude has enriched a truly important debate, for it is the very right of homosexual people to direct their own lives, emotions and sexuality that is in question.

Yet if these objections to the "construction of a gay identity" are valid, it is also true that desire cannot be denied a name, and certainly not for mere reasons of methodology. From the simple fact that something resembling homosexual desire exists, it has to be referred to by some kind of designation. Otherwise we will merely return to the time of suffocating and hypocritical invisibility which only reinforced the mechanisms of repression. Besides, it seems significant that – at least in Brazil – this anti-identity attitude started to develop when the gay movement began to attract the wrath of the Establishment. Moreover, the discussion has slipped into linguistic niceties which verge on the ridiculous when taken from the lecture-halls of the universities which created them and introduced into daily life. An example is the proposal to substitute "I am homosexual" (*sou homossexual*) with a reticent "I am at this moment homosexual" (*estou homossexual*). It should be added that this intellectualised (and not wholly contemptible) position indirectly conforms to macho gay fashion, whereby (basically male) homosexuals seek now more than ever to live within the social norms and, in an alarming cult of misogyny, steer aggressively clear of contact with effeminate stereotypes. Despite this effort by gay men not to be filed under the category of *bicha* or "queer", the media have definitely discovered homosexuals. A conscious return to the closet, therefore, will not save queers from ideological manipulation.

Although forced by the objectives of this book to refer to the gay identity, I am aware that I am skating on thin ice. However, it seems to me absurd to abolish this reference to identity simply because reflection has not yet resolved the terms of the problem. For practical reasons, therefore, "homosexual desire" here refers to a very wide range of expressions of love between members of the same sex, even when these expressions do not come under the narrow definition of "homosexual" as created by medico-scientific debate and used by the media at this moment in history. Thus, for example, the word "homosexual" can only be applied very inadequately to the expressions of affection and to the sexual relations between men that occur in various tribes indigenous to Brazil. Here customs are dictated by motives quite alien to the Western urban culture which coined the definition of homosexual and compartmentalised sex. Thus, because there do not seem to be alternatives in the current stage of discussion, I consciously run the risk of being imprecise. When confronted by this same dilemma, Michel Foucault commented, "What is important is *not to be* homosexual but rather to *furiously seek to be* gay" (my emphasis). "To ask ourselves about our relationship to homosexuality is above all to desire a world where these relationships are possible, more than simply to desire a sexual relationship with someone of the same sex."[1] Foucault refers to a state of coming-to-be and being-in-change which seems to me very interesting precisely because it does not claim that homosexuality is a condition in the sanctuary of normality, nor does it refrain from fomenting the nuances of desire which can continue changing indefinitely within the space of a labyrinthine definition. Meanwhile, I remember once in Aracaju (north-eastern Brazil) hearing an interesting and very astute term used by the locals to refer to a gay man: "doubtful". Gay men are exactly that: doubtful – the ones who cause doubt. In other words, they are those who confirm uncertainty, who open a space for difference and who constitute a symbol of contradiction confronting the bounds of normality.

It is in the context of this coming-to-be homosexual that I would like to penetrate, so to speak, Brazil.

To Be or Not To Be Brazilian

"It is not rare for the sociologist who wants to understand Brazil to have to become a poet," said Roger Bastide, a French anthropologist. Why? Because he "no longer knows which conceptual system to use. None of the ideas which he learned in Europe or North America are valid here. The old is mixed in with the new. Historical eras are entangled with one another. Terms such as 'social class' or 'historical dialectic' do not have the same meaning, do not refer to the same concrete realities. It would be necessary (...) to discover concepts that were to a certain extent liquid, (...) that were modelled on a living reality in perpetual transformation."[2] The same bewilderment when one is confronted by Brazil returns when the question is asked: what does it mean to be Brazilian?

To start with, the question of a Brazilian identity or national character runs up against the undisguisable nationalistic impulse which inspires it. This merits at least a word of caution. In Brazil there is currently a serious re-evaluation of nationalism as a disease endemic to Latin America and probably to Third World countries in general. The basic criticism is that such nationalism results in an arbitrary conceptualisation which eliminates individuals, classes, ethnic groups and their differences in order to unite them in an abstract and monolithic representation called "the people". This is particularly noticeable and paradoxical in the case of Brazil. How can we speak of a national identity in dealing with a country which, compared to the Eurocentric world, has existed for less than 500 years and which only came to life as an autonomous political entity little more than 150 years ago?

Over the last four centuries the Atlantic side of South America has continually spread, politically speaking, to create vast frontiers. Within these arbitrary demarcations exists a people for whom Portuguese has by chance become the mother-tongue (or, maybe, stepmother-tongue). Lost inside enormous distances, this people lives in search of itself, for it does not exist as such. The concept of nationhood has been conscientiously worked on since the formal declaration of Brazilian independence in 1822. The intention has been to create the idea of a fatherland that would function as the most important of the socially undefined and diverse groups which live within the remote Brazilian frontiers and thereby encourage the dominant groups to take advantage of the recently claimed nationality. Afterwards the concept of nationhood oscillated at the whim of the British, interested in Brazil's consumer potential. Later it was the turn of the United States, which, in order to control the southern part of the continent, came to see Brazil as a kind of underdeveloped alter ego. Bombarded by influences and interests of every kind, this country called Brazil owes its fragility less to the fact that it is a patchwork quilt than because it tries to forge a hazardous identity.

I remember an experimental Brazilian film by Julio Bressane, which magnificently explains the perplexity of this "homo brasiliensis". In an interview, the principal character (an archeologist ironically called Brasil) says, "I was, am and will be the *caraíba*" – "stranger" in Tupi, an indigenous language. The archeologist goes to a desert island in search of ancient inscriptions to be deciphered; once there he comes across earthenware snakes, toads and lizards and a straw jaguar all in the middle of the real jungle. Foreign to itself, Brazil's identity has come from imitating others. Its national character has arisen as a parody of foreign reality.

To study Brazil is to plunge into an enigma of superlatives. It has the largest virgin forest in the world, the Amazon. Its problems, however, are almost insuperable, as it has the highest foreign debt on the globe. From the point of view of territory, Brazil is the fifth largest nation in the world, with 8,511,000 square kilometres – a little under the United States. In other words it is an area 35 times larger than Great Britain and 15 times the size of France. To give a clearer idea of this enormity, the state of Amazonas alone is six times larger than Britain and is almost all virgin forest. São Paulo, the country's most industrialised and most populous state, alone covers an area similar to that of Britain. 120 million people, the sixth largest population on earth, live in the immense territory of Brazil, which is almost half the land mass of South America. São Paulo, capital of the state of the same name, is the sixth largest city on the planet.

Meanwhile Brazilian superlatives also occur from the point of view of deprivation. According to INAN, the National Institute of Food and Nutrition, the country has about 21 million people in a permanent state of hunger and malnutrition, a factor responsible for 40% of infant mortality, which is in the order of 80.3 deaths per thousand births and reaches 130 deaths in the north-east. Nutritional levels for the majority of the population are continuing to fall. As for income, in 1981 67.3% of the country's wage-earners were paid no more than three times the legal minimum wage and received 31.4% of the national income, while the top 5.7% were paid ten or more times the legal minimum and received 29.2% of the national income.

Meanwhile, almost indifferent to this picture of degradation, the goverment has already brought the country into the nuclear age with an ambitious and megalomaniac project to construct various nuclear power stations. The first of these is ready to enter service and generate electricity for which, the technocrats admit, there is no demand, since Brazil already has electricity in excess. Furthermore, this first power station (Angra 1) has been built between Rio de Janeiro and São Paulo, the country's two largest cities – which suggests the particularly frightening idea of a nuclear accident and the absolute impossibility of evacuating the two metropolises in time.

Considered by the Portuguese as a temporary transit-point, Brazil became a nation – a colossal and contradictory nation – almost by historical accident. Contradictions and misunderstandings have characterised it since its chance discovery in 1500 and its disorganised colonisation from that moment on. For a start, it is known that the Portuguese sailors anchored there in the belief that they were near India, whose spices interested them much more than vague unknown lands. And when the clerk of the fleet, Pero Vaz de Caminha, informed the King of Portugal that they had discovered a place "where everything that is planted grows", he did not realise that behind these fertile coastal lands lay one of the most arid regions in the world. These, due to the monoculture of sugar, would become the most underdeveloped region in the whole western hemisphere, almost rivalling the tragedy of starvation which took place in Biafra. And, with all this still taking place in 1983, floods, probably provoked by disturbing the ecosystem, covered the extremely fertile states in the south of the country and caused inestimable damage.

It was purely by chance that Brazil came to speak Portuguese – not Spanish, as many people think. And to give another example of how chance has affected Brazilian history, our independence was proclaimed by the heir to the Portuguese throne who, angry with his father, tore the ribbons of Portugal's colours from his clothes and cried "Independence or Death!" Scholarly works do not, of course, mention that a good part of his ill humour was due to the diarrhea he was suffering from, and which had forced him to stop repeatedly on his journey from Rio de Janeiro to São Paulo. Moreover, Brazilian independence owed much to the British navy which offered the new country its fleet (not for nothing, of course), thus helping it to free itself from Portuguese imperialism. The British, horrified by the barbarous custom of bringing slaves from Africa (a trade it had earlier encouraged), would even enter Brazilian waters in pursuit of slave ships. The Brazilians, who had already sent all their gold to British coffers through Portugal, were now encouraged to free their slaves – because the expanding British economy needed to increase exports and therefore needed citizens who were free enough to buy its products.

Another fatality of this history of surprises were the snakes which, contrary to what the European imagination frequently supposes, no longer live in the streets of Brazilian towns as they did perhaps a century ago. Today, thanks to the rapid process of industrialisation and the consequent devastation of the environment, the remaining snakes have taken refuge in the limited forestry reserves which have often been reduced to barely 10% of the various Brazilian states. The Amazon forest itself is in a phase of accelerated "colonisation", with the federal government handing its territory over to multinational mining companies and making sporadic threats to pull down its trees and sell the wood on the international market to pay the country's enormous foreign debt. This factor can also be seen in the fact that, contrary to the trend before 1970, 67% of the population are currently concentrated in urban areas and this number is growing, as a result of the agrarian policy of the large ranches whose priority is once again to export their products.

Brazil illustrates perfectly the saying: "Do as I say, not as I do." For example, the friendliness of Brazilians is often talked about. The assertion is made even more insistently when one learns it is intended to mask the many popular rebellions which have spattered the country's history with blood. It also covers the no less violent assaults by Brazil on its neighbours' territories, some of which, with or without the aid of diplomacy, were very successful. Baron Rio Branco, who established the agile style of Itamaraty (the Ministry of Foreign Affairs), is also well known; biographers said of him that "frontier disputes were his favourite pastime". Thus the state of Acre was taken from Bolivia with the later promise of compensation by a Bolivian railway which Brazil never constructed. There was the famous War of the Triple Alliance against Paraguay in 1865, through which Brazil "received" 60,000 square kilometres of land from the defeated country as spoils of war. Still in the nineteenth century, there were occasional assaults on the territories of Venezuela, Peru and Argentina. Today the Brazilian frontier has informally advanced about one hundred kilometres into Paraguay in the region of Alto Parana; the same is occuring in Uruguay, whose borderlands – very cheap thanks to exchange rates – are being acquired in large numbers by Brazilian farmers. To cast more doubt on the myth of Brazilian cordiality, it is important to remember that in 1983 Brazil became the world's sixth largest exporter of arms – manufactured to earn foreign exchange in trade with Arab countries and the Third World in general as much as to defend national security. Moreover, in the framework of national production the Brazilian war industry is even more important: at present arms are the country's third largest export, being surpassed only by coffee and soya.

Even the Brazilian flag illustrates the idea of compensating for something lacking by displaying it. In the centre of the flag there is a band on which can be read the resounding phrase "Order and Progess" (*Ordem e Progresso*). General de Gaulle showed his disbelief on a visit to Brazil in the 1960s when he said, "This is not a serious country." Indeed can a country be serious when it uses the concepts of *racial democracy* and *coloured nation* as instruments of official racism? In this "racial paradise", blacks see themselves relegated to the status of an inferior caste and rarely break out of the economic limits of the shanty-towns – all under the protection of a supposedly liberal Constitution. On the other hand the samba (Afro-Brazilian music) and Carnival (permanently bound to the ancient negro drums) have been made official and claimed as typically "ours". Also of African origin are *feijoada* (a Brazilian dish par excellence) and *candomblé* (the blacks' religion, now an obligatory tourist item). To prove the lack of racism the last census intended simply to omit the category "colour" – because, after all, the Constitution states that all Brazilians are free whatever their colour. This proved impossible for reasons which included protests from militant black groups. The results, however, revealed some facts which racial democracy does not explain: in 1940 there were six times as many whites as blacks while in the 1980 census there were nine times as many. The number of coloureds obviously grew, giving the impression that interbreeding had improved. Yet the percentage of whites also continued to grow, which suggests that the process is more a whitening of blacks than a darkening of whites. In a country which was predominantly black during the period of Portuguese colonisation, whites now compose 55% of the population. The number of mulattos has grown (38%), but this does not sufficiently explain why only 6% of the country is now black.

The same must be said of the Indians – Brazil's first inhabitants and its most legitimate heirs. It is reckoned that at the time of the Discovery there were between 2 and 5 million natives living in Brazil. Today the number of Indians is between 120,000 and 220,000 in the whole country. Of the 230 tribes supposedly in existence in 1900 only 140 remained in the 1950s. Throughout the centuries the indigenous peoples have been decimated by diseases brought by the whites – smallpox, influenza, tuberculosis, venereal disease. They are often slaughtered as their territories are systematically invaded by ambitious whites, when not appropriated by the federal government itself – which has a specific body to control Indians (FUNAI, the National Indian Foundation). With the native reservations not always demarcated or respected, their hunting grounds have diminished and their arable lands have been depleted, when not absorbed by large ranches; starvation has arrived. For these reasons it is not uncommon to see Indians in the interior of the country begging far from their lands. Often forced by necessity to migrate to the cities, they lose the last traces of their culture and survive undernourished, usually condemned to be the last members of tribes in extinction.

Yet we have an Indian chief in Congress: Deputy Mário Juruna, a Chavante.

The State of Coming-To-Be

Brazil is known as a place "where you can get anything done", something obviously reflected in local gay life. So, for example, there are no anti-homosexual laws either in the Constitution or the Penal Code (see Chapter Three). The police, however, carry out periodic raids and constantly humiliate homosexuals in public places. Indirect reasons are thought up ("indecent assault" or "loitering") to set off a repression which stems from the basic authoritarianism of the Brazilian social structure and one of its truest reflections: machismo. Nonetheless not even these truculent national chauvinists who prop up the family and propriety can be taken seriously. They frequently persecute in openly gay men the spectre of the very desire which torments them. I have learnt from different sources that a police commissioner noted for recent violent attacks on the gay ghetto in São Paulo would, on the pretext of arresting vagabonds, seize boys loitering in the streets and take them to his office with intentions that were hardly connected with the fulfilling of the law. In addition, during the police persecution which almost closed the gay paper *Lampião* in 1979, it was learnt that the federal agent responsible for the repression had a less than admirable past – he probably feared that the "gay press" would reveal it in a gossip column. I also remember the case of a gay friend who was inexplicably attacked, beaten up and whose life was threatened one day in the street by a plain-clothes policeman whom he did not know and had hardly looked at. This friend told me that the policeman's attitude reminded him more than anything else of someone who was assaulting him sexually. In north-eastern Brazil, where machismo is often the cause of tragedy, there are many ultra-masculine homosexuals (closeted, of course) among the police; the number of married men there with a double sex life is also surprising. I met a young man in Bahia who had a macho lover. Their meetings always followed the same pattern; they drank beer in a bar, spat to one side in a manly fashion and talked about their latest female conquests – while groping each other under the table. They always ended up in bed together in the nearest hotel.

I suspect that Brazilian machismo is, to a certain extent, an effusive form of seeking out homosexuality rather than a means of rejecting it or simply warding off queers. The macho dons this armour to defend himself from something which fascinates him. This is more or less the same way the refrain "Order and Progress" is blazoned across the Brazilian flag, to conceal the country's inner leanings towards chaos and disorder. Exactly as in the paradoxical case of the national macho, the Brazilian longing for both order and chaos can be said to be an almost inseparable mixture. It inclines towards the dark with the same longing with which it inclines towards the light. The *New York Times* once said of Brazilians that for them "no belief is so rigid that it cannot be bent and no enemy so hated that he cannot be embraced". On the other hand, certain analysts of the "Brazilian character" claim that its tendency to mix opposites is really the result of its basic trait, ie. the tendency to conciliate, which gives the appearance of good judgment, if not of cordiality. They are also referring, however, to another tendency which, as the result of disputed historical events, is said to have become endemic among Brazilians: indolence, which has, it is said, led fatally to lechery. These authors like to quote the testimony of foreign travellers who have visited Brazil at different times. This is, furthermore, in itself another of our tendencies – to call on the evidence of Brazilianists. I think there is a plausible explanation for this; if it is pointless to define the terms of "Brazilianness", it is also true that we Brazilians are only sure of what we are when face-to-face with foreigners.

Meanwhile, how can we understand the exuberant explosion of eroticism in the midst of extreme poverty? It stems indisputably from the same oscillation between light and dark, life and death, love and hate, which, despite being opposites are as close to each other as the two ends of a horseshoe. There are plenty of examples of this in Latin America. I once met a Spanish missionary who confessed he was scandalised to discover that the Indians in Colombia liked to spend part of their meagre income on fireworks which they happily set off on religious holidays. The priest said that it was years before he could understand something foreign to contemporary European culture; in Latin America emotions are expressed in the language of passion and lust for a life which is lived regardless of risk – perhaps because of the daily and palpable proximity of death. Being superfluous, passion signifies "in this historical era, a momentaneous attempt to overcome the utilitarianism of the culture and, thereby, the quantitative and instrumental character of cultural organisation". Just as public orgies took place during the medieval plagues of Europe, so the Brazilian Carnival – with its explosions of the sexual instinct – might also constitute "a habitual response to collective catastrophes and social threats".[3] In these three days of sensual excitation and collective delirium the pleasure principle emerges supreme and rules – or the restraints offered by reason lose their meaning; at that point everything can and does happen. This break from common sense is so great that even the police, who are usually very violent, act with caution, in fear of those seeking revenge or of outbursts in jail. In Carnival instinct does not excuse itself; people dance, sing, have sex, fight, steal and kill each other in a unique whirlpool movement that might have given Freud precious data for his unfinished "metapsychology". Continuing along the same lines of the relationship between squalor and sensuality, I should recall the flourishing culture of the north-east, one of the most exuberant and original in the country, with its popular dances, singers and improvisers,* its rich dialect, artisanship, sense of humour and literature, all born in one of the poorest, driest and longest-suffering regions of the planet.

This indisputable taste for lechery, richly present in Brazilian life and history, can thus be seen at the heart of the squalor. The *bunda*, for example, the backside, this exuberant part of the human body, enjoys an almost privileged place in the context of local eroticism, impressing even those who are accustomed to the country's mores – and that on the streets as much in bed. The presence (discomforting to many historians) of homosexual practices in their most perverse and uncontrolled forms in this world of play has scandalised foreign travellers, as well as very often fascinating and seducing them to the extent of fomenting inner disorder.

If, as Michel Foucault would have it, to practise homosexuality is to be in a state of becoming, then the homosexual experience does not seem incompatible with the characteristic coming-to-be of a nation as enigmatic and incomplete as Brazil. For the same reason it would be imprudent to make definite claims about this experience. Any attempt at the historical systemisation of homosexuality as experienced by Brazilians will be less the history of permissiveness arising from the mechanisms of social control (from the Inquisition and police censorship to psychiatry and academic science) and more the insurrection of vestiges of an uncontrolled desire which flourishes underground, in the backyards of the provinces and the public conveniences of large cities. What is written here, therefore, claims to be neither a scientific nor complete work but an impressionistic (and sometimes sentimental) journey through the homoerotic intestines of Brazil.

*The *repentista* or "improviser" is a traditional figure in north-east Brazil. A *repentista* is someone who comments on events in song and on guitar, generally in a kind of singing duel/argument with another *repentista*. The winner is the one who can improvise most and best [Trans. note].

CHAPTER ONE

Brazil Seen From the Moon

"South of the Equator no sin can there be:
let's launch a new sin, full steam, sweaty and free."

from a song by Chico Buarque and Rui Guerra

"I seem to be in Sodom, or even worse..."

When Brazil was discovered in the sixteenth century, Europeans considered the Indians they found there either the purest of angels (nurturing the Renaissance myth of the "noble savage") and/or beings "worse than beasts of the jungle". ("Animals with a human face" were Villegagnon's words in a letter to Calvin.) For the Renaissance freethinkers the Indians were human beings and should be respected as such; for the slave-traffickers or fanatical missionaries they were no more than wild animals. According to von Martius, a German naturalist who travelled to Brazil at the beginning of the 19th century, the Indians were physically and morally decadent and at the end of their civilisation. As biological evidence for this, he pointed out that although the native men were tall and muscular, their penises were generally small and only became erect with difficulty. Furthermore, he considered them to be sexually cold, in contrast with their women who, according to the scandalised report of Gabriel Soares de Souza, a sixteenth-century Portuguese, were demanding, passionate and sexually active from the age of twelve to seventy. Some naturalists saw in this difference between male and female the reason why Indian women preferred the white colonisers. Gabriel Soares noted that to increase the size of their modest male parts, the forest-dwellers covered the penis with the poisonous hair of an animal which made it swell and lengthen to such a point that not even the Indian women could tolerate its penetration. This traveller, who wrote a treatise on life in Brazil and its landscape, also suggested that another indigenous custom, that of wrapping up the penis, was less for protection than display, an observation corroborated by Margraf, a Dutchman, in 1648. The latter states that in taking over Guanabara Bay in 1555, Villegagnon, the French commandant, barracked his soldiers on an island to keep them away from the Indian women, whom he called "wild bitches" because of their sexual appetite. Soldiers who disobeyed the order could be whipped and even executed.

The fact is that sexual codes among the natives had nothing in common with the Western puritanism of that period. Virginity, for example, was ascribed little importance and the celibate was even censured. In 1556 André Thevet, a Frenchman, noted that Indian men offered their daughters to strangers in exchange for any trifle. A year later, Hans Staden, a German traveller, wrote that a defeated enemy had the right to sleep with his captor's wife and daughter before being put to death. José de Anchieta, a Portuguese Jesuit who came to Brazil to convert the Indians and to found new cities, admitted that he had never heard of any woman being killed by her husband because of adultery or jealousy. In 1587 Gabriel Soares wrote that Indian women even arranged lovers for their own husbands. Moreover, polyandry was as frequently observed as polygamy among the aboriginals. Joan Neuhof, a traveller who visited Brazil in the eighteenth century, claimed to have known a chief called Janduí who was 120 years old and had fifty wives. Various foreign chroniclers also refer to the fact that the Indians liked to relate their sexual exploits in public, with no shame and probably a good deal of fantasy. All this appeared very astonishing to the Christians, who from the very beginning had been deeply shocked (or amazed) by the forest-dwellers' tranquil nudity.

But none of the licentiousness of the inhabitants of this tropical paradise shocked the moralists of the time more than the "abominable sin", "sodomy" or "defilement" – names given to the homosexual act which, according to Abelardo Romeiro, a prudish historian, "has been spreading among the people of Brazil for centuries like a contagious disease." Such horror was understandable; for Europeans – Catholic and

Protestant alike – sodomy was one of the four *clamantia peccata* ("sins which cry out to the skies") of medieval theology. In 1587 Gabriel Soares de Souza stated that "the savages (...) are devoted to the abominable sin, which they do not revile. He who serves as the man is considered valiant and they speak of this exploit as if it were a feat of valour. In their villages in the interior there are some who have public tents for as many as wish them as public women." In other words, there was even something resembling our prostitution. In 1576 another Portuguese – Pero de Magalhães de Gândavo – also observed that the Indians "surrender themselves to the vice of sodomy as if they did not have the reason of men". In 1578 Jean de Léry, a Frenchman, wrote that, when arguing amongst themselves, Brazilian Indians insulted each other with the word *tivira* – the synonym of "queer" in Tupi, its literal meaning being "man with broken behind".

Centuries later, in 1859, Avé-Lallement, a German researcher travelling through north-eastern Brazil, noted that there were no true men or women among the Botocudos but rather men-women and women-men, for their physical constitution did not differ much from one sex to the other (unlike the occidental-patriarchal system, which is responsible for the models of strength in men and frailty in women). Travelling through central Brazil in 1894, Karl von den Steinem, another German, wrote that in the *baito* (men's house: only men were permitted to enter, after several initiation tests), it was quite natural for youths of the Bororo tribe to have sexual relations among themselves, as well as being devoted to some extremely delicate tasks. According to Steinem:

> How elegantly and with what detail the men worked could be seen principally in the making of arrows. There were many small skills in that activity which might have been more naturally entrusted to a woman's delicate hands. The decoration, for example, was made of minute and multicoloured feathers, which were placed on the floor one by one and meticulously arranged. And there could not be so much gossip and laughter at a spinning-wheel as there was in the *baito*! Certainly there would be little femininity when, for some variety, two of the workers suddenly stood up to offer the spectacle of a wrestling-match, which was followed with the greatest interest by the others. They would rise, fight, knock each

> other down and then continue their work or lie down to rest. Very often couples in love could be seen amusing themselves under a communal red blanket.[1]

The amazement of the Christians can be imagined when they discovered that the natives' medicine was frequently administered by sexual intercourse between the witch-doctor (*pajé*) and his patient, anal intercourse included. It was also common for the *pajé* to transmit his knowledge of medicine to his disciples through the sexual act.

Confronted by what Europeans considered this "moral weakness", which they clearly attributed to paganism, it is not surprising that the Portuguese of the time identified the natives with the practice of homosexuality.[2] The conquerors called the Indians "buggers" or "heathens". The first term (from the Middle Ages) and the second (from the Bible) were applied indifferently to the heretic and to the practitioner of sodomy – for the "abominable sin" was almost always associated with the greater sin of disbelief or heresy. But if the Europeans professed horror at pagan debauchery, they also became fascinated by it in that it symbolised liberation from their guilt. For the colonists, who came from a Europe being decimated by rival doctrines and under the strict watch of the Inquisition, "the passionate temperaments, the immoral customs and all the unremitting growth of virgin nature were an invitation to a dissolute and unrestrained life in which everything was permitted" – in the words of the historian Paulo Prado.[3] For Simão de Vasconcelos, a Portuguese chronicler, the seventeenth-century colonists were in no way different from the Indians, "because although they are Christian, they live as the heathens do". Pierre Moreau, a French traveller in Brazil in the same century, stated that during the short period of Dutch colonisation of Pernambuco, "everyone led a scandalous life: Jews, Christians, Portuguese, Dutch, English, French, Germans, blacks, Brazilians, mestizos, mulattos, mamelukes and creoles".

The truth is that among foreigners who came to Brazil there was a – perhaps silent – consensus which transcended nationality and doctrine: it was that of *infra equinoxialem nihil peccari* – "there is no sin below the equator". It seemed that the tropics placed Christian moral duties in parentheses. Thus in the seventeenth century the city of Recife (capital of Pernambuco) was considered the largest centre of prostitution in the

Americas; its brothels were frequented by sailors and soldiers, but also by local dignitaries, councillors and members of the colonial administration. Many of the prostitutes of the time were famous: Sara Hendricx from Holland, for example, who is said to have arrived by ship dressed as a man to escape the vigilance of Calvinist preachers. Pierrre Moreau wrote that the incidence of incest and unnatural sin, "for which many Portuguese were condemned to death", was high there. The same author refers to the case of a Dutch captain who, convicted of practising sodomy, was first exiled to the island of Fernando de Noronha (off the Brazilian coast), then sent to prison in Amsterdam. Such facts were, moreover, confirmed by Vincent Soler, a Calvinist preacher who lived in Recife in the same period and who claimed in a letter: "I seem to be in Sodom, or even worse." Herman Wätjen, in the seventeenth century, also refers to the many cases of sodomy in Pernambuco. Manuel de Nóbrega, however, a Portuguese Jesuit, seems to have been the first to note the wide and indiscriminate diffusion of homosexual practices in Brazil. In the mid-sixteenth century he wrote that many colonists took Indian men as wives "according to the custom of the land".

The practice of prostitution, considered uncontrollable, could also be the measure of permissiveness in colonial Bahia and Rio de Janeiro. Foreign travellers wrote that Portuguese ladies in both cities dressed up their slaves to prostitute them in the streets as another form of income. After spending three weeks in Rio in 1828, Victor Jacquemont said that he had never had the displeasure of seeing people as indecent as the Brazilians. In Rio de Janeiro as in Recife it was common to find prostitutes installed in the same buildings as respectable families. Yet it was not only in the large towns that the well-behaved European travellers were scandalised. Saint-Hilaire, who visited Brazil in the first decades of the nineteenth century, said that he came across prostitutes even in the small towns of the interior. And in the middle of the nineteenth century Edward Wilberforce, an Englishman, wrote that in Guarapari (in the hinterland of the state of Espírito Santo) he surprised a couple in the middle of intercourse in daylight, on a hammock on the veranda of their house; a child was playing underneath. For him this was perhaps at least evidence of bad taste.

The debauchery among the clergy and in convents (see Chapter Two) also became well-known from the scandalised reports of foreign travellers. In 1845 Count de Suzannet declared that "there is nothing more despicable than a Brazilian priest". Not even the austere Calvinist preachers appear to have escaped this kind of amnesty from sin once they had stepped onto Brazilian soil. It is said that in Recife, during the Dutch period, many Protestant pastors were drunkards and lived in concubinage, sometimes with more than one woman. Wätjen refers to one of them in particular: Daniel Schagen, who was suspended from evangelical office for consorting and living with prostitutes. All this caused Father Antônio de Jaboatão, an eighteenth-century missionary, to admit that in Brazil "the devil has already cast his anchor and it is stuck fast in men's hearts".

The situation does not appear to have changed much with the flight of the King of Portugal, João VI, to Brazil in 1808, nor after independence in 1822, with the establishment of an Empire in Brazil. It is said that Emperor Pedro I (Dom João's son) had various mistresses even after marrying the daughter of Francis I of Austria, Archduchess Dona Maria Leopoldin. One of these lovers is believed to have been the wife of the Portuguese commandant of the garrison in Rio de Janeiro at the time. Furthermore, shortly after proclaiming independence, the then Prince Pedro is said to have spent a night in a brothel on a journey to São Paulo. On visiting Bahia as Emperor he took a retinue of 233 people, including his wife and official mistress, who was later to be made a marchioness. As for his son and successor, Pedro II, who was considered shy and chaste, the Austrian diplomatic representative to Brazil, Baron Daiser, said in 1840: "I believe that the young Emperor's morality is still intact. But immorality of every kind is so widespread in this country and the vices – hardly acknowledged as such – are so diverse and so many that I fear for the immediate future."

Does Baron Daiser's fear make sense? It would be best to consult those foreigners who still come to Brazil today – "a republic full of people saying goodbye", according to the poet Oswalde de Andrade.

Venus Reclining, Uranus at Street Corners

In the middle of the Brazilian political upheaval of 1961-62, a gigantic Argentinian gentleman, almost 2 metres tall and with childlike eyes, arrived in the city of Recife to take up his post as teacher of Stage Direction and Design at the theatre school of the local University. His name was Tulio Carella, a teetotaller of about forty who had left his wife in Buenos Aires to plunge, as he put it, "into the land of burning coal" – recollecting that the name *Brasil* comes from brazil-wood, a native wood so called because it produces a resin as red as coal.* The facts and impressions of his journey were scrupulously noted down in his diary (later published), which constitutes one of the most disturbing accounts of the sudden transformation (or madness) of a stranger in the tropics. Carella, a Catholic and a profound believer in mysticism, thought that the Powers of Fire, with their dual aspect of destruction and purification, simultaneously producing light and darkness, were in a process of development in Brazil. Poetically, he proposed that the name of the country be the United States of Fire. Such reflections seem truly prophetic when his diary is read, as the following facts show.

Carella had already been seduced on Brazilian territory, by a woman who burst into his hotel room on one of the stop-overs of his flight. In Recife he dived into a reality where poverty, luxury and revolution were inextricably bound together – in the country's poorest and most explosive region. In his diary he wrote: "What is noticeable in this town is the mixture of the metropolitan and the wild, the progressive and the archaic." His elegant bearing, foreign clothes and unusual height, together with the different language he spoke – Spanish – made Carella an object of curiosity in the streets. Men, especially blacks and mulattos, greedily pursued and tried to touch him. At first he was afraid. He saw eyes undressing him. He felt the urgent shock of the stranger in Sodom solicited by its inhabitants. However, he did not exactly consider himself the Messenger Angel in the Biblical story of Lot. On the contrary, he was a stranger who wanted to break out of his shell and surrender to this tropical Sodom's enchantments. He believed that there, "as among the birds, the male is the more attractive". Above all, he was fascinated by the black men. They "have shining skulls, the colour of polished steel; they are lascivious and cruel. The sea's aphrodisiac air makes them gentle and bloodthirsty. (...) For me they are an inexhaustible source of wonder. To have one near me produces a kind of happiness and at that moment I want nothing else. (...) This is Africa in America."

**Brasa* (Span. & Port.) means both "burning coal" and "ardour" [Trans. note].

The city's sensual heat seemed to dilute his blood; the air had the scent of honey and was "splendid for the sex glands". The university professor with pretensions to philosophy noted that merely to think of bodily functions made him aware of needs that had previously been forbidden. He went for a walk along the quays in the port. The youths of every skin colour walked by, fingering their sexes or displaying their backsides under their tight trousers. They argued over him among themselves. While he was watching a religious procession in the street, men groped and pinched him. A black gently took his hand and whispered flirtations in his ear. Carella became alarmed; he was discovering that these pursuits pleased him. He fled into a bar. Harassed, he went into the toilet, and found several men displaying their erections. He fled again, although even more fascinated, and entered the toilet of another bar. There a blond youth sucked his cock. That produced in Carella a change that was both physical and mental; he felt lighter and happier. "My existence has been lost or changed. I seem to be someone else. I begin to feel myself a prisoner of a series of attractions that I have never imagined before." He remembered an inscription he had seen in the ruins of the whorehouse in Pompei: "Here happiness reigns." And he associated it with Recife, where "everything is erotic energy, bodily contact, Venus reclining and Uranus at street corners".

Carella was fascinated by the presence of blacks more than anything else. They "walk as if dancing". The very word *negro* acquired an erotic connotation: "If I repeat it constantly it is because I hear it like a musical note, a lulling sound, an embrace. (...) I think that not blood but sunlight, the vital substance of the tropics, runs in the veins of blacks. (...) Here they resemble swans and wear their rags with an indescribable majesty." He was also fascinated by the blond negros typical of north-eastern Brazil and known locally as *sararás* – they have the characteristic physiognomy and woolly hair of blacks, but due to a congenital abnormality characterised by the absence of pigmentation, their skin is light and their hair blond.

Carella learnt that there were boarding-houses "only for men" in the city and he was persistently invited to them. He was, however, afraid. He tried to find his earlier peace of mind, which had been shattered by the insolence of those men. He went into a church where three masses were being celebrated at the same time. He only found a temporary peace. Trying to pray, he found he could not: the negros stuck in his mind. He went to a post office, sat in a bar, entered a shop; in each of these places men importuned him. Watching a television in a shop window, a group of men positioned themselves strategically; Carella followed the manoeuvre of a handsome negro fondling the buttocks of a youth apparently absorbed by the screen. Returning to his room, Carella rediscovered a pleasure from infancy – he stripped completely. "To be nude is one of the ways to regain Paradise."

So the streets of Sodom became the paths of Paradise. Carella began to surrender to the men's opportuning, already feeling part of it all. From the notes in his diary it seems that his erotic interest became more important than anything else he had come to do in the city.

> I walk to the Santa Rita quay. I sit on the railing. It's late. It's not long before a negro appears, looks at me and begins to urinate, pretending to turn away. When he finishes, he sits down near me. He is burly, strong and, in the half-light, only his teeth can be seen clearly. (...) He takes my hand and caresses it, admiring its light colour. Then, gently, he raises my hand to his thigh, to his already hard prick. His laugh is fascinating and he tells me we are brothers. If I want, we will meet tomorrow. I want to. (...) It's ridiculous, but I feel as if I were twelve years old.
>
> Sudden and violent rain; I take shelter in the door of a shirt shop; a mulatto with green eyes gets hard simply seeing me, but because he is with two companions he limits himself to making his erection more comfortable.
>
> A negro was aroused when I looked at him and did not try to hide his swelling prick; on the contrary, pretending to joke, he rubbed against one of his companions, but without taking his eyes off me. In the pissoir at the Market an old man with a beard smokes a pipe and shakes a great rod as if he wanted to excite a casual spectator.
>
> A television shop window. A young lad leaves an old man and stands next to me while a delicious little negro sighs and pants on the other's side. A third watches me, signing with his arm that I should follow him. As I don't obey, he returns and insists. His features are perfect. In the dark street he pretends to urinate and shows me his penis,

> which is very big. (...) We enter a boarding-house, where there are no free rooms. Going down the stairs he embraces me, kisses me, rubs against me, pulls out his dick, which he puts into my hand, and ejaculates. He admits that it is the second time he has come. The first time was when he showed me his penis in the dark street.

When he had an attack of diarrhea, Tulio Carella considered it God's punishment. As soon as he was cured, however, he could not resist returning to the streets, the quaysides, the toilets in bars, in order to hear whispered declarations of love and experience the delicious sensation of being the object of desire of so many men. It was then that he met a young *sarará* of 22, whose nickname, from his herculean manner and body, was King Kong. They talked. Almost point-blank King Kong informed him that he had "23 centimetres by 4 in diameter", a fact which he said normally drove women wild. Carella took him to his room on Good Friday and examined him with the maddened eye of desire. And he did not resist. He gave himself to the centaur while a procession passed outside singing hymns. In his diary Carella wrote some of the most beautiful pages of homosexual erotica that I know. (He writes in the third person, calling himself Lúcio Ginarte, perhaps from some vain precaution.)

> King Kong proceeds with caution. Little by little he slides down Lúcio's back until meeting a convex prominence where he settles. His stroking is at first gentle, then harder, becoming alive, deliberate. (...) He has decided. With a boldness that astounds Lúcio, he unbuttons his shirt and pulls it off, then does the same with his trousers. He is completely naked and displays himself with pride, knowing it would be difficult to find a body more perfect than his own. And because Lúcio hesitates, he pulls him up, helps him undress. Lúcio sees his own body and King Kong's in the dressing-table mirror. The meagre light is enough to delineate hills and valleys. They compare members, which are almost the same size. But King Kong does not understand prolonged foreplay: he wants to screw immediately. He turns Lúcio round so that his back is to him and, without wasting time, lays the gland against the naked flesh. Lúcio, who has been distracted for a moment by the bodies in the mirror, rebels; he could never take that prick. He tries to pull away, but King Kong holds

him as he continues pushing uselessly into the narrow entry. Lúcio squirms in pain and succeds in getting away, but is pulled back by the indisputable strengh of those steel muscles. A second attempt fails and Lúcio suffers and refuses, but he can no longer control the excited male who holds him with one hand as the other rubs spit on his penis. King Kong enters again; his fingers have become iron pincers. Lúcio feels both fear and attraction. Will this cylinder of hard flesh succeed in penetrating his body? Some of King Kong's great lust communicates itself to him. King Kong is now an obsessed monster, possessed by an angry erotic passion, implacable, unable to control his reactions. He is blind and dumb except for some guttural noises and heavy breathing, the indication of his unyielding purpose. Only the sense of touch means anything and in the contact of mucous membranes he seeks the return of lost tranquility. He has to enter this pale, alien body in order to communicate with the white gods who inhabit it, even if he has to tear it and make it bleed. He applies more saliva, spreads the buttocks and takes him with his stiff member. It seems unlikely he will achieve his goal. Lúcio gives a cry and pulls away. King Kong roars, seizes his victim again, puts his rod in the right place, pushes, pushes harder when he realises that the flesh is beginning to give. It dilates slightly before the continuing pressure, allowing the hope that the act might be completed. He breathes deeply and pushes with a terrible violence; Lúcio, feeling himself invaded, strangles a cry. The rapist's hands drive into his chest, producing a new pain which in no way distracts from the other; they counterbalance, complement and cancel each other. He is totally infected by King Kong's violent lust. He forgets his modesty, prudence and morality. He is compelled to surrender, anxious to feel and enjoy this gigantic instrument. He relaxes and helps the stallion penetrating his entrails with movements that hurt and do not hurt. First the glans, then the rest, all slowly disappear past the dilated anal sphincter. One last thrust completes the work; King Kong owns and subdues his body. King Kong knows he has touched the depths and triumphed. His claws turn to silk; instead of grasping, he caresses Lúcio's chest, his back and his belly. Resting his face on one of Lúcio's shoulders he relishes his partner's groans more clearly.

Lúcio suffers, but through some interaction in the order established for each sensation the suffering is also delight. The rapist begins to move, at first slowly and then with greater force and speed until he reaches a steady and accelerating rhythm. The interlocked bodies can be seen in the mirror moving in cadence, with the long, piston-like withdrawal and entry of the huge virile member which is tearing him apart yet making him experience previously unknown sensations. The silence becomes stronger (their panting is part of that silence), jubilant and grows into something like song. Lúcio reaches out behind to stroke that marvellous body, to appreciate it better and more. At that moment King Kong groans and, immobile, reaches orgasm. Lúcio, unable to tolerate any more, masturbates and shares the other's pleasure. Their breathing slows. Their hands, no longer possessive or caressing, slip away, tired and grateful. Happily they let the tension drain, staying quiet together for a few moments before separating. King Kong withdraws his member – it has lost its rigidity but not its length. Lúcio sighs with relief and nostalgia. They wash in the basin and dress. (...) King Kong's face is lit with a pleasant smile. Sitting down, he picks up the pencil again and asks if Lúcio is content. Lúcio answers, omitting half the truth: "It hurt a lot." With a proud expression, the other writes: "It hurt *but* you liked it."

Guilt-ridden, Carella argued with himself. Afterwards, he sought out King Kong again. Carella knew he had got engaged and would marry sooner or later. He gave King Kong money, which he spent on prostitutes, retrurning with a sore. Unable to have sex, he asked Carella to hold his prick discreetly in the street at each shop window where they stopped. Carella held back from the more stable relationship that he wanted because he was still being importuned and fought over by the men of the town. "I am followed by a great train of youths and men as a bridal gown is followed by a great train. (...) I can't shake them off; they cling like leeches." It all began again, irresistibly, libidinously. "Something makes me enter the pissoir in a bar. A young negro is there with a hard-on. He takes my penis as I take his; he ejaculates at that moment, filling my hand with sperm." Carella confessed in his diary that "workers, mulattos, barrowboys, negros, ragamuffins and urchins arouse desire in me and desire me". He learnt that the average human lifespan in the region was 37 years and that infant mortality reached 75%. For that reason he almost never saw old people in the streets. He saw that life passed "as lightly as a spark in those ephemeral bodies" and concluded that "perhaps awareness of this brevity disposes them to pleasure and they take advantage of it when they can". So did he, Carella, take advantage when he could, perhaps driven by this sense of fatality. "I turn slowly. He kisses my back, then sinks and kneels again, kisses my buttocks, spreads them with his hands and voraciously licks my hole. It is not the first time that I have been caressed in this way, but it has never been done with such enthusiasm, perfection, constancy and duration – more than half an hour of licking and sucking." He also learnt sado-masochistic pleasure; he struck and was struck. Bodies disfigured by the diseases of squalor began to attract him and he was fascinated by the monstrous testicles of those with elephantiasis. There was no longer a distinction between beauty and horror for him.

Tulio Carella spent almost two years in Recife, submerged in its constant climate of orgy – in the streets, in bus queues, in bars and parks, at shop windows, in rain and sun. In his long diary he admitted that he knew only two countries with such a rich sexual activity: Italy and Brazil – where sex was as much to satisfy needs as to be rewarded by pleasure. Indeed, he was having sex every day, more than once a day, admitting: "I can't stop now. I'm impelled by an earthly force stronger than any resistance I can put up. I'm falling into an abyss. (...) Here I am in middle age, soliciting like a whore – frenetically and insatiably." The casual human landscape drew him against his will: "A boy, with a hard and enormous member like a tentpole, walks by hand-in-hand with his mother." Or: "Bus. Throughout the journey a dark youth rests his sex in my hand. As for me, I rest my hand on a sailor whose arse stands out in a harmonious curve." His integration in Recife's sensual atmosphere was complete. "To sense myself surrounded by this incessant desire makes me happy. (...) I have gained a lot in coming to this city. I feel I have been freed. (...) I have shed my country and my old habits like the shell of a ripened fruit. I think that another me is being born." Then his diary ended with a wounding confession: "I was like a man raised to set light to women's cunts, but I make men's pricks burn like torches."

Perhaps because his presence in the city at a politically

explosive period was too noticeable, Carella was arrested by the Brazlian military, on suspicion of smuggling arms from Cuba for the rebellious farm-workers of Pernambuco. He was interrogated and tortured for a long time, and once taken up in a plane where they threatened to throw him out if he would not confess his subversive crimes. The police had received information that he often walked the quaysides at night and met people suspected of being subversives or guerrillas. Looking through his apartment, they came across his diary and read it carefully. Then they saw their mistake; they had arrested a queer instead of a Cuban guerrilla. Carella was released and warned to say nothing about his arrest, or obscene extracts from the photocopy of his diary that they were keeping would be published. Shortly afterwards he was called in by the university rector and dismissed from his post. The rector, who had been informed of everything by the police, was not inclined to accept in his school someone who "lived chasing men and, what is worse, negros". Humiliated, Carella returned to Buenos Aires at once, where it was said that he fell sick with nostalgia for Brazil. It was 1962. It is vaguely known that he separated from his wife and that he died of heart failure in 1979. Apart from the first volume of his *Diary*, published in Portuguese translation, there is an edition of Tulio Carella's poems dedicated to the city of Recife, the Sodom which had welcomed him so hospitably.

*

In the same year in which Carella left, another foreigner arrived in Brazil, this time from Belgium. His name was Conrad Detrez; he was a 25-year-old Catholic seminarist who had come to help with the work of evangelisation in Brazilian factories and shanty-towns. Little by little Detrez distanced himself from the priestly ministry, becoming a member of an urban guerrilla group led by Carlos Marighela, a Castrist revolutionary who was later killed by the army. Arrested and deported from Brazil in 1967, Detrez returned to Europe where, in collaboration with Marighela, he published an essay on the liberation of Brazil. He became famous for his autobiographical novels, receiving the Prix Renaudot in 1978, for the very book in which he tells how his homosexuality blossomed in a Brazil shaken by guerrilla warfare and "heavily eroticised".

After being seduced and losing his virginity to the female sacristan of a proletarian church in the state of Rio de Janeiro, the young Detrez went on a spiritual retreat in a monastery in São Vicente, a seaside town near São Paulo. There he discovered he was next to a barracks. He watched the half-naked soldiers exercising on the beach. He meditated on Christian love and planned to found a religious order of contemplative and celibate workers. One afternoon his attention was taken by two soldiers – one white and the other black – who stripped naked, swam and fell arm in arm on the sand under the setting sun. Conrad watched the idyll, seeing their hardened pricks, a fact which disturbed him deeply. To escape worldly temptations and dedicate himself to his evangelical mission, he went to live in the house of a young priest on a hill in a shanty-town by the city of Rio de Janeiro. Fernando, a black from Bahia and an activist in the Christian workers' movement, lived in the same hut. Soon afterwards the young priest left with a Catholic woman activist with whom he had fallen in love.

Fernando and Conrad stayed on, trying to keep their faith in Christ's teachings. But Carnival came and Fernando decided to go and enjoy himself for the four days of celebration. It was when Conrad went out into the streets in search of his friend that he had his first experience of collective madness. At first he only watched the sweating crowds, where men and women of every colour, wearing almost nothing, groped and kissed each other. Then he was seized and swept away by a group of revellers in the sensual and hypnotic rhythm of the drumbeat. When Conrad came to, it was night and he was lying beside a woman on a beach. Both were naked and they made love among the waves. When the sun rose, however, he repented and fled in search of a church, but found them all closed. He looked for Fernando again and found him at a ball where hundreds of youths were dancing together to the sound of a thunderous orchestra. In that atmosphere Conrad lost his head, jumped on Fernando and kissed him on the mouth. They made love right there, against a wall. Realising that he was in love with his Brazilian friend, Conrad began to cry. In ecstasy the two returned to their hut in the shanty-town. Conrad himself wrote:

> My friend brusquely pulled me between his legs, spread my buttocks and penetrated me. I roared with pain. My skin and flesh were being torn. I bled, shouted that I loved him, that he was killing me, that it was hurting, hurting a

> lot, that I was surrendering to him. My sperm flooded over me, my blood ran down my thighs. We slept, ate, made love in the smell of dried blood and sweat; we spent two days in a confusion of tears and games, of very gentle and dangerous embraces, sitting, lying, standing, breaking every rule, committing every excess that our imaginations could conceive – excesses that would have led us to death if Carnival had not come to an end.

With the advent of Lent both went to confess. They promised to reform and made plans to convert the working class to Christianity. In the chapel where they had gone to worship they hardly brushed against each other before they found themselves once more, and against their will, embracing, kissing and clasping each other. In the end they made love in the very chapel, in front of their God. So their lives went on in the midst of broken promises and a passion that was becoming more and more disturbing. During the day they preached and politicised the workers, risking violent reprisals from the police. At night they returned home tired, pulled each other onto the bed and made love. Troubled, they made advances to two women workers in the same group, in an effort to overcome what they called their "mad love". They plunged frenziedly into political activity against the dictatorship. Yet nothing worked. Whenever they were alone they wanted each other's bodies. Fernando, in despair, decided to return home; Conrad threatened to kill himself. He howled in solitude. He suffered. Then he began to read about the Cuban revolution. After studying Marxism-Leninism, he joined the clandestine political movement, cured of Christ and Fernando. The military arrested and tortured him; in prison a truncheon was pushed up his backside. He wanted to die.

In both his books and interviews Detrez has made acute observations on homosexual eroticism in urban Brazil, as well as commenting on the relationship between Catholicism and Brazilian machismo. He notes that machos keep their distance from the pratice of religion because, for good or bad, they are aware of the homerotic dimension of this exuberant religion in which men become so interested in another male that they will worship him in a temple. According to Detrez something similar takes place during Carnival. In the four days of revelry and licentiousness men very commonly cross-dress and have sex with each other, even if their lives are "straight". It may be true that after this break they return to their daily routine but Detrez sees it as indisputable proof of the bisexual potential of Brazilian men – which is also evident in other patriarchal societies, Arab or Latin.

Conrad also refers to the same *machista* ambiguity in the relationship between politics and homosexuality. His experience with guerrillas in Brazil made him realise that political activity and the desire for power play a very important role in asserting the militants' virility. It could not be admitted that a homosexual (ie. a man usually considered weak) would want to exercise a power reserved for machos. In such a context Detrez was naturally obliged to conceal his homosexuality. Moreover, he writes that in these clandestine groups he met a significant number of lesbians, who often disputed leadership with the heterosexual machos. He sensed a great deal of homoerotic ambiguity among the guerrillas, starting with the cult of Castro and Che Guevara. He tells of a guerrilla who, probably boasting, claimed in front of his companions that he followed Castro "because he found Fidel good-looking". It is worth remembering that in the sensual religion of a country like Brazil the face of Che Guevara (killed in guerrilla warfare in Bolivia) served to some extent as the image of the crucified Christ – a fact which Detrez considers very typical of Latin-American history, where Christ has sometimes appeared as a guerrilla. Still in the context of the ambiguity between politics, religion and homoeroticism, Detrez saw that the working class's interest in politics often arose from an emotional involvement. He considered this natural, partly because he had been awakened to the Brazilian reality by his loving relationship with Fernando. As he himself admitted in writing: "It was thanks to my homosexuality that I discovered the working-class question, poverty and social injustice; thanks to it I rose up against fascism."[4]

*

It is not improbable that, during his stay in Rio, Conrad Detrez met Allen Young. This 23-year-old journalist from the USA had arrived in the city in 1964 on a study scholarship from the Fulbright Commission. Their politics were similar, for Allen was then a Marxist, an anti-Vietnam-war activist and an unconditional admirer of socialist Cuba. His stay of almost two years in Brazil, at a time of great political upheaval (the military had just taken power in a coup d'état) revealed to Allen a little-explored dimension of himself – his attraction to men. It was in Rio de Janeiro, he wrote, that he first said to himself "I am a homosexual", and it was in that city that he first experienced pleasure in making love with another man – until then his behaviour had been both secretive and frightened. He stopped psychoanalysis, his "cure" taking place, he says, in the contacts he made with the homosexuals of Rio, whom he met everywhere – cruising in the streets, in cinemas, bars, saunas and on the local beaches. He confessed that he was often shocked by the compulsive behaviour and alienation typical of the gay ghetto and he suffered deeply at the suicide of a Brazilian friend, a gay man as closeted as he was at the time. Nevertheless, he was happy; he seemed closer than ever to homosexuals and many became his friends.

At the beginning of the 1970s Allen, now an activist in the American gay movement and with new critical perspectives, returned to Brazil. His old homosexual friends now seemed to him to be prejudiced against limp-wristed queens, unswerving believers in monogamy and most definitely in the closet. They even asked Allen not to come out to straight people. Meanwhile, Allen says, among the heterosexuals with whom he was actually living there were sympathetic reactions to his homosexuality. He believed that if anti-gay machismo existed in Latin culture, it could be eradicated simply because – unlike Anglo-Saxon culture – Latin culture has never pretended that homosexuality does not exist. It was true that the separation of sexual roles among Brazilians seemed to him very pronounced, with a clear hierarchy in which the *bicha* ("queer") submitted to the *bofe* ("stud"). It was difficult for him to accept a notion prevalent among the Brazilian proletariat – the macho fucks the *bicha* without being reduced to the *bicha*'s status, much less being emotionally involved. Most important for the macho is the active part played in the relationship, and Allen believed it was a typical way in which Brazilian men could express their homosexuality without running into greater risks on the social level. He was also surprised by the complicated racism of his homosexual friends, many of whom considered themselves to be progressive. A black friend, for example, was gratified by his non-racist attitude but confessed to being racist himself, since he did not like the Japanese (there is a large population of Japanese origin in Brazil, especially in São Paulo).

Allen's experiences led him to the conclusion that a homosexuality lived as the American gay movement intended – openly and freely from sexual roles – was not tolerated in Brazil. This would explain the innumerable cases of violence against homosexuals. Allen also refers to a more subtle violence on the linguistic level; slang words are very often based on prejudice against *bichas* and women, both of whom are always considered passive. With this in mind, Allen supposed that an eventual gay movement in Brazil would have problems not only with the police but with the traditional left as well – a prophetic observation, as will be seen in Chapter Five.

*

In the 1980s another Argentinian, this time a poet and student, wrote down his impressions of gay life in urban Brazil, thus giving an idea of how it had evolved. Nestor Perlongher classified himself as a "fugitive tourist" from the Argentinian dictatorship – which was interesting, because in the previous decade I had gone to Argentina to escape from the Brazilian dictatorship. It also confirms the impression that history in Latin America turns as inevitably as an eternal wheel.

For Nestor Brazilian cities are – unlike the "ultra-repressive Argentina" – a "promised land of promiscuity, flirtation and everyday variants of debauchery". On his first night in Brazil (in São Paulo, where he still lives), he was enchanted to be dragged from nightclub to nightclub arm-in-arm with a mulatto. A few days later a boy from the slums hit him over the head with a bottle – in order to rob him of a pair of glasses! As soon as the wound healed, Nestor returned to his self-appointed task, fascinated by the ease of sexual contacts. In one day he had sex with three men, on another with five; once he beat his own record by having sex with eleven men in just one day. He sometimes went out to send a letter but never reached the Post Office. He had sex in hotels, in familiar and unfamiliar bathrooms, even in a shop, invited in by a boy who worked there.

Nestor refers to the extreme ambiguity of the city, the country's largest (9 million inhabitants) and a veritable showcase of all the contradictions in Brazilian life. In the centre of São Paulo prostitutes, transvestites, thieves, rentboys, clones, migrants from the north-east, an Americanised middle class and men from the suburbs jostle together and furiously cruise. The police, who are also to be found there, occasionally strike out, arresting those suspected of vagrancy simply because they are not carrying identity documents. There are also innumerable cinemas in the city, such as the cavernous Art-Palácio, in whose corridors, according to Nestor, one can slip dangerously on the fresh sperm spattered on the floor.

He also mentions his experiences in Rio de Janeiro, where one night, in a dark street frequented by homosexuals, he saw a fat mulatto wearing shirt and shoes but no trousers and showing his erect rod to passers-by. What seems to have fascinated him the most, however, was the city of Salvador, capital of the state of Bahia, which he considers mythic, pre-capitalist and the most African of Brazilian cities. There, where luxury lives side-by-side with the most obscene poverty, Nestor sees the *bicha* as an institution and homosexuality as naive and archaic. But he also believes that the Africanity of Bahia lives off more than sex; there is also an insidious racism. A black transvestite told him of the time he went to look for work as a dancer in a nightclub. The owner turned him down, saying: "Black girls don't dance here; they work in the kitchen." Until a short time ago there was an activist group of black homosexuals in Salvador that denounced the exploitation by whites who use them as sex objects but who prefer other whites in long-term relationships. This discrimination and poverty obviously create situations of revenge. A youth Nestor once took to one of the cheapest hotels mugged him – with the silent complicity of the manager, himself a notorious homosexual. Such a situation filled him with fear – but also with delight, for the bodies he desired in his fantasies were black. Precisely because they are associated with the most sordid poverty, Brazilian blacks have always been a component of sadism in white fantasy. It was not by chance that Nestor fell for a *filho-de-santo* (an initiate in the Afro-Brazilian religion of *candomblé*); the initiation rites tend to be particularly bloody, with hens and other animals being sacificed and their blood poured over the head of the young devotee. This all takes place in the midst of sensual dances of mystic origin in which bodies often twist lasciviously as they are possessed by African divinities. There is carnality in this mysticism.

Carnality and mysticism: two elements which run through Brazilian life and confer it with the gift to disturb, as the examples I have found and cited here confirm.

CHAPTER TWO

The Holy Inquisition Discovers Paradise

"The least pain,
Lord Visitor
of the Holy Office
who was sent to us
by the Holy See,
is to be buggered
in the right place."

Hermilo Borba Filho (1972)

In a wonderfully indecent musical comedy about the development of Brazilian patriarchal society, the playwright and novelist Hermilo Borba Filho includes a scene with the Inquisitor interrogating defendants in sixteenth-century Brazil. A man has just confessed to having had sex with a male slave, taking turn about. "And how many nights was this?" the Inquisitor asks. "Many, my Lord," the man replies candidly. As punishment, the Inquisitor orders the culprit to marry. To his surprise, he is informed that the man is already married. "And where is the wife?" A woman with an enormous backside appears before the Inquisitor and confesses to having been sodomised by her husband every night for the forty years of their marriage. When the Inquisitor asks how she feels, the woman shows him her backside and answers: "Can't you see, my Lord?" The Inquisitor hands down sentence: husband and wife must go to prison where they will be obliged to copulate "only from the front", at which the man exclaims: "How cruel!" while his wife, astonished, asks: "Do people get any pleasure from the front?" The Inquisitor calls the next defendant. A youth enters and confesses to having experienced "unparalleled delight" on sodomising a delicate slave. When the Inquisitor asks if he has done it often, the boy immediately confesses: "More than a thousand times." At that the Inquisitor, annoyed, stands up and protests against the sinners' levity: "For just one Jewess, I don't know how many buggers!" He leaves his post while the stage is invaded by sodomites singing the "Buggers' Anthem", which claims that it is much better to take it up the backside than to go to war or obey the government.

Beginnings: Hearts in Exile

When in an almost feudal manner the Portuguese King João III gave the Captaincy of Pernambuco to Duarte Coelho in 1534 and the Captaincy of São Vicente to Martim Afonso de Souza in 1535, he not only handed these two subjects a share in the recently discovered Brazil but also detailed instructions on how to administer justice in these parts of the new colony. As military commanders and governors of their respective provinces, both had the right of life and death over "slaves and heathens, as over Christian peasants and free men". The letter from the King specified and stressed four instances of punishment; if the crimes of *heresy*, *treason*, *sodomy* or *counterfeiting* were proven, the governor/commander enjoyed the authority to condemn to death any individual without appeal. If the defendant was a "person of higher rank", however, the governor could, if he wished, absolve the death penalty and sentence "ten years of exile and up to one hundred cruzados fine".

João III certainly had reasons for being so explicit in regard to the new colony. One of the commonest punishments in Portugal was exile to Brazil. The "Ordinances of the Kingdom", which contained the laws and penal code of the time, specified crimes and indicated very severe punishments (more details in Chapter Three). About 200 types of offences – among them witchcraft, homicide, rape and sodomy – were punishable with exile to the colonies, Brazil included. The first Portuguese colonists sent to the Americas, therefore, were generally murderers, thieves, fugitive Jews and people considered debauched and deviant for having committed fornication, sodomy, bestiality, pimping and idleness (masturbation). As a result Brazil was forced to become a focus of liberality and promiscuity, attracting adventurers and rogues interested in easy riches as much as in naked Indian women and other tropical delights. It was this amalgam of explosive elements that led Duarte Coelho to write anxiously to the King asking him to stop sending exiles to Brazil, for he considered them "worse than poison". The situation does not seem to have changed much with the passing of time. In the eighteenth century the Bishop of Pará protested in a letter to the Court that "the wretched morals of this country remind me of the destiny of the five [Biblical] towns, for it seems that I dwell in the suburbs of Gomorrah and in the neighbourhood of Sodom".

It should be remembered also that Portuguese sexual morality was that of the Mocarabs (Christians in the Iberian peninsula who had lived under the Moors), who were considered more liberal than the Protestants of the north or the Catholics of Castille. Among the Portuguese the Catholic liturgy was said to be more social than religious – "a lyrical Christianity" with phallic and animist relics of pagan religions. One indication of this moderated theocracy is the absence of great cathedrals on Portuguese territory, unlike Spain, where the many imposing religious temples are evidence of its unifying Catholicism. In Portugal mysticism was part of social life – oxen were taken to church for the priests to bless; infertile women raised their skirts to rub against the legs on the image of St Gonçalo; suspicious husbands went to question the "cuckold rocks" while nubile girls spoke to the "marriage rocks". The Virgin Mary even appeared scandalously pregnant, as in the swollen-bellied image of Our Lady of O – still extant in Brazil. It is true that the climatic influences of the tropics should be added to these moral and religious features, for social conditions in Brazil undermined continence, asceticism and monogamy. In the context of the old colony's patriarchal regime, boys and adolescents were transformed into over-excited males, which is why their sexual initiation took place when they were as young as 12 or 13.

Gilberto Freyre, the sociologist, believes that homosexuality (which he calls the "cult of Venus Urania") was popularised in Brazil by those European colonists (whether Portuguese, Spanish, Italians, Moors or Jews) who discovered fertile territory for its expansion in the Indians' sexual morality and the unfettered conditions of colonisation. He recalls that sodomy flourished freely in Renaissance Italy, from where it spread all over Europe, Italian homosexuals being questioned by the Inquisition in Spain in the sixteenth and seventeenth centuries. Furthermore, there was a large Italian colony in Lisbon, responsible (according to Freyre's theory) for the spreading among the Portuguese of "Socratic love" (sic). Many Portuguese sodomites are known to have been exiled to Brazil, some being subsequently interrogated by the Inquisition. Cited as equally favourable to the dissemination of homosexuality in Portugal is the fact that in the fifteenth and sixteenth centuries Portuguese sailors made long sea voyages, on which they came across and were influenced by oriental countries with a rich erotic life, such as China.

Slavery, Piety and Eroticism

The colony's population was made up of more than Europeans and Indians. Brazil would have been very different without the presence of black slaves, first transported from Africa by Portuguese and English merchants between 1542 and 1546. The trade was so prosperous that by the seventeenth century slaves were sold on credit. In 1630 the state of Pernambuco imported about 4,000 slaves as labour in the sugar industry, while in the eighteenth century the state of Bahia alone imported more than 25,000 individuals annually. Since all the relevant documentation was burnt after the Abolition of Slavery (1888), the total number of Africans brought to Brazil is not known with accuracy, but historians calculate the total brought to work on the sugar plantations and in the gold mines as 16 million in three centuries of the slave-based regime. Travelling through Brazil between 1842 and 1845, Prince Adelbert of Prussia reported that 2,936,000 of the country's 3,116,000 inhabitants were black. Such predominance was so noteworthy that Charles Darwin, who visited Brazil in 1822, claimed that it was "a country of slavery and, furthermore, moral degradation".

Everything in Brazil was done by slaves. The most beautiful of the women inevitably became their masters' concubines and sex objects and bore them bastard children. The erotic life of the sons of the sugar-mill owners began with female slaves. Young black boys might also be sexual playthings – in fact the white youth's initiation into physical love was often the submission of his black playmate, who was commonly, and not without cause, known by the nickname of "punchbag". In these circumstances the slave-based Brazilian regime tended to make the white masters more idle and debauched, as they spent their days stretched out on hammocks and used a black man's hand "for the most intimate details of the toilet", according to

Gilberto Freyre. It was not surprising that, served like princes by their slaves, white men came to have the delicate hands of women and feet of boys – "a sometimes exaggerated beauty, smallness and delicacy of the feet and hands, degenerating into effeminacy", according to the reports of Richard Burton, who took the generally large feet and hands of the English and Portuguese as comparison. In these soft bodies, however, supreme importance was given to the penis, which ideally was "arrogantly virile". Some patriarchs sent spies to discover the genital dimensions of prospective sons-in-law, without which knowledge the marriage was not permitted. An *Instruction Manual for Landowners*, published in 1839, advised slave-buyers to avoid purchasing those with small or misshapen sexes, since it was believed that a well-endowed member guaranteed fertility and greater virility. Even if misplaced, such a criterion and preoccupation are indisputable evidence of great intimacy with the masculine sex and of the existence of a truly phallocratic cult in Brazilian society of the time. Then, as today, men customarily scratched their genitals in public to display their virility (much like the gesture of spitting contemptuously to the side).

In this atmosphere of intense sexual activity venereal disease flourished freely, through a prostitution that was as much domestic (with slaves) as professional (in brothels) – hygiene being notable in neither case. In 1864 Dr Frutuoso Pinto da Silva of the Faculty of Medicine in Bahia called the attention of parents, teachers and supervisors to the problem of morality and sexual hygiene in Brazilian colleges. Great advances were said to have been made there by gonorrhea, syphilis, onanism and pederasty – and "pederasty seems to walk in stealth making its pernicious conquests in the midst of youth", according to the doctor. Moreover, some authors believe that homosexuality flourished in Jesuit colleges among the many orphans which the priests had brought from Portugal. In the mansions as much as the slave quarters syphilis had become the Brazilian disease par excellence. It was transmitted by the owners to the female slaves and by the latter to the sons of the owners – as much by suckling as by sexual initiation, since black wet-nurses fulfilled both functions at different stages in the white boys' lives. Interestingly, syphilis was taken as a sign of virility; it was supposedly common for men to display the scars on their bodies with pride; youths without these marks were mocked and considered virgins or less masculine. It is also worth remembering that it was commonly believed that the syphilitic could cure himself if the virus was transmitted to a pubescent girl (especially a black adolescent) during sexual intercourse – which meant that black women were contaminated even younger. Another theory was that white babies, born syphilitic because of their parents, passed the disease to the wet-nurses when being fed – so much so that certain doctors of the time demanded proof of the *infants'* physical health. These extraordinary aspects of Brazilian life suggest that civilisation arrived side by side with syphilisation, a result of the uncontrolled miscegenation between Indians, Europeans and Africans.

Meanwhile, it is interesting to note how such a disposition towards the erotic went hand-in-hand with the strictest and most resounding practice of Catholicism. Even when wasted by venereal desease and scarred by syphilis, each and every man went to tell his beads and hear the usually interminable litanies chanted by blacks and slaves in his house or in church. It was customary to go out with rosaries, relics, scapulars, bags and medallions of saints around one's neck. Litanies were sung in the street at nightfall. Contemporary foreign travellers refer to daily religious festivals, with processions and choral singing for popular entertainment. Sir George Keith, visiting Brazil at the beginning of the nineteenth century, claimed never to have seen so many processions as in Rio de Janeiro. At household altars prayers were said in the morning, at meal-times and at night, duties attended by the householder, his family, servants and slaves without distinction. There were prayers for everything: protection against disease, storms and thieves. Certain illnesses were treated with Holy Oil from church and everyone fasted rigorously on the days ordered by religion. The cult of the Sacred Heart of Jesus with its appeal to patience and resignation in the face of hardship was very popular; Gilberto Freyre ironically observes that the cult's popularity was proof of and reflected the basic sado-masochism inherent in relations between men and women, whites and slaves in colonial Brazil. This mixture of perverse carnality and fanatical mysticism also indicates the links between religious sensuality and moral laxity, as will be seen.

The Hedonistic God

It can be imagined, as some authors would have it, that contemporary demographic needs were directly responsible for this unscrupulous sexual conduct. Yet this explanation lacks flexibility, forgetting, for example, that lovers were free to hand – the white man had only to reach out in order to fondle his slaves. Even priests did not escape these circumstances. Since the sixteenth century a large number of the clergy (except the irreproachably celibate Jesuits) had lived with Indian and black women. In a country where religion theoretically obliged its ministers to maintain a rigorous chastity, it was very common for priests to have natural children by their slaves. No one, therefore, was surprised to be introduced to a mulatto as "the son of Father So-and-so". The concern of the Bishop of Pernambuco can be understood when, in 1738, he recommended priests not to have female slaves of the parish under the age of forty in their houses. On the other hand, since it was fashionable to have a priest in the family, it is understandable that the ministers of the Holy Church were not ordained exclusively to serve religion; whoever was called to the priesthood indeed assumed the duties of patriarchal society.

Foreigners travelling or living in Brazil at different times unanimously condemned the appalling reputation of the country's clergy. Froger, eighteenth-century traveller, wrote that many priests had public mistresses. In 1768 La Caille, a French priest, admitted to being scandalised by the licentiousness of the clergy in Rio de Janeiro. In 1728 Le Gentil de La Barbinais referred to some Bahian monks who dressed as female slaves to meet the women they were having affairs with. This did not help them stay out of the public eye, for they were better known by their lovers' names than by their own. Still in the eighteenth century, there is a report that various priests in São Paulo, consumed with jealousy, quarrelled publicly over the amorous favours of Maria Putiú, a famous mulatta. It is a fact that throughout Brazil there were priests who led a more discreet marital life, maintaining "housekeepers" or "godmothers" and raising numerous "godchildren" or "nephews and nieces" with an ill-concealed parental care. Burton claimed that this did not surprise the parishioners, who were accustomed to the idea of celibacy being purely theoretical. The situation was such that Luis dos Santos Vilhena, a famous professor of Greek in Bahia, complained in a letter to the King of Portugal at the end of the eighteenth century that the wealth of the numerous priests living with black and mulatta women ran the risk of falling into the hands of their coloured bastards ("usually corrupt men", he said) and could therefore be lost.

There were also references to clerical scandals concerning

indiscreet homosexual liaisons. In a letter to the Count of Oeiras in 1761, the Bishop of Rio de Janeiro denounced the debauchery of the clergy in São Paulo, where there were "dissolute masters in concubinage with disciples". He mentioned in particular Father Manuel dos Santos, living with Antônio José, a student and future cleric; Father Inácio Ribeiro, living with Inacinho, a musician; and a certain Pedro de Vasconcelos, the lover of Joaquim Veloso, both connected with the Church.

In this hedonistic climate which not even the clergy escaped, it was common to fall in love in the religious temples, where participation in the ceremomies often served as a cover for forbidden meetings. La Flotte, a French traveller, said that he received "enchanting invitations" during a church celebration in 1757. It was true that since white women were so confined to their homes, love affairs and adulteries could only begin in church, a veritable escape valve for the vigilated society of the time. Furthermore, in the convents perfumed nuns wore the most delicate undergarments, silk stockings and shoes encrusted with gold and diamonds. According to John Barrow, an Englishman who travelled through Brazil in the eighteenth century, syphilis was even devastating the monasteries and the known remedies of the time were taken there secretly. In the seventeenth and eighteenth centuries it was said to be common for young men to circle the convents in search of lovers. The atmosphere was certainly propitious, for many of the nuns were young women from good families who had been encloistered for losing their virginity before marriage; others were widows and unfaithful wives who had been forcibly sent there. As if that were not enough, these women were served by a battalion of slaves who did all the manual work – in the Convent of Exile in Bahia there were 400 slaves for 75 nuns. It can be imagined how idle this made monastic life. Information also exists about numerous profane festivals in the convents, with pastoral dances and even Carnival revels, enabling the Brides of Christ to break their vows of chastity without even leaving the sacred space of the convent.

The Punitive God

Frightened by the spectre of the Reformation, the Roman Catholic Church had retaliated with the Counter-Reformation, laying siege to heresies and deviant customs. Both the ecclesiastical and royal authorities in Portugal tried to find more effective means of controlling the Brazilian colonists who, finding themselves so far from the Court, naturally tended to neglect the commands of God and King. The Tribunal of the Holy Inquisition, which was active in Portugal from 1536 until 1765, seemed more than adequate to achieve this aim of instilling discipline. On various occasions, therefore, the General Council of the Inquisition sent its Commissioners to Brazil on formal visits. Sometimes their presence was requested by the colonial authorities themselves, as in 1645 when the Superior of the Society of Jesus wrote to the Portuguese Council protesting the "great scandal on account of matters of Judaism, such as witchcraft and the abominable sin. In particular there is information that a man by the name of Francisco da Rocha has said that the Apostles of Our Lord Christ and Christ Himself were misers, sodomites and intriguers."[1]

Once in Brazil, the Visitors of the Holy Office aimed to suppress moral turpitude and possible foci of political treachery as much as abuses on the level of faith and doctrine. Indeed the Inquisition scarcely disguised the fact that its objectives were linked to temporal power. National churches might be subordinate to the Pope but in practice they obeyed the kings and the dominant class of the countries where the Inquisition functioned. Political control of Inquisitorial trials was the object of much dispute, for the possessions of the accused or condemned were confiscated – in part or totally – and handed over to the Crown. Accusations could also be a means of harassment between political enemies in the same dominant class – as in the case of rich Jews, who were persecuted and dispossessed in the name of the Catholic faith.

An ecclesiastical version of civil justice, the Inquisition kept watch for innumerable types of crimes – Jewish, Lutheran or Muslim practices, any heresy, including blasphemy and breaking religious laws, witchcraft and sorcery, bigamy, heathen custom (such as nudity and painting the body, particularly tattooing in the style of the Indians) and sodomy. There were cases such as that of Diogo de Teive, a Portuguese teacher and humanist, who was sentenced to two years' imprisonment for eating meat on Fridays. Punishments varied and included flogging, public penance, fines, total or partial confiscation of goods, exile, forced labour in the galleys, life imprisonment and death at the stake. In the last case the condemned prisoner was handed over to the secular tribunal because the Church refused to carry out the sentence that it itself had given.

From the incomplete research made so far into the vast documentation available, it is calculated that in almost 300 years of activity the Inquisition tried around 40,000 people in Portugal and its colonies, burning 1,808 at the stake and sentencing 29,560 to other punishments. Until 1821, when the Portuguese Inquisition was officially closed, Brazil was always subordinate to decisions of the Inquisition in Lisbon. In fact little is yet known about the Inquisition's activities in the colonies. It is accepted that the first Visit of the Holy Office to Brazil was in 1591 at Bahia; in 1593 it moved to Pernambuco, where it stayed until 1595. The proceedings followed a regular pattern. There was an Auto-da-Fé, which began with a religious ceremony of great pomp and continued with a sung mass in the church where the Edicts of Faith and Grace were published. At the end of the ceremony the local dignitaries swore fidelity to the Lord Visitor. The Period of Grace followed, several weeks in which people could voluntarily confess their crimes in order to earn the Tribunal's mercy and mitigation of the eventual penalties. This was also the time for the public to accuse those who had sinned against the Catholic faith and morals. In other words, people were encouraged to denounce each other.

Any citizen had the right and was indeed obliged to make accusations, by anonymous letter to guarantee secrecy if desired. The Edict itself proclaimed that denunciation was the duty of "any person, man or woman, cleric or contemplative, free or not, of whatever state, condition, dignity and pre-eminence, including fathers and mothers and any other relatives present or absent, companions, consorts, participants and consentors of the said crimes and errors."[2]

The resulting climate was naturally one of crude vigilance and control. In the Denunciations of Pernambuco for 1593 a young girl called Ana told how she had heard noises in the neighbouring house and had gone to spy through the front door. She had then seen Maria Rodrigues committing the abominable sin with a coloured girl of eleven or twelve years of age. There was the bizarre case of Manoel Dias who "lifted his leg and made great wind before the image of the Virgin" in church at vespers, as João da Rosa, who had witnessed the deed, told the Visitor. The climate engendered by the accusations is made more than clear by the story of Baltazar da Lomba, an unmarried homosexual of fifty, known for "sewing, spinning and kneading dough like a woman" and denounced in Paraiba in 1594. As well as the general accusation of committing sodomy with various Indian men, Baltazar was specifically accused by a slave who had seen him "committing the abominable sin with a black man on some grass outside the house". Another accuser told the Inquisition that "in the dark and at an opening in the door, he placed his ear and listened and heard the said Baltazar da Lomba with an Indian with the name of Acauy, twenty years old, and perceived that they were both in a hammock and perceived the hammock scrape and them panting as if they were at the abominable deed and heard from the said Indian some words in his language which meant 'Do you want more?' as at the end of committing the sin and the said Baltazar said then that they should go out to urinate" (*Denunciations of Pernambuco, 1593*). In fact accusations even succeeded in achieving punishment for crimes of omission, as in the case during the Visit of the Inquisition to Pernambuco in 1593, when the youth Mateus paid a fine and public penance for having failed to denounce the blasphemer João Nunes. Another case was that of a certain Pedrálvares who, during the Visit of the Inquisition to Bahia in 1591, was punished, made penitent and publicly flogged for not having denounced his wife, a supposed heretic.

The confessions of the guilty came after the accusations and were aided by so-called bailiffs, people contracted by the Tribunal for the specific purpose of gathering information and uncovering suspects. For the interrogations the Inquisitors used prepared lists with 71 types of crimes, into which 200 types of defendant could be placed. The accused and condemned belonged to every social stratum as well as the most diverse occupations. There were governors, doctors, poets, lawyers, chemists, great and petty merchants, soldiers, mill-owners, miners, labourers, artisans and many priests as well as slaves, Indians, women and others considered second-class citizens. As for the crimes, the Inquisitors' greatest preoccupation was with those concerning the Catholic faith. Apart from the Protestant Reformation and related heresies, which the Church jealously opposed with all its spirit of orthodoxy, there was also the danger of Jewish practices. In Spain and Portugal a large number of Jews had been obliged to convert to Catholicism (the so-called New Christians). New Christians were suspected of continuing to profess the Jewish faith in private and therefore merited the Inquisition's special vigilance. As well as crimes against faith, there were those against morality and customs. It seems that these rarely merited the death penalty, although the Ordinances of the Kingdom recommended death at the stake in cases of sodomy. Sentences for moral crimes could certainly be severe, eg. prolonged exile to the Portuguese colonies in Africa or forced labour in the galleys – which was synonymous with death, since few returned alive. Yet although only those convicted of heresy were normally sent to Lisbon by the Inquisition, references exist to Brazilians sentenced there for the "crime of lewdness", as happened to Manuel Pinto de Almeida and Pedro Pais Leme.

The Ludic Sinners

In 1605 the Holy Office visited Rio de Janeiro. It returned to Bahia in 1618, concentrating its activities in Salvador, at that time the colony's capital; the Visit lasted until 1620. In 1646 the Holy Office ordered new enquiries in Bahia, this time without the presence of a special Visitor; the local clergy took his place. It is said that the peak of the Inquisition's persecution in Brazil was in the eighteenth century, but there is still little information available. Inquisitorial trials are also known to have been held in Paraíba, Pará and Maranhão.

Altogether it has to be admitted that the Inquisition was obliged to be more lenient on Brazilian soil; the size of the colony and the instability of a life constantly threatened by innumerable natural dangers reduced social pressures and imposed an atmosphere of greater tolerance. The Inquisition's horrendous dungeons in Europe became ordinary prisons in Brazil, with windows overlooking the street through which prisoners begged alms when there were processions and could even talk to passers-by. Moreover, because punishments did not seem very serious, Brazilian sins were less from heresy than from roguery. It is understandable why Hermilo Borba Filho's Inquisitor, cited at the beginning of the chapter, was so impatient. Paulo Prado, a historian, was surprised at the percentage of sexual offences revealed in the 1591 Visit to Bahia. Of 120 confessions, 45 referred to sexual transgressions, demonstrating "in what atmosphere of dissolution and aberration the inhabitants of the colony lived", practising "sodomy, tribadism and erotic pedophilia, products of the most unrestrained sexual hyperesthesia, only appropriate in large centres of population".[3] In this Visit, sodomy was the second most practised of all crimes, being surpassed only by offences of blasphemy, the latter often displaying a fertile and acid imagination. (Eg. the case of a certain Francisco Pires, who was denounced for having said that if he had to wait at the door of Paradise for as long as he had to wait for the end of his parish priest's sermon, he would prefer not to go to Paradise.) Of the 203 confessed crimes, 37 were for the sexual sin of sodomy, ie. 18% of the total. These included sexual practices between two men, two women or a man and a woman (in the last case specifically anal coitus). The scale of the practice of sodomy in colonial Brazil is revealed by the calculations of the anthropologist Luís Mott, who claims there were 111 sodomites among the 557 accusations and confessions in the Visits to Bahia and Pernambuco in 1591 and 1593 respectively – ie. 21% of the total of committed offences. In the Second Bahian Tribunal (1618-20), 62 penitents (56 men and 6 women) appeared before the Inquisitors and 16 acts of sodomy were confessed. Comparing the confessions in Bahia in 1591 and 1618, a rise in the number of sins of sodomy and blasphemy can be seen, perhaps because society had become freer and social control less efficient. It should also be remembered that the dissolute clergy certainly had little authority to exercise moral vigilance over the population.

The greatest incidence of the abominable sin in confessions and accusations seems to have occurred among whites, perhaps because the Inquisition paid them more attention. As for age, the highest number of cases was in the 13 to 20 age group and the second highest among 21 to 30-year-olds. The youngest of the confessing sodomites was a 16-year-old from Bahia, Bastião Aguiar. He stated that when he was ten or eleven he had slept in the same bed as his brother Antonio Aguiar (a year older) and then "once or twice, alternately, they had sinned with their dishonest virile members, by their back passages, beginning by wanting to penetrate, yet they had not penetrated and he the penitent had not been old enough to achieve pollution" (*Confessions of Bahia, 1591-92*). His brother, Antonio Aguiar, confessed in turn to having had sexual relations with another partner, a mestizo called Marcos, who was between seventeen and eighteen years old and a servant in the house. One night, as all three were sleeping in the same bed, the penitent lying face down, "the mestizo lay over him and placed his dishonest member in the back passage of the penitent, performed in him from behind as with a woman from the front, committing and effecting the sin of sodomy. By the same method he, the penitent, threw the said mestizo onto his belly and he, the penitent, placed himself upon him and behind him, sleeping with him carnally as a man with a woman and this happened to each of them some fifteen or twenty times in the space of a month" (*Confessions of Bahia, 1591-92*).

The oldest of the known penitents was a Portuguese priest called Frutuoso Álvares, who was exiled to Cape Verde (Africa) for "indecent contact" and then to Brazil for repetition of the crime of sodomy. He was then 65, had a white beard and was parish priest of Matoim in Bahia. He confessed to having committed "the vileness of lewd contact with some forty people, more or less, embracing and kissing them" (*Confessions of Bahia 1591-92*). Father Frutuoso Álvares seems to have been a famous pedophile;[4] he confessed that even during his exile in Cape Verde he had committed the abominable sin with two boys. During his exile in Brazil he had had sexual relations with many adolescents aged between twelve and seventeen, being arrested several times and freed from lack of evidence, apart from once having to pay a fine. One of his sexual partners, Jerônimo da Parada, a seventeen-year-old student, confessed to the Inquisitor that on two distinct occasions he had "placed before him his nature together with that of Father Frutuoso Álvares". A few days after this sin, the same Jerônimo reported that the said priest, having come to Salvador, was given hospitality in his grandmother's home "and when they were alone, the said priest said to him that they should do again as they had done at other times and that he, Jerônimo, answered that he did not want to. Then the priest gave him a coin and because he was not content with one coin, he gave him another coin. Then both removed their trousers and lay on the bed and after having done in front as at other times, the said cleric lay with his belly down and said to him, the penitent, that he should put himself on top of him and he did so and slept with the said cleric carnally from behind, committing the sin of sodomy, placing his lewd member in the back passage of the cleric as a man does with a woman by the natural passage in front and this sin was committed having pollution one time only" (*Confessions of Bahia, 1591-92*). Among priests at that time there was also the case of Cônego Bartolomeu de Vasconcelos, who was infatuated by the blacks of Guinea and who was known as a passive homosexual.

The case of Pero Garcia, the owner of a large sugar-mill in Bahia, in the same confessions is especially strange. A married man, it was only at the age of 42 – "overcome by the appetite of the flesh" – that he began homosexual activity, committing the sin of sodomy with four partners, among them a free mulatto and two slaves. It was said that his relationship with Joseph, the mulatto, was so well-known and steadfast that the other servants called Joseph "the master's concubine". Joseph's testimony to the Inquisitor seems to confirm that his relationship with Pero Garcia was a serious affair. "According to his recollection they committed the abominable sin together in the master's bed once or twice at night, after the evening meal, and the other times were in the morning and in the afternoon after lunch, both being in perfect reason and not accustomed to being otherwise" (*Confessions of Bahia, 1591-92*). Pero Garcia also confessed to having sodomised Jacinto, a boy of six or seven years old, once or twice.

As for pedophilia, apart from the already mentioned Father Frutuoso Álvares, João Fernandes, a mestizo of twenty, confessed to having sodomised Bartolomeu Pires, who was thirteen, when they both slept in the same hammock "with shirts and without drawers" (*Confessions of Pernambuco, 1594-95*). And let us not forget Mateus Duarte, a 50-year-old free mulatto who "has been held in prison in Salvador for a year and a half, accused of having committed the abominable sin of sodomy, according to public knowledge, which says that he attacked a white boy of seventeen and that the said boy did not consent and cried out" (*Confessions of Bahia, 1591-93*).

The records of confessions clearly show how much the Inquisitors liked detailed answers with the variations and number of abominable sins committed. Their insistence eventually brought to light some apparently long-standing loving relationships, such as that of the New Christian Diogo Afonso and his lover Fernão (both adolescents), who used to make love "in the fields and on the riverbanks". They attested to having sinned together more than 200 times between 1591 and 1592. There was also the interesting and painful testimony of Antonio Rodrigues. A married man, he appeared twice before the Inquisitor in Pernambuco in 1594, the second time to confess the exact number of times he had had sex with Damião Gonçalves, saying that "it was more than the said twenty times, in a hammock and in the plantation house and in the plantation field". In order that their individual confessions should not contradict each other, Antonio confessed that he had arranged previously with Damiao and also with Domingos Pires – with whom he apparently had a brief relationship – the number of times that they had had sex together. This testimony gives an idea of the climate of anxiety and fear created by the Inquisition, if one considers the manner in which Antonio betrayed the pact with his two friends, beating his breast and crying, after repenting and promising to mend his ways in the presence of the Inquisitor.

The known confessions and denunciations also include numerous cases of lesbianism in colonial Brazil. Filipa de Souza, for example, cited in various reports which prove the diverse number of her lovers, was well-known in Bahia in 1590 for speaking "endearments and loves and lewd words even better than if she had been a ruffian in his lair" and for having burst into a convent. Among those she boasted of having had affairs with were Paula Antunes, Maria Pinheira, Maria de Peralto and Paula de Siqueira, some of whom were also heard by the Inquisition. There was also Guiomar Pinheira, a 38-year-old mestiza who, also in 1591, told how she had been raped while still an adolescent by Isabel Dias in Oporto (Portugal), where, she said, young girls used to play sexual games together. Luiza Roiz was also well-known at the time, for she liked to importune the black slave women in Salvador, Bahia.

Obviously, and judging from the facts reported in Inquisitorial documents, homosexuals were also to be found among the local aristocracy. Captain Martim Carvalho, for example, Income Treasurer of Bahia around 1590, had a young male lover who accompanied him on journeys into the interior. The affair between the two became so public and scandalous that the captain, after a hearing before the Inquisitor, was sent to Portugal where he must have been severely punished. There was also a certain João Queixada, who lived in the house of the Governor of Bahia and who confessed that he used to copulate with the pages of the Cathedral Dean while still living in Lisbon. The most notable case among the Bahian aristocracy, however, was that of Diogo Botelho who, according to an ex-lover's testimony, was "sometimes active, sometimes passive". Well-known throughout the city as a sodomite, Botelho was Governor of Bahia and First Captain of Brazil between 1602 and 1607. According to Luís Mott, the anthropologist, he built the famous Fort of São Marcelo, a jewel of colonial baroque architecture which can still be seen in the Bay of All Saints facing the city of Salvador.

Although Indians appear very seldom in the Inquisitorial Confessions, there are some cases, such as that of Joane, who lived on the island of Maré in Bahia in 1590 and who was accused of *tivira* (or *tibira*). Joane had become very well known as a homosexual; "as well as committing the abominable sin with many others, acting as a female, particularly with the Indian Constantino with whom he lived as if they were man and woman, the said Joane serving as a woman and the said Constantino as a man" (*Denunciations of Bahia, 1591-93*).

Among blacks there were interesting cases such as that of Francisco Manicongo, a cobbler's apprentice known among the slaves as a sodomite for "performing the duty of a female" and for refusing to "wear the men's clothes which his master gave him". Francisco's accuser added "that in Angola and the Congo, in which lands he had wandered much and of which he had much experience, it is customary among the pagan negroes to wear a loincloth with the ends in front which leave an opening in the rear... this custom being adopted by those sodomitic negros who serve as passive women in the abominable sin. These passives are called *jimbandaa* in the language of Angola and the Congo, which means passive sodomite." The accuser claimed to have seen Francisco Manicongo "wearing a loin-cloth such as passive sodomites wear in his land of the Congo and he immediately rebuked him" (*Denunciations of Bahia, 1591-93*).

Being slaves, blacks obviously ran the risk of being exploited by their masters, men as much as women. Inquisitorial records report innumerable examples of a markedly sadomasochistic tenor in sexual relations between master and slave. In Bahia in 1590 Felipe Tomás, a Portuguese Jew, was accused of having fled Pernambuco after the death of "a boy, his servant, whom he killed for they had both been accused of committing the abominable sin of sodomy". Felipe was also accused by his slave Francisco, who had escaped from the house in order not to be assaulted by his master, "who would order him to be in shirt and without trousers while he was writing at night". Also in Bahia at the time Gaspar Rois, thirty years old and foreman of the mill at Pirajá, was accused of having committed "the abominable sin with Matias, aged twenty-five, his black native from Guinea with whom he did it several times, attacking him and violating him and for love of him the said negro had fled him". The most striking testimony of rape by a slave-master was reported in the Records of the Holy Office Tribunal in the state of Pará in 1763, where a slave called Joaquim Antonio an unmarried negro of twenty-five or twenty-six, told how he was forced into the sin of sodomy by Francisco Serrão, his master's son:

> On the ground floor of the house in which he lived, at the hour of noon, the penitent was sitting on the stair which led to the upper floor of the said house, when he was called by the said Francisco Serrão to the said ground floor. And he the penitent went to learn what was ordered of him and he made him enter the said room and closing the door and taking the key ordered him to sit on the bed in which he used to sleep. However, the penitent hesitated, which made him take the said penitent and throw him onto the said bed, telling him to put his face on it and stay with his back upwards. Immediately he made him take down his trousers. The penitent at once understood the evil aim the said Francisco Serrão had in these actions, because at that time servants of the said mill had complained that he had assaulted them by the posterior part. Seeing that the door was closed and there was nowhere for him to escape to, fearful of some severe punishment, he agreed to what he wanted. Presently the said Francisco Serrão sought to introduce his vile member into the posterior passage of the penitent with all force. The penitent being unable to tolerate it, he shook him as he could without being able to consummate his depraved desire other than outside the said passage, covering his legs with the semen that he spilt. Once the said action was concluded he told the penitent not to tell any person and gave him four coins, promising that he would give him still more money. And the door being opened for him, the said penitent went out and fled far from him so that, having escaped from the first, a similar or worse peril should not befall him. And the said Francisco Serrão remained in evil humour with him, so that he often had him severely flogged on other pretexts. And having heard from many people that this case belonged to the Holy Office and that it was good to give account of it to discharge his conscience, desiring to discharge his own,

> he presented himself. He added that the same Francisco Serrão was accustomed to committing the sin of sodomy and as such he is held and reported to be among almost all or the greater part of those who are in the service of the said mill. And the following have complained and complain that he has committed and consummated the sin with them, the blacks João Primeiro of the Mixicongo nation, João Valentim of the Mixicongo nation, Garcia of the same nation, all three being unmarried and Domingos José of the same nation, married to the black woman Francisca, and also complain José Domingos, Manoel Bixiga, Florêncio Domingos Antônio, Miguel José, Miguel da Costa, all of the same nation and João de Angola, of the Kingdom of Angola, now married. And while alive the blacks João Gomes, Domingos Beicinho, Afonso and Pedro complained, followed by the youths Florêncio and Antonio, children of the nation of Angola, in the service of the same mill. The complaints of the above-named being repeated among the slaves, the said deceased Manuel Fagundo and Pedro revealed that the sins of sodomy had been committed, for they showed to the informer their rear parts and he saw them swollen in the entry to the passage and spilling blood. The said Pedro was the first to show himself in the said way and then the said Manuel Fagundo and lastly the black Antonio showed himself in the same way and they all complained that the said Francisco Serrão had made swellings and bruises with his member. Among the said slaves at the said mill those who saw and learnt of this vile conduct are certain that it was the cause by which the said blacks João Gomes, Domingos Beicinho, Afonso, Manuel Fagundo and Pedro died, because soon after the said acts and the said swellings they fell so ill that their lives ended. As a result those who remain live with the fear of dying from the same cause. For this reason they flee from the said Francisco Serrão whenever it is possible.

The violence of such relationships was often provoked, even anticipated, by the very fear of being punished, as in the case of the mulatto Fernão Luiz in Bahia in 1590. He, "having committed the abominable sin with a boy from the Islands, in order not to be discovered, killed the said boy and his father and mother with poison which he gave them in a chicken to eat". There were obvious reasons for such fear; numerous individuals were publicly humiliated or censured for sexual perversions. In such cases punishments varied widely. Less harsh penalties included compulsory fasts, special prayers, solitary detention, the wearing of sackcloth and payment of fines. Thus a certain Domingos Pires in Pernambuco in 1593 was condemned as a sodomite but sentenced only to penances of prayer and fasting as well as being required to stay and receive instruction in a monastery for one month. In cases considered more serious there was the sentence of exile to other cities or states in Brazil or to countries in Africa, as well as forced labour in the galleys, the number of years varying according to the degree of guilt. In the same Inquisition in Pernambuco in 1593 a certain Jorge de Souza, aged seventeen, was exiled to Angola for five years, where he received instruction from the Jesuits – all for having committed the sin of sodomy. There was also the case of Marcos Tavares, an unmarried mestizo of twenty-two, in Bahia in 1590. Accused of committing the abominable sin, he was condemned to take part in the Auto-da-Fé barefoot, with a rope round his waist, and be publicly whipped, after which he was exiled from the city for ten years – a penalty considered light because the accused was still young when he committed the crime.

The Penitential Grand Finale

After the defendant had confessed and been interrogated, it was common practice in the Inquisition for the Visitor to prepare the accusation and to hear the defence procurator and the prosecution and defence testimony (which was always secret). If there were doubts during the trial, the Inquisitor could call for torture in order to define the extent of the confession. Only then did the Inquisitorial Tribunal give sentence, which varied according to whether the acused was considered *incompetent* (under age), *contumacious* (absent), *feigned* (pretending to repent), *persuaded* (continuing in error), *false* (confessing only to avoid the penalty), *revocative* (contradicting oneself in the confession) or *relapsed* (recidivist, after having been absolved or reconciled with the Inquisition). The sentences were read out in the Tribunals or in public Autos- da-Fé, which were held in the town square, with or without ceremony, and eagerly attended by the whole population. Imagine yourself in the public square of the town of Olinda in Pernambuco at the reading of the following sentence:

The Visitor of the Holy Office, having seen the documents, declarations of witnesses and the confession made after his arrest, sentences the sodomite Salvador Romeiro, who confessed that he had already been arrested on the Island of São Tomé and sent under guard to Portugal where he rowed in the galleys for having committed the vileness of the sin of idleness [masturbation]. Moreover it is shown that after this the accused committed at many and different times the horrible and abominable crime of sodomy, being sometimes active and sometimes passive, with little fear of God and forgetful of the salvation of his soul. Moreover the accused is proved to be well-known and infamous as a sodomite and committer of such vilenesses, in which case the laws and ordinations of the Kingdom order that, in whichever way it is done, he be burned and turned to dust by fire in order that his body and burial are memory no more and that all his goods be confiscated by the Royal Crown even if he have descendants or ancestors and that sons and descendants be disinherited and infamous as those who commit the crime of lèse-majesté. Regarding, however, the victim with mercy, for which he pleaded, confessing his guilt after arrest with many proofs of repentance, the accused, Salvador Romeiro, is condemned to go to the Auto-da-Fé barefoot, bare-bodied, with uncovered head, with a rope around his wasit and a lit candle in his hand and be publicly whipped through this town and banished to the galleys of the Kingdom for eight years, where he will go on board in the ordinary manner and on which he will serve the Kingdom for the said eight years, rowing without recompense, making penance for these horrible and abominable crimes and he will pay the costs of this trial. Olinda, Captaincy of Pernambuco, 4th August 1594. Heitor Furtado de Mendonça, Visitor.[5]

CHAPTER THREE

Systems of Control and Repression: Our Brave New World

> "Our weed still flourishes everywhere against bars. Let there be scenery and let there be greenery in this cell, and let here the same desire and the same rage burn into gold. Love is ice in flames."
>
> *M. D. Magno* (1978)

As the driving force behind the ideas of patriotic tradition and the trustees of covenants with western civilisation, the ruling classes in Brazil have seemed very defensive and particularly vulnerable to the spectre of deviant desire. They have become susceptible to homophobic panic to the same extent with which they call for strict observance of moral principles – "which are the soul of nationality", in the words of the Cardinal Primate of Brazil, Dom Avelar Brandão Vilela. In the concept of the ruling class I am including both the growing middle class, who are keen to rise on the social ladder, and the country's intellectuals, who are not only privileged in benefitting from the framework of culture, but who generally also lay the ideological basis for domination of the masses – even when invoking progressive ideas and intentions.

In Brazil it is also these classes who, with more or less subtlety, set out schemes to repress the population sexually. Sometimes erecting a dense wall of theoretical justifications (as do the adherents of psychiatry), sometimes merely disseminating ideas of naturality and normality in homeopathic doses, the ruling classes are linked directly to the activities of the

Inquisition, the Penal Code, Police Regulations and the state censorship which, in the past and present, have all tirelessly persecuted Brazilian homosexuals. To this end, they even make use of distortions in the country's history, retold in accordance with moralistic and prejudiced principles. Thus in 1982 the then Minister of Education and Culture, General Rubem Ludwig, spoke out with President João Figueiredo in announcing a campaign against the escalation of pornography because, he claimed, eroticism has no roots in the cultural traditions of Brazil. As a result sex shops were closed, cinema and television censorship became more strict and bishops from various dioceses organised boycotts of those TV channels which broadcast programmes considered "improper" for Christian homes. Singled out were the innumerable homosexual characters and situations which the permissive boom had brought to the screen – "threatening the emotional integrity of our children", in the words of one indignant viewer.

Unfortunately, oppressive attitudes do not stem only from the notoriously conservative sectors of the country. A recent book on natural medicine (much in fashion nowadays in "advanced" Brazilian circles) labels male homosexuality (lesbianism is not even mentioned) as a curable "psychic or somatic pathology" and gives a long list of the various types of treatment offered by macrobiotics, acupuncture, homeopathy, phytotherapy, shiatsu and hatha yoga, while recommending – in the "special advice" section – that sweet and artificial foods (soft drinks, ice cream, chocolates, chewing gum, sweets, etc.) be avoided so as not to "catch" homosexuality.[1] Another example: during the tense pro-amnesty demonstrations in 1979, a Trotskyist newspaper in São Paulo drew attention to the names of more than 400 of the military dictatorship's torturers. As well as such descriptions as "drug addict", "traitor" and sexual maniac", various of the supposed torturers' names carried the qualification "homosexual", the quite tendentious and sexist implication certainly being to add another bourgeois-decadent attribute.

The Scandal of the "Homosexual Indians"

The consternation which many Brazilian intellectuals feel when faced with homosexuality (fear of the call which they hear within themselves?) blossoms at the periodic "discoveries" of

Brazilian Indians "addicted to pederasty". As well as foreign travellers (as we saw in Chapter One), highly regarded anthropologists and researchers of the present day confirm that homosexual activity occurs as a cultural component of many Brazilian tribes: Darcy Ribeiro among the Cadiuéu, Thomas Gregor among the Mehinaku, Lévi-Strauss among the Nhambiquara, Florestan Fernandes among the Tupinamba, etc. Nevertheless, the belief is still common that the Indians in Brazil contracted homosexuality like influenza and venereal disease, from whites. In 1974, for example, national newspapers and magazines created a scandal when a certain official of FUNAI (the state organisation for Indian matters) was denounced for having perverted Indians of the Kren-Akarore tribe by offering them his backside. Despite verging on the ridiculous, the tenor of the news did not suggest any note of irony, as can be seen from the words of Edilson Martins, a reporter who invoked not only his own experience among the Indians but also the testimony of those well known to be experts on the interior, such as the Villas-Boas brothers, who were "unanimous in confirming the non-existence of homosexuality among our aborigines". According to the same reporter, "this practice has been introduced by civilised elements", who passed on, in addition to homosexuality, alcoholism, tuberculosis, prostitution, "indeed the wellspring of *physiological and social afflictions*" (my emphasis) which Indians inherit on coming into contact with civilisation.[2]

For more information I sought recent and more direct sources. After coming across anthropologists who were made reticent by "such a delicate subject" as indigenous homosexuality, in 1983 I met and interviewed Sérgio Domingues, a philosophy student who works for FUNAI and lives in the north of the state of Goiás among the Kraô Indians in one of their eight villages, each of which has 150 to 250 inhabitants. According to Sérgio, the Kraô are the least warlike and most poetical of the Timbira cultural sub-group to which they belong. They are sensitive and affectionate even in front of strangers; they cultivate cordiality and the spoken word and dislike bravery, which for them is a negative personality trait. The shaman or witch-doctor – whose delicate mannerisms are also to be seen in such tribes as the Canela, Guarani and Bororo, of the same cultural family – is almost indistinguishable from the other Indians, due to the delicate nature of the whole tribe. In the village the men indiscriminately wear shorts or go naked;

the women used to wear a miniscule grass skirt but now prefer to tie a cloth round their waist. The whites who live there are prohibited by FUNAI from going naked among the Indians.

Sérgio claims almost never to have seen any special friendship between men and women; in any case this fondness is not as great as the affection – which is indeed very common – which men have for each other. Single men all sleep together in the open air in the masculine area of the village, the *kó* (central patio), where women fear to enter except at times of celebration. On the other hand, the men do not generally enter the female area, the *ikré* (house), except after marriage. It is in the *kó* that the men meet twice a day – before leaving for the hunt and on return – to plan the community's activities. At these meetings groups of men pile up, with heads resting on the chest or shoulders of others. It is also common for two youths to sit very closely together, with the one behind embracing the waist of the one in front. Hours are spent combing each other's hair and they also like to caress each other's genitals. In daily life in the village it is common to see two youths walking hand in hand without there being any specifically erotic connotation. Nevertheless, there is much sexual intercourse at any hour of the day or night – men with men as much as men with women. Single men of between fifteen and twenty are especially active in the former. Sérgio also states that at night he was often woken by the sounds of unmarried men groping each other in the *kó*, where they sleep clutching and embracing each other. When they wish to have sex, the youths prefer to go into the forest.* Sérgio became the friend of a handsome Kraô of fifteen who tirelessly and with explicit gestures invited him to "make *cunin*" – "I put it in your backside and then you put it in mine." This boy like to walk hand in hand with Sérgio and was the one who introduced him to the tribe's ritual dances. He once interrupted a Portuguese lesson which Sérgio was giving the young boys and, in public, displayed his erect penis and invited him once more to make *cunin*, while he and the other Indians laughed in amusement. Another time he went to the hammock

*Sérgio relates that it is the custom of the Mehinaku (also part of the Timbira family) to prepare areas of the forest as love-nests. He was once walking in the forest with an old Mehinaku when they stopped to rest in a hut. Before settling down, the old man cleaned the area and explained, quite normally, that it was the place where *mentuaiê* (unmarried men) came to "make *cunin*" (have sex) with each other.

where Sérgio slept at night and made the same invitation. But when he put his arm over the shoulder of a FUNAI driver, he was thrown off. "This isn't the time for a man to embrace me," the white man retorted, irritated.

There was another Indian male in the village, who was twenty and who cooked and took part in all the women's social life. He sometimes wore the same cloth round his waist as the women and he liked to help in the painting of the men's bodies – a predominantly feminine task. The FUNAI officials called him the "gay Indian", but Sérgio says that he did not have any more sex with men than the others in the tribe. Moreover, he did not suffer any discrimination in the village on account of his strange habits. The Indians, indeed, did not seem to place great importance on such a difference, even when it occurred outside their circle. Thus the head of a FUNAI office near the village was known to be gay and often mocked by his colleagues, but the Indians considered him a white man on a par with the others. If they were not very deferential to him, it was because he was an official of the federal government, for which Indians generally have little sympathy. This demonstrates how sexual roles among the Kraô are only relatively rigid. For example, it is not uncommon for men to wear round their waist the cloth characteristic of women; this is often done playfully, to imitate women and laugh. Nor is sexual intercourse between men exclusive to the unmarried. Sérgio was once driving with a group of Indians. Since they had to spend the night on the road they all slept together in the back of the truck. That night he felt an erect penis rubbing against his back; it was a married Indian insistently inviting him to make *cunin* and bodly pushing his penis between Sérgio's thighs. When Sérgio said that he was tired, the Indian gave a deep laugh, turned on his side and went to sleep. However, Sérgio almost never received overtures from men when he was accompanied by his wife, an anthropologist who would sometimes visit him in the village.

Insofar as he could tell, Sérgio had the impression that the women did not demonstrate as much affection among themselves as did the men, perhaps because they only met together in the fields and their social life focussed on the children and work. In Kraô mythology it was a goddess who originated agriculture and so while men hunt, women plant and gather. This work is directly linked to the feeding of children, also a primordially female task. Yet even if the women's function is fundamentally reproductive, for that very reason their role is very important to the Kraô, for whom it is inconceivable not to have children. Generally they have many offspring. When Sérgio arrived at the village with his wife, the Indians were persistent in asking about their children and were amazed that they did not have any. Furthermore, it is for reasons of fertility that married women do not have exclusive sexual partners; during pregnancy they often have intercourse with several men, for it is believed that the child is the result of an accumulation of sperm in the womb – which is why children called various Indians "father".

Sexuality does not seem to be restricted to the very narrow functions among the Kraô. By occupying a very important ludic area, it oscillates between desire and pure play. This even distinguishes them from other tribes of the Timbira sub-group, such as the pragmatic Xavante, who usually prepare one boy from a young age to take on the sexual and social functions granted to women. As an adult this Indian accompanies the other men on distant warrior and hunting expeditions and fulfils all the tasks performed by women, whose presence there is not allowed. Because of his importance on such occasions, he enjoys great prestige among the tribe.

The above information comes from a white man who declares himself a contented heterosexual. I think it constitutes an adequate response to those whites who, even when admitting they are opposed to ethnocentricity, deny the indigenous cultures the possibility of including forms of affective-sexual relationships looked down on or gratuitously condemned by Western civilisation.

From Sodomy to Tacit Silence

When someone becomes aware of the different call of their desire, they generally have to overcome centuries of repression to arrive at the epicentre of their self. When I meet closeted gays, especially the extremely defensive ones who abound in the intelligentsia, I think that their secrecy is perhaps the result of a secular terror rooted in something like the collective subconscious. It is not absurd to imagine that innumerable, repeated and violent prohibitions on deviant sexuality have perhaps instilled in homosexual desire an archetypal panic, almost at heartbeat level. In the case of Brazil, this began with the Western inheritance from 1500 onwards. Although not restricted to homosexuals, the crime of sodomy was generally associated with love between individuals of the same sex, as indicated in the so-called Ordinances of the Kingdom of Portugal, in whose books all Portuguese laws, from the Constitution to the Civil and Penal Codes, were compiled from the time of the Renaissance. The Ordinances were always composed of five books, the last of which was a compilation of the classifications which define crimes, penalties and guidelines for judicial proceedings. It is important to point out that in "matters which involve sin" and caused disagreement among the lawyers, the Ordinances ordered recourse to Roman and Canon law, which demonstrates the importance tradition and the Catholic religion had in the matter of legislation. To give an idea of their severity, they determined that "whoever denies God and His Mother will have his tongue pulled from his throat and be burnt", a punishment also imposed for the crime of treason to the Crown.

The oldest of these various compilations were the Afonsine Ordinances, proclaimed in the reign of Afonso V and published in 1446. Their source was Roman and Canon law as well as the "Book of Laws and Dispositions", which collected the medieval laws of the territories which later came to constitute Portugal. It already (Book V, Section 17) listed the penalty of burning for sodomy – "of all sins the most vile, unclean and foul" and the cause whereby "God set the Flood upon the earth". The Manueline Ordinances (published in 1521 in the reign of Dom Manuel) and the Philipine Ordinances (petitioned by Philip I but only published in 1603 in the following reign) were based on the Afonsine Ordinances, but reformulated and brought up to date.

The Manueline Ordinances, in force in Portugal at the time of the Discovery, were the oldest Penal Code applied in Brazil. They placed sodomy on the same level as lèse-majesté. As well as burning at the stake, the confiscation of the condemned man's goods and infamy on his children and descendants were added to the punishment. The Philipine Ordinances, however, had a greater importance, for they were in force for more than two hundred years and continued to be so after independence, being adapted and brought up to date in 1823 for the Imperial Constitution. Chapter XIII dealt with persons "who commit the crime of sodomy and with beasts". "Any person, of any rank, who in any way commits the sin of sodomy, shall be burnt and made dust by the fire so that his body and burial never have memory and all his goods shall be confiscated by the Crown of our Kingdom, even if he have descendants, in which case his children and grandchildren shall be unworthy and infamous as the children of those who commit the crime of lèse-majesté." Unlike the earlier Ordinances, women were no longer excluded from the law, "for some commit the sin against nature with others and in the manner with which we have spoken of men". As a further innovation the Philipine Ordinances proclaimed that in those cases where individuals of the same sex only masturbated each other, the penalty would be exile to the galleys. According to the law, whoever knew and did not denounce a sodomite would lose all his belongings and suffer perpetual exile from the Kingdom. On the other hand, the person who denounced a suspected sodomite had the right, if the crime was proved, to receive half of the criminal's belongings; if he owned nothing, the Crown itself would reward the accuser with 100 cruzados. To allow witnesses to speak freely before the Tribunal, it was guaranteed that their names would be held in secret in the records. In addition the accuser could opt to make his denunciation in public or in private.

As for the accused, the law allowed for the possibility of torture to make him denounce other suspected sodomites. As in the case of crimes of lèse-majesté, counterfeiting and witchcraft, punishment for sodomy was not susceptible to mitigation or mercy, even if the criminal was a noble or official of the Crown – positions which generally conferred immunity or privileges when other crimes were concerned. In the Philipine Code there was also a penalty for men who appeared "in women's garb" and for women "in men's garb", as for all who used make-up "except for festivals and games". In this last case the penalties varied from public whipping to three years of exile as well as a fine which the accused had to pay to the person who had denounced them before the law.

There were also ecclesiastical statutes in colonial Brazil, distinct equally from the Inquisition and from secular justice. They considered sodomy a crime and "heinous sin, detestable and horrible, provoking the wrath of God and execrable even to the Devil himself". Thus in 1707 the Statutes of the Archbishopric of Bahia (then the capital) proclaimed in its paragraph 939 that "the man who dresses in women's clothes will pay 100 cruzados and will be arbitrarily exiled from the Archbishopric in accordance to the scandal he gives and the effects which result".[3]

The Imperial Constitution, proclaimed shortly after independence, generally brought the Philipine Ordinances up to date. However, a new Criminal Code was prepared and ratified in 1830. Influenced by Jeremy Bentham and the Napoleonic (1810) and Neapolitan (1819) Codes, this Penal Code assimilated all the most advanced criminal legislation of the time. Unlike such countries as Great Britain, the United States, Germany, Austria, etc., in Brazil the juridical expression of sodomy (or its equivalent) disappeared from legislation. This Code seems to have been so important that it strongly influenced the Spanish Penal Code and thereby the Codes of many Latin American countries. This was all, of course, an echo of the French Revolution which, paradoxically, came to fruit in a tropical Empire – a contradiction which is certainly not surprising given the absurd patchwork quilt that Brazil has always been. However, crimes "offending morality and good custom", when practised in public, did come up in the Imperial Code. Without being explicitly mentioned, homosexuality was to be classified (in practice or in theory) under this very vaguely worded infraction from that moment on. Indeed, in Brazilian legislation this subject seems to have been considered so unwholesome that it has been surrounded by tacit silence – a typical situation in provincial societies where not even public opinion exists. As a result, matters of this nature easily end up in the hands of the police. Furthermore, in the Imperial Code crimes against morals and good custom were to be found in the section of "Police Crimes" and were at that time punishable with ten to forty days' imprisonment and a fine corresponding to half of the time. This Code also stated that minors under fourteen could not be held criminally responsible; culprits up to the age of seventeen were to be placed in special correction houses. In addition, those under twenty-one who committed a crime were given a reduced sentence because of their age. As can be seen, although there was an age of majority, it was very fluid. As for the corruption of minors, the idea (but not the concept) is apparent in cases of rape or seduction (with carnal coitus) of an "honest women" of less than seventeen years. Still further, the criminal would receive no punishment if he married the victim, her honour thereby being saved.

In the Republican Penal Code of 1890 the same juridical expression still appeared, but was now "crime against the security and honesty of the family" or "assault on modesty". The prescribed penalty was raised to between one and six years in prison in the case of sexual violence, including the so-called corruption of minors. It was apparently the first time that the juridical expression "under-age minor" was explicitly mentioned and rigorously defined. In the case of a simple and public "obscene act or gesture assaulting propriety" the penalty was also more severe than in the Imperial Code, varying from one to six months in prison. The punishment (from 15 to 60 days) for those who cross-dressed, wearing "clothes inappropriate to their sex" and "in public in order to deceive" was maintained in the Republican Penal Code. When the Code was reformed in 1932, prohibition of circulation on national territory of leaflets, books, magazines, newspapers, engravings, etc. which offended public morals was added to the chapter on "assault on modesty". The prescribed penalty was relatively harsh – from six months to two years' imprisonment as well as a fine and loss of the object where the offence occured (which meant, in practice, that publications could be seized on a judge's orders). In the following Penal Code (proclaimed in 1940 and still in force) the crime of assault on modesty was maintained for when the obscene act took place in public or the obscene object was exposed to the public – which included cinematic, phonographic or theatrical performances, with six months to two years' imprisonment or payment of the corresponding fine. The crime of corruption of minors (from fourteen to eighteen) was also kept, with a penalty of one to four years in prison.

The Birth of the Hygienic State

The system which modernises is also the system which sophisticates its control. If lawyers at least appeared to be leaving the foreground, their place did not remain unoccupied. With the advent of pragmatic, liberal and positivist doctrines associated with the French and American Revolutions on the one hand and the Industrial Revolution on the other, new spokesmen arrived with the snares of a more subtle and more scientific power. Hygienists were the first agents to specialise in this form of control – which was rigorously divided into categories – followed by medical lawyers and psychiatrists, as will be seen.

Since the 1830s the liberal and civilising state had been aware of the high rate of infant mortality and the appalling sanitary conditions in the partiarchal households of Brazil. From the idea that the fatherland (recently inaugurated by independence) needed healthier children, the conviction arose that the old patriarchal family was incapable of protecting its members' lives. This household thus had to be modernised and supplied with scientific prescriptions and more efficient health and educational care, for, as Dr Joaquim Pedro de Mello said in 1846, "in no manner can society refrain from demanding that parents respect their offspring's future, directing it according to the precepts required by the sound principles of rational hygiene".[4] But if the liberal state's first aim was to prepare the families of the ruling classes for new times, the rest of the population was not free from interference. As the state strengthened its influence on society, the less favoured classes were gradually being hygienised by campaigns of moralisation and collective hygiene as well as philanthropic assistance. This all helped to maintain the social pact and, with it, the normalising influence of the family unit – which constituted the basic nucleus of the bourgeois state emerging in Brazil.

It was through hygiene specialists that the state trespassed on family life. With free passage to this area formerly impenetrable to science, the medical hygienist could impose his authority on several levels. The citizen's emotions and sexuality, as well as his/her body, came to suffer interference from this specialist whose hygienic standards were intended to improve the race and thus make the fatherland great. From the idea of a healthy body, faithful to the ideals of the racial superiority of the white bourgeoisie, the imposition of a hygienised sexuality created rigorous models of moral conduct within the family. In this sense marriage was restructured and its legitimacy augmented by the sexual pleasure which was the right of the couple within the bounds of a strictly conjugal sexuality. The objective was a greater cohesion of married couples and a perfection of legal matrimony – which granted "the safest guarantees for moral and physical life". As a corollary, the standards of reproduction would be improved, since attacking extra-conjugal sex was one way of reducing the high incidence of venereal disease in the old patriarchal family.

The idea of the "fatherland" was, of course, at the centre of these justifications. The improvement of the reproductive standard was a guarantee of better children for the fatherland; thus it would not be an exaggeration to say that the right to orgasm really became a civic obligation. As this patriotic pragmatism became effective in the middle of the nineteenth century, sexual roles became clearly limited, with masculinity and femininity identified with paternity and maternity respectively. Whatever found itself outside these regulatory standards was abnormal. From this point on, doctors of the time were insistent in their condemnation of celibates, libertines and homosexuals, all held to be irresponsible citizens and opponents of social and biological well-being in that they deserted the supreme role of man-the-father. The libertine was reproached for exposing himself to venereal disease, the cause of physical and moral ills in the social sphere as much as the domestic. According to Dr Macedo Júnior (1869), promiscuity provoked "weak fevers, fainting fits, paralysis, apoplexies, convulsions, dementia, gout and all the diseases which Pinel classified under the five orders of neuroses", as a result of the "excessive losses of semen".[5] Meanwhile, the bachelor's dissolute morals and lack of discipline made him more susceptible to insanity and a shorter lifespan than married men. Fonseca Viana, a hygienist, wrote in a thesis in 1842, "the isolated life and the burden of vexations without a companion to console and mitigate sorrows almost always engender hypochondria, tuberculosis and many other maladies".[6] If being a bad father (like the libertine) or refusing to be a father (like the bachelor) constituted serious failings in the hygienic code, then it was even more serious to refuse a man's "natural" vocation, as in the case of a sodomite or *bagaxa* – prostitute.

Perhaps as a legacy of the not very remote period when the immoral content of – "this subject" prevented it from being dealt with in public,[7] the treatment of such deviants was only indirectly referred to, and linked above all to upbringing in infancy. For educational purposes, medical hygiene drew preventive measures from pederasty, which it presented as a warning and negative example. As a result it was easier to take charge of infancy and impose a scientifically programmed upbringing whereby small boys had to apply themselves to physical exercises in order to avoid effeminacy, and learn to love work so as to avoid a dangerous moral indolence. Pederasty was also used as a kind of shock treatment for adult sexuality: men either obeyed the precepts of hygiene or lost their masculinty, as could be proved by the pederast's "execrable appearance". This reinforced medical control and, automatically, the role of the hygienist, who thus profited doubly from the anathematisation of the sodomite.

Hygienic ideology, therefore, was a step forward from the methods of the Inquisition, whose control had been relative.

The aim was now to exercise control in the name of science, which presided over everything with an aura of neutrality. Although the hygienic-bourgeois model contributed to the eradication of the bestial punishments of the colonial period, it had its price in that it helped to create a self-oppressed, intolerant and well-behaved citizen, entirely at the disposition of the state and fatherland. The new order ushered in by hygienic normalisation used the doctrine of science to exercise a therapeutic control as a substitute for the old religious control. In progressively distancing itself from the world of law (secular or religious), hygienist ideology set its references in the land of the norm. Citizens now owed allegiance less to God than to the doctor and, instead of Christian dogma, the standard of normality reigned. It was through this breach that psychiatry could enter and refine scientific control over people of deviant sexual practice.

Enter Homosexuality

Wide experience with madness throughout the nineteenth century had already given psychiatry sufficient know-how to classify deviations from the norm no longer as crimes but as illnesses. As a sick person, therefore, the pederast was not to blame for his transgression. From the legal point of view, this came to mean that the pederast could not be punished, which was to have unforeseeable consequences. For its part, in seeking psychiatric assessment, the law granted legitimacy to and made neccessary psychiatric custody, using as a bridge legal medicine, which also sought to impose itself with a scientific statute. The insane and minors were already considered "irresponsible" under the Imperial Penal code (Articles 10, 11, 12, 13), it being left to the judge to decide whether or not they should be placed in "houses destined for them".

Following the European example, scientific attacks on "sexual perversions" began to abound in Brazil from the middle of the nineteenth century. Initially to their distaste, sectors of medicine and the law came to admit the existence of "sexual acts against nature" – *nefanda Venus* in the language of Roman law, still used by specialists of the time. In a book published in 1894, José Viveiros de Castro, a lawyer specialising in criminal law, used psychiatric concepts to present historical facts on "sexual inversion" from ancient history to his own day. He warned that "there has been a great development of pederasty among us", adding that even "anal onanism with women, anti-natural coitus, is becoming a habit with those youths who represent here *le monde qui s'amuse*".[8] He then referred to "more than one notable Empire politician", who were accused of being "some active, others passive" in this vice. Without naming him, Viveiros de Castro cited a certain politician well-known for appearing in public with his lovers, for whom he arranged good posts, granted large allowances and, more than once, helped to marry. In deliberately neutral tones, Viveiros de Castro alluded to the great moral and political qualities of this man who had been nominated state governor but whose name had been vetoed in a three-cornered list for senator, where he competed with "two nonentities".

To make these analyses viable, a rigorously scientific definition was necessary. It was then that the clinical figure of the "homosexual" arose, a term originally coined in 1869 in Germany by Dr Karol M. Kertbeny, and since then widely used by science, Brazil included. The inauguration of homosexuality as a scientific category was intended to result in more rigorous and less subjective specifications. In the words of Leonídio Ribeiro, a medico-legal expert, it "then came to be studied in the light of science, where it was verified that the subject was an anomaly characterised by a preference, from the sexual point of view (. . .) which an individual manifested in an active, passive or mixed manner for another individual of the same sex".[9] So defined, "the practices of sexual inversion could not continue to be considered haphazardly as a sin, vice or crime, since it had been demonstrated that, in the majority of cases, it concerned sick or abnormal individuals who should not be punished, since they lacked, above all, treatment". After releasing the insane from prison, medicine would also help "these poor individuals, many of whom are victims of their perversions and anomalies".[10] This point of view was shared by Dr Viveiros de Castro, who based his arguments on European authors and concluded that the law should only punish those pederasts who were debauched and addicted, particularly when they corrupted minors; "but when it is a case of uranism, ie. an individual stricken with congenital or psychic inversion, punishment would be truly cruel, because they cannot escape these inclinations, which are integral elements of their personality".[11] Thus methods change, but not the specialists who define illnesses and prescribe treatments.

According to Viveiros de Castro, the causes of the homosexual anomaly could be "erotic madness" resulting from sexual psychopathies in mentally alienated individuals, hereditary defects in glandular development, unhealthy living, alcoholism or excessive onanism, or circumstances favourable to acquisition of the vice such as prison, age or impotence. He claimed that homosexuals suffered from a psychic alteration called "effeminisation", which was characterised by the following behaviour:

> Like women they have a passion for the *toilette*, ornaments, ostentatious colours, lace, and perfumes. (...) They depilate themselves carefully. (...) They give themselves feminine names – Maintenon, Princess Salome, Foedora, Adriana Lecouvrer, Cora Pearl, etc. They are capricious, envious, vindictive. (...) They go quickly from ferocious egotism to tearful sensitivity. Their endowment is falsehood, accusation, cowardice, obliteration of moral sense. The anonymous letter is the most exact expression of their courage. They do not enter professions which require manly qualities, but prefer to be tailors, dressmakers, launderers, starchers, hairdressers, florists, etc. (...) Their jealousy is a mixture of endangered sensuality and wounded *amour propre*. Cases have been told of pederasts who, in attacks of jealous rage, have torn with their teeth their companion's belly or ripped the skin from his scrotum and member.[12]

Lesbians, which he called "tribades", were classified by Dr Viveiros as congenital and addicted madwomen. As causes in the development of "tribadism", he pointed to disgust provoked by the sexual aberrations that a man demanded of his partner, life in boarding-schools, modern literature and modern education, "which brought women out of the silent half-light of the fireplace into the tumultuous upheavals of the world, opening up unknown horizons, initiating them into the secrets of vice and awakening indiscreet curiosity".[13] Furthermore, he claimed that "when the addiction is of long duration, its cure is almost impossible, because the nerves in the genital parts have become hyperesthetised and the pleasure experienced far exceeds that granted by the embraces of natural love".[14]

After 1930, the formation of a group of medical lawyers headed by Leonidio Ribeiro led to methods of identifying criminals based on the fascist theories of Lombroso, an Italian, and the results of training at the Polizei-Institut of the Third Reich in Berlin, being imposed on Brazil. Along with criminals, the insane and prostitutes, homosexuals were meticulously studied, even the photographs taken when they were arrested. In 1935, for example, a team headed by Leonidio Ribeiro studied the morphological constitution of 184 homosexuals in the Anthropology Laboratory of the Institute of Identification in Rio de Janeiro. For his work in the field of criminal anthropology, Leonidio Ribeiro was awarded the Lombroso Prize in Italy and the results of these experiments with homosexuals were published in the pages of an Italian specialist magazine edited by Lombroso's disciples. Keen to detect endocrinologically so-called "signs of intersexuality", many researchers believed that male homosexuals had predominantly female pubic hair, pelvis and waistline, as well as an excessive development of the buttocks and lack of hairs on the thorax. But they stumbled over the discovery in gay men of an "exaggerated development of the penis, which we do not know whether to attribute to ethnological reasons or also to endocrinous imbalances".[15] Dissatisfied, the specialists went further in search of more direct evidence, such as relaxation of the sphincter, lack of folds or diffuse folds in the anus, the presence of ulcers, fissures and hemorrhoids. However, the brilliant conclusion to the investigation of the equally famous medical lawyer Afrânio Peixoto claimed that the only indications of pederasty that could be effectively proved, apart from blennorrheas and rectal cancers, were the "epidermic results of irritative friction" such as hard skin, carbuncles and condylomas, "common in passive pederasts".[16]

This same obsession with identifying the pervert and his perversion led doctors to encroach boldly on such thin ice as that of artistic creation. Insofar as art was considered *morbigenous* ("capable of making healthy people sick"), it was necessary to unmask it, from a psychiatric point of view, to counter its effects. Thus in 1926 there appeared a psychopathological study on the life and work of the writer João do Rio, who had died in 1921 and had been well-known as homosexual. Written in the most authentic parnassian style by Inaldo de Lira Neves-Manta, a psychiatrist (who also defined himself as a psychoanalyst), the book claimed to prove the strange theory that the pages of great beauty produced by João do Rio were the result of the excessive sensibility with which "sexual inversion" had endowed the writer. For that reason

Neves-Manta gave a positive answer to the question: was João do Rio's work not "the result of a hallucinatory state"? That was nothing unusual, for, according to the author, the work of many extraordinary writers, from Goethe to Wilde, was believed to have been engendered in such states. João do Rio's traits, both physiological ("a neurarthritic with all the complications that entails") and psychological ("he was really a mass of united dysgeneses and sublimated degenerations") were then dissected in detail and it was argued that "he suffered the consequences of glandular malfunction and a hyperthyroidal constitution". Since, according to Neves-Manta, "the individual is as healthy as his endocrine system", both João do Rio's "sexual neurosis" and his art were the result of poor glandular performance.

The final conclusion, although not surprising for specialists of the time, is astonishing in its audacity: neither free will nor artistic creativity really exist, since both are determined at random by glandular or psychic dysfunction. In the end, Neves-Manta asks with poorly concealed arrogance, "what responsibility falls to the strong (...) handsome, welcoming palm tree if it is born crooked?"[17]

On Course for the Judicial Asylum

If it is true that in Brazil the attacks of psychiatry on homosexuals have never resulted in the creation of institutions, this does not mean that, since the 1920s, the suggestions of a growing psychiatrisation of homosexuality have not been periodically repeated by the country's medico-police authorities whose concern is the defence of the "healthy society". In a thesis in 1926 on sexual perversions, Viriato Fernandes Nunes, a medical lawyer, admitted that if "the psychic functions of these criminals [pederasts] have been disturbed" that was no reason for society to allow them "a freedom from which they may profit to commit new crimes".[18] Consequently, it is not right – Aldo Sinisgalli, another medical lawyer, added – that society "remain exposed to the reactions of their morbid tendencies," since homosexuality signified "the destruction of society, the weakening of countries". If it "were the rule, the world would soon come to an end".[19] Thus society must use means of repression which, while not slipping into the excesses of the past, "safely prevent the repetition of these crimes", considering "scientific norms very different from that primitive empiricism", according to the same Dr Nunes. In the words of Leonídio Ribeiro, here is "another social problem to be resolved by medicine".[20] As sick people "are *irresponsible because of their illness,* it would be unjust, incoherent and absurd to apply punishments," reiterated Aldo Sinisgalli. (My emphasis.) Thus Afrânio Peixoto categorically insisted that "instead of anathematising and pouring brimstone and sulphur over the Sodom and Gomorrah of unnatural vices, it would be more intelligent, having understood this error, to try and correct it".[21]

In such a case, how should modern society protect itself? Through specialists, Sinisgalli said. "For inverts, treatment; that is what they need. Let the doctor and educator be charged with the cure of organic and psychic ills *since these ills lie within their competence.*"[22] (My emphasis.) How to treat homosexuals? Suggestions followed various tacks. Above all prevention through an education which fortified character and taught respect for society. If the illness was a proven fact, there had to be recourse to endocrinology for the use of "organotherapeutic extracts", ie. applying the essences of various animal organs to the human organism in order to correct the glandular malfunction. Unfortunately, however, Aldo Sinisgalli claimed that pederasty "is a plague which strikes everywhere" and at all times, "thriving despite everything and everyone." Thus many specialists discussed more drastic methods, since simply leaving perverts at liberty "would be even more outrageous", in the words of Fernandes Nunes. Put them in psychiatric hospitals? No, because there would be the risk of their vices being transferred to the other patients. Lock them up in prison? Also no, because that would prevent doctors from treating them. And so Dr Nunes himself proposed, in the 1920s, the establishment of an institution whose sole purpose would be the confinement of homosexuals, "guaranteeing society the security of their seclusion and giving the criminal the medical help that he needs".

Such a suggestion, which still has its adherents in the Brazilian system of criminal psychiatry, was repeated and developed towards the end of the 1930s by Aldo Sinisgalli, who was thinking of an institute similar to the Judicial Asylum then in existence, but devoted exclusively to pederasts. There they would receive medical treatment and re-education by a body of specialised teachers so that the state could "resolve this social problem scientifically and in a humanitarian fashion."[24] The specialists talk very vaguely of the aims of this correctional institution. It would almost certainly be their responsibilty to decide what types of pederasty were criminal and in what conditions it became a "social problem". Sinisgalli made an exception for "honest inverts" who "try to dominate their abnormal instincts and satisfy their abnormal desires in secret"; they did not deserve any punishment, since they were not responsible for their illness.[25] These were obviously the same specialists who would give a definition of a well-behaved pederast.

Disagreeing that homosexuals were merely ill and not morally depraved, other sectors of Brazilian medicine preferred to tighten the screw, as could be seen from the First São Paulo Week of Legal Medicine in 1937. Since a wide reform of the Penal Code was being proposed at the time, various lawyers and doctors present requested that it include "means to punish all practice of homosexuality, no matter what form it might take", as suggested by the chairman, José Soares de Melo, a lawyer. He was seconded by Professor Tavares de Almeida, who simply sought "jail for the pervert and the asylum for the insane".[26] The reformed Penal Code would thus legally prescribe the imprisonment of pederasts considered dangerous to the social fabric. Moreover, according to Soares de Melo, as a security and preventive measure the state could segregate an individual even before he committed a crime, in the same way that an alcoholic and epileptic might be interned as potential criminals. He added, "the same is true of the homosexual, who, being dangerous to state and society, can and should be segregated"; thus "I hope that the Republic's future Penal Code has a clear mechanism to punish the practice of homosexuality".[27] To sum up, punishment would be preventive, before the crime occurred, so that to be homosexual would automatically mean to be criminal.

These ideas seem to have had strong supporters in the thirties. So much so that the Legislative Commission drew up a proposed Penal Code with a chapter specifically on homosexuality, article 258 of which specified that "libidinous acts between members of the male sex will be punished when they cause public sandal, both participants being detained for up to one year". In dealing with abnormals, "the judge may, on medical advice, substitute the penalty with a means of security appropriate to the circumstances".[28] This innovation was not introduced into the new Penal Code of 1940, which is still in force today. This does not mean, however, that the specialists have respected the outcome. In fact many lawyers simply behave as if such modifications had been introduced. Based on the authority of psychiatric findings whose "scientific analyses" discover fascinating pathologies and create unimaginable monsters, judges have much material to justify punitive sentences which scarcely conceal the most archaic prejudices. Yet, since combatting and controlling homosexuality is also a social problem, the interaction of science with the police apparatus is inevitable. Thus in Brazil various systems of control and repression have combined against homosexuality, leaving the dividing line between the intervention of criminal psychiatry and police action tenuous, as will be seen from the following cases.

Febrônio and Chrysóstomo: Outlaws in a Country Without Laws

The cases of Febrônio Índio do Brasil and Roosevelt Antônio Chrysóstomo de Oliveira give an idea of how the manipulation of homosexuality by the criminal psychiatric establishment has evolved. The first began in 1927, the second in 1980, more that fifty years later. Febrônio Índio do Brasil (an enchantingly resonant name, even frankly totemic) was condemned as a "moral lunatic" – a concept which, in the eyes of lawyers and psychiatrists, can cover any violation of the established norm. Blaise Cendrars, a French poet who visited Brazil in the 1920s, interviewed Febrônio in prison, where he found him in solitary confinement and completely naked. Cendrars described him as a mulatto with wavy hair and sad eyes, "small but herculean", very gentle and talkative. These physical traits can be partially confirmed by the photographs of Febrônio to be found in books and archives. Nonetheless, the governor of the jail where he was imprisoned claimed that Febrônio's gynocomasty (excessive development of the masculine mammary glands) and "wide pelvis, suggestive of the feminine type" were Lombrosian signs of his homosexuality and madness. Who was Febrônio? On his arrest in August 1927, charged with the rape and death of a minor, Febrônio – then 32 years old – had already had several run-ins with the police, mostly in his life as a wanderer. After running away from home – his father was a butcher who liked to beat his children – Febrônio taught himself to read. Coming to Rio de Janeiro when he was fourteen, he was arrested for petty theft and sent first to a correction school and then to a house of discipline. In those institutions he acquired the reputation of an insubordinate and read about faith-healing, surgery and dentistry. The others feared him for his powers of witchcraft. Later, in prison, Febrônio read the Bible voraciously. Comparing himself to the prophet Daniel, he began to foretell the future. When free again he travelled throughout the country, opened dental surgeries in various towns from north to south and practised medicine clandestinely in São Paulo and Rio de Janeiro.

On returning to Rio, then the federal capital, he proclaimed himself the prophet of a new religion and called himself the "Prince of Fire". He claimed to hear voices and have terrifying visions where the devil put him to the test and beat him. He began to see a Blonde Lady, who gave him the mission of announcing to the world that God was not dead. To do this Febrônio had to brand himself and ten chosen young men with the cabalistic sign D.C.V.X.V.I. – "a tattoo which is the symbol of the Living God, even when made with violence," he said. He then wrote his gospel, *The Revelations of the Prince of Fire,* a book of 67 pages published in 1925, all the copies of which were burnt by police order. Febrônio also had tattooed on his chest "This is the son of light". After being imprisoned on a charge of murder, the police began to suspect that he had committed innumerable other crimes. Blaise Cendrars, however, saw the question differently. Saying that God had taught him to "prophesy and proclaim Life with the voice of Death", Febrônio was in fact revealing his roots in African and indigenous witchcraft. The murders – if he had really committed them – were not acts of madness but authentic ritual sacrifices. For Cendrars, this was Febrônio's attempt to identify with his totem. He did not simply want to spill but to absorb his victims' blood, which was why he drank it and rolled over the corpses, as he claimed. Like most African witch-doctors, he was probably from the Buffalo clan, to which blacksmiths, judges, surgeons and butchers also belonged. His surgical operations, dental extractions and tattoos were the very path of totemic identification. Which was why, according to Cendrars, white law and science were not equipped to judge Febrônio; instead of seeing him as the first example of a "classic sadist" in Brazil, they simply judged him monstrous and mad, thus losing the opportunity of understanding the mysteries of a typical initiation rite.

The prison governor confirmed that Febrônio would abandon

himself to "the vice of pederasty" in prison. It was said that Febrônio, when free, chose his victims from door-to-door salesmen, news-vendors and shoe-shiners, having also attracted a student at military school, a cabin-boy and a young recruit. Presenting himself as the heir to an immense fortune, he gave them presents, treated them kindly and promised them work. Then he took them into the forest where he had his visions and where he was arrested beside a corpse, naked and with a bloody sword in his hand. It appeared that he read his victims extracts from his gospel there and tattooed them, before penetrating them and beheading or disemboweling them. This did not always happen; according to Álvaro Ferreira, an eighteen-year-old, Febrônio forced him to have anal sex and then, after tattooing him with the sacred letters, let him go. Although he had admitted one of his crimes, Febrônio soon strongly denied the validity of his confession, saying that it had been obtained by torture. To save Febrônio from prison, his lawyer, who had only recently graduated and was only twenty years old, denounced the torture and alleged that his client was mentally ill and should be interned in an asylum and not sentenced to prison. Starting with the idea that sadism and homosexuality were linked and referring to Febrônio's criminal religiosity, the lawyer presented him as a "moral lunatic" no more responsible for his acts than a blind man for his blindness – a very common argument at the time. Febrônio was therefore taken from the hands of Justice and flung into the grip of Psychiatry, to receive the "fairest and most scientific" treatment, in the words of Leonídio Ribeiro, the doyen of Brazilian medical lawyers.

Heitor Carrilho, the expert who studied Febrônio in the Judicial Asylum for a year, referred to his sadistic homosexuality as a case of "constitutional amorality" with instinctive sexual perversions. The conclusion of this report, which was presented to the judge, was that Febrônio was a sick man who was criminally irresponsible, but also highly dangerous. He therefore believed that Febrônio should "remain interned for life for the good of society, in an establishment appropriate for psychopathic criminals".[29] Thus locked away in the Judicial Asylum as a specific character type, Febrônio made insistent and regular efforts to prove not only his innocence by his sanity. In 1933 he wrote directly to the judge of the 6th Criminal Circuit of the Federal District, requesting a new examination by experts. The judge refused, claiming that the director of the asylum would not fail to inform him when "the patient was cured, if that were possible". A year later Febrônio twice made the same petition, once through his two brothers, who assumed all responsibility for his acts and for his continuing treatment in one of their houses. After examination by the same specialist Febrônio was considered as ill as when he was first looked at, so much so that his brothers would not be able "to restrain his anti-social tendencies". Some months later Febrônio's brother Agenor wrote to the judge again, claiming that after eight years of internment in the asylum Febrônio was no longer violent and even let himself be attacked by people weaker than himself. He referred to the fact that his brother had never been formally found guilty and protested dramatically that while the powerful committed errors with impunity, there were "other unhappy people who sometimes commit no kind of crime" but who "die locked up in prison".

The judge did not consider this appeal, claiming that Febrônio himself had written his brother's letter. However, the truth of Agenor's observations (or of Febrônio himself) was confirmed by the inadvertent testimony of Dr José Egon Barros da Cunha, who visited the Judicial Asylum around 1934. Febrônio was brought to be his guide, "a docile degenerate who offers no danger" thanks to the efficacy of the treatment, as the then medical director said. Dressed in a drill suit, with a tie and "scrupulously polished" yellow shoes, Febrônio had become an unpaid prison functionary. While showing the doctor around the establishment, Febrônio told him of the horrendous crimes committed by the other internees, which he claimed were sickening and deserved the death penalty, as if Febrônio himself were not part of that world – which gives an idea of how much he had been tamed.[30] Nevertheless Febrônio escaped in 1935, to be recaptured the following day. In 1936 he filed a writ of habeas corpus, which was refused. He wrote a letter, also signed by his brother, which referred to the "principles of human solidarity, which tie the sacred bonds between Justice and the poor sons of men". He said he was tired after almost ten years' confinement and requested a new psychiatric examination, with the hope of being transferred to a penal colony, where he would have more freedom. A new examination was made by the same specialist, Heitor Carrilho, who confirmed the results of his first findings, adding that Febrônio now had paranoid ideas and believed himself to be an instrument of the gods "for the realisation of reforms and social transformations".[31]

From a dangerous madman, the psychiatric system now transformed Febrônio into a reformer or revolutionary. Nonetheless, he returned to his task some months later with another request for transfer in a letter signed by his brother Agenor. The reply might have contributed to the fact that from then on Febrônio ceased to fight; the judge said firmly that "his place is in the Judicial Asylum, from where he can only be released when science takes the responsibility for his complete cure".[32] Thereafter Febrônio was silent. In the years which followed, medical reports witnessed the decline of a man broken by electro-shock and chemotherapy, until he was transformed into "the relic of the Judicial Asylum", in the words of Dr Ulysses de Carvalho, another specialist. The last medical report on Febrônio was in 1956, thus marking 29 consecutive years of confinement in the same asylum. The two specialists showed that they were moved: "Whether or not he committed a crime is unimportant, the maximum imposed on any criminal has been served; in our country the maximum penalty for any crime is thirty years in prison." Yet in 1982, Peter Fry, an anthropologist, found Febrônio Índio do Brasil still alive at eighty-six in the same Judicial Asylum, where he had been interned for 55 years! According to Fry, he is one of the oldest and longest-held prisoners in Brazil – without ever having been sentenced for the crimes he is said to have committed.

*

Although taking place much later and in a completely different context, the trial of Antônio Chrysóstomo has surprising points in common with that of Febrônio, showing how the psychiatric system, now aided by new and more subtle means of repression, has changed little insofar as homosexuals are concerned. A quite well-known journalist in Brazil, especially as a critic of popular music, Roosevelt Antônio Chrysóstomo was also one of my editorial colleagues on *Lampião*, a monthly gay liberation newspaper published between 1978 and 1981 and labelled by public opinion as the "voice of Brazilian homosexuals" (see Chapter Five). In Rio de Janeiro in February 1979 Chrysóstomo adopted a little girl of three called Claúdia, whose mother was mentally handicapped and who had been begging on the streets. She was always to be seen at the door of the building which housed *Lampião's* editorial offices. A year and a half after the adoption Chrysóstomo's neighbours in his building began a campaign against him. First a woman neighbour and a maid testified before a children's judge that he had maltreated and raped the girl, because when they had given her a bath they had seen that her vagina was "red and swollen". According to Aguinaldo Silva, a journalist, they, with the collusion of people connected with the Communist Party and fellow-travellers, formed a kind of anti-Chrysóstomo committee, whose methods included phone calls to other editors on *Lampião* threatening to involve the newspaper in scandal if Chrysóstomo was not immediately confined in a psychiatric clinic.[33] Shortly afterwards, Claúdia was removed from Chrysóstomo's custody and taken to a branch of the National Foundation for the Welfare of Minors (the state agency responsible for orphans and delinquents), where she lived from then on.

At the request of the judge the girl was examined and legal doctors reported that her hymen was intact. Chrysóstomo was nevertheless indicted, now accused of "maltreatment of a minor" and "use of a minor for criminal purposes". Nor did the campaign cool down. There was anonymous pressure, from the press included, which exploited the case with sensationalism under such headlines as "she was a serving-girl, in the midst of orgies". In an obviously planted story, a quality newspaper in Rio de Janeiro announced that the "rapist" had been arrested. On the day after the false report, Chrysóstomo in fact received a remand order, accused of being a "pedophile, in a city where there are thousands of abandoned children".[34] In his request for remand, the prosecutor had included an issue of *Lampião*, to give "an exact idea of the personality of those who read such a newspaper and, a fortiori, of those responsible for it".[35]

In all this it became clear that Chrysóstomo was causing bad feeling in the building. As well as going through a period of alcoholism, he was openly and proudly homosexual. He used to take boys back to his apartment, where he was living with a lover. Among the accusations heard in court, a woman neighbour reported that there were many parties in Chrysóstomo's flat: "there were never women present (...) because she never heard a woman's voice on those occasions"; from this she concluded that "the climate in which the little girl was living was not proper for her development".[36] A psychologist also gave evidence as the "spokeswoman" for the girl, then four years old. Having interrogated her beforehand, she "translated" the interview into adult language – obviously running the risk of placing her own interpretation on the little girl's short and vague words. Through the mouth of the psychologist Claúdia accused her adopted father of taking off her clothes to touch her and of locking her in her room. A maid recently employed by Chrysóstomo also made some accusations, stating that coming to work one Monday, she had found empty whisky bottles and sperm stains on the floor of the apartment. As a Jehovah's Witness (one of the most conservative and puritanical religions in Brazil), it is questionable if this woman would have been able to distinguish dried sperm stains from chance stains of fat, milk or candle-grease on the carpet. She also said that she had seen Chrysóstomo kissing the girl on the mouth – a not uncommon occurrence in the Brazilian middle class, although still shocking for someone as strongly religious as a Jehovah's Witness. Another neighbour speaking for the prosecution said she had seen a bruise on the girl's head and a cut on her leg, facts which she linked to Claúdia's constant crying to deduce that they were evidence of beating by her adoptive father.

In the middle of the hearing, Chrysóstomo's trial was suddenly made in camera, so that it could no longer be attended by the public, an unusual event in Brazilian law. Examined at length by two state psychiatrists, Chrysóstomo was considered a well-spoken individual who had no mental anomaly, but who displayed "personality problems". As a homosexual, he suffered from paraphilia – repeated sexual activity with a non-consenting or improper partner. According to the report, "given the alcoholism and sexual deviation" present in Chrysóstomo, he had probably taken the girl "as a kind of symbol for activities that were indecent and contrary to morals and good behaviour".[37] After eight months in prison without being found guilty, Chrysóstomo was finally judged and sentenced to two years and eight months' imprisonment (for violent attack on moral decency), plus two months and twenty days (for mistreating a child) and one year preventive imprisonment (for being a social danger). The total sentence was several months higher than the minimum penalty, giving the impression that the aim had been to deliberately prevent Chrysóstomo obtaining remission or parole. Given the irregularities of the trial, such a hypothesis is not absurd. It is enough to say that the judge's sentence was based on the evidence of the neighbour who had first denounced Chrysóstomo. He did not, however, take into consideration the fact that, when called to repeat her accusation months later, the same witness tearfully apologised and embraced Chrysóstomo in public, claiming that she had been pressurised into accusing him by other neighbours who wanted to evict him from the building.

I went to visit Chrysóstomo in Rio de Janeiro. As a journalist, he was serving his sentence in a special prison inside military police barracks, where he had some privileges such as being able to cook in his cell (the prison food was inedible) and receive telephone calls – despite having to live with ex-policemen of the Death Squadron* who were also imprisoned there. The Chrysóstomo I found had aged, particularly from losing several teeth as result of a mouth infection; prison bureaucracy made it difficult for him to see a dentist. He took me to his cell, which he shared with three other men. To reach his bed, he had to walk on boards on the floor, which was flooded by the rain that in some places fell through the roof. The place was like a shanty-hut, with clothes drying on a line, bunks and a few old pieces of furniture.

From there Chrysóstomo was moved to a filthy prison without explanation, not even his lawyers knowing where he was. He was placed in a cell of 50 square metres with 62 other prisoners who paddled in the water which drained from latrine and sewer. He was finally moved one more time, to a penitentiary. Retried on 17 March 1983, he was found innocent on the grounds that the earlier trial had been based on conjecture rather than evidence. After one year and nine months of imprisonment, Chrysóstomo was set free.

*

In my opinion, comparison of Febrônio's and Chrysóstomo's cases leads to some somewhat surprising conclusions. Both were punished by the law without sufficient grounds or legal explanation. In practice, Febrônio was condemned to life imprisonment – a punishment which does not exist in the Brazilian Penal Code. Chrysóstomo, on the other hand, suffered imprisonment without being sentenced, a result of the order of preventive imprisonment – a judicial instrument strongly contested in the juridicial arena itself and anyway only used with individuals considered to be extremely dangerous, a fact recognised by the very judge who ordered it. A great

*Right-wing murderers [Trans. note].

favourite of the Brazilian police, preventive imprisonment is, for this very reason, characterised as a method of police kidnapping.

Between Febrônio and Chrysóstomo can be seen an evolution in the control of citizens by the criminal-psychiatric establishment. With Febrônio homosexuality was consolidated as an illness, continuing a process begun in the nineteenth century. The victory of the principle of the *unimpeachability* of the so-called mentally ill considerably aggravated this tendency on the penal level. If in the hands of the judge the condemned man served a limited sentence which included the possibility of parole or reduced punishment, in the hands of the psychiatrist the "moral lunatic" does not even have a sentence which establishes timespans or limits against which he can appeal. His liberty depends directly and exclusively on the omnipotent opinion of the doctor, who can force him to continue the "treatment" for the rest of his life – as in the case of Febrônio, who served almost double the limit of 30 years' imprisonment for a crime. Furthermore, the idea of illness extended to the public, particularly through the press, which fully exploited every detail of the case and bestowed on Febrônio such descriptions as "raving lunatic" and "delirious black", possessor of a "dissipated imagination", ignorant and lacking in education. There was even a Carnival song all the rage in the 1920s:

> I went to the forest, woman
> to look for wood, woman
> I saw an animal, woman
> with only one eye!
> It wasn't an animal,
> not at all.
> It was Febrônio
> in baggy pants...

Pedro Nava, a memoirist, believes that the "one eye" is a clear reference to the anus; the "baggy pants" were the latest fashion and therefore popular among gay men of the time.[38] The most concrete result was that the name of Febrônio became an adjective. In Rio slang of the thirties *"febrônio"* was a synonym for "queer". In other words, psychiatry succeeded in transforming the case of one individual into a "universal principle",[39] directly touching the awareness of anonymous collaborators, so effectively that it even modified language. Meanwhile the psychiatrist who defined and several times confirmed Febrônio's "moral lunacy" was rewarded with the directorship of the asylum and attained such prestige in his field that his name was given to the establishment, now called the Heitor Carrilho Judicial Asylum.

With Chrysóstomo the means of control made an important and Orwellian advance in achieving not only the consensus and collusion of the criminal-psychiatric-police establishment but also the connivance of sectors of so-called public opinion. Perhaps with the acceleration of the mechanisms of permissiveness and a result of increasing urban violence, the system of repression has tended to receive the collaboration of growing sectors of the population whose values and privileges are under growing threat. Indeed, in my opinion the determining presence of neighbours in the initiation and direction of punishing the "criminal" Chrysóstomo is evidence of a growing *fascisisation* of the middle class. Rather than specialised and strategically placed moralisers (who create the rules of conduct), we now have a multiplication and infiltration of anonymous moralisers who are the real development of central control. As in Don Siegel's horror film *The Body Snatchers* (in Brazil it was given the significant title of *Vampiros das almas* – "Vampires of the Soul") – control has become the consciences of individuals and its agent is no longer detectable: it is in your neighbour, perhaps in yourself.

The most frightening aspect of the Chrysóstomo case is that he was persecuted with the collaboration and approval of representatives of official progressive opinion. Thus it was a woman known to be linked to the Communist Party and with feminist pretensions who orchestrated Chrysóstomo's accusers, on the flimsy pretext that "that monstrous rapist's child" had to be protected.[40] Whether by coincidence or not, several secondary spokespeople were also linked to the CP, some of them in the press. *Veja,* the most important conservative magazine with a national circulation, at the time a bastion of camouflaged members of the CP, mustered sensationalist arguments against Chrysóstomo, claiming he organised orgies in his home and, in a serious state of alcoholism, once stayed "48 consecutive hours in a bar in the centre of the city, seated in his feces and urine".[41] In the *Folha de São Paulo,* considered the most progressive mainstream newspaper in the country, a feminist refused to contribute material on Chrysóstomo, saying that "he was guilty on paper". The Journalists' Union of Rio de Janeiro also hesitated for some time before attesting to the Court that Chrysóstomo had been a journalist for more than 20 years. Even more shocking and displaying the lowest level of consciousness and self-esteem was the fact that the Brazilian gay movement almost totally and deliberately ignored the Chrysóstomo case, cutting relations with *Lampião,* which Chrysóstomo kept contact with, for as long as the episode lasted. It was only several months before the conclusion of the case that parts of the gay liberation movement decided to set up a kind of committee for Chrysóstomo's freedom with the support of bodies connected with the defence of human rights in Brazil. Nonetheless a long letter – a frightening document – was sent by a well-known gay activist in Rio de Janeiro, an open enemy of Chrysóstomo, to each of the organised groups in the country and innumerable independent homosexual activists. It argued that the gay movement would lose its credibility in the eyes of the public if it took a position favourable to Chrysóstomo, for the reason that it was not his homosexuality which was on trial but the ill-treatment he had inflicted on a minor. Taking on the role of the judge, the writer presented a long list of condemnatory proofs.

Such facts make one reflect on the mere appearance of modernity to which Brazilian progressivism is very often reduced, as it camouflages traditional values that have never been eradicated. As well as revealing typically provincial quarrels, the attack on Chrysóstomo came down to such conservative ideological motivations as the excellence of the family and the innocence of children, in defence of which the beliefs of otherwise opposing political colours were assembled. Pedophiles and other deviants obviously constitute adequate targets for these new champions of normality. It is enough to remember that the queer who adopts a child can represent a threat to the hegemony exercised by the heterosexual couple and nuclear family who, in our societies, still hold the monopoly on children. Furthermore, it does not seem to me absurd that Chrysóstomo's persecution symbolises, through complicated guilt mechanisms, an attempt to exorcise the fantasies of rape and pedophilia which the accusers prohibit in themselves. Do-gooders alleviate their own guilt through a scapegoat, and are able, for a time, to sleep in peace.

CHAPTER FOUR

The Ambiguous Art of Being Ambiguous

"I'm not here to clarify anything.
Whatever I can confuse, I'll confuse."

Ney Matogrosso (1983)

Reminiscences of the Transvestite Scene

Unlike today, when the profession of actor/actress enjoys great prestige, even if on the fringes of society, in eighteenth-century Brazil the theatre "grovelled under the sign of infamy", in the words of Valdemar de Oliveira, a theatre historian. The Portuguese showed great contempt towards actors, whose profession they considered to be the most shameful possible. So much so that actors were denied the Christian burial which was allowed even to bandits and criminals. In the reign of Dona Maria I, Pina Manique, the Chief of Police, presented a report in which he informed the Queen that comics and impresarios were "the most inferior of the vulgar crowd". As a result, a decree was published in 1780 prohibiting the presence of women on the stage, to prevent their being abused by such rabble. The decree also prohibited women from entering theatre wings, dressing-rooms and auditoria; furthermore, to avoid other circumstances favourable to licentiousness, the use of curtains in boxes was also forbidden.[1] That the decree was effective could be seen from the absence of actresses from Antonio José de Paula's theatre company, which visited Brazil from Portugal at the end of the eighteenth century. It is nonetheless very probable that this prohibition followed tradition. Since the catechistic plays of the Jesuits in Brazil, the rare feminine roles had been played by men, eg. the role of an old woman in Fr José de Anchieta's *At the Feast of St Lourenço* as played by Indians in the sixteenth century. It is also known that the *Ratio Studiorum* – a rule-book published by the Society of Jesus in 1599 – forbade feminine roles in its college theatres, with the exception of the character of the Holy Virgin. The justification was to prevent the young men of the time from being distracted or plunged into passion.[2]

It must be admitted, however, that the absence of women on the Brazilian stage in colonial times was not simply the result of Dona Maria's prohibition. Although the decree was only revoked in 1800, there were reports of theatre companies in that same period – in Rio de Janeiro, São Paulo and Porto Alegre – which were unusual in including women. It is known that there were various actresses in a company formed in Rio de Janeiro between 1779 and 1790 on the order of the Viceroy himself. Among them were Joaquina da Lapa (known as Lapinha) and Maria Jacinta (known as Marucas) – and it can be imagined from their nicknames that they were not only popular but had a certain affinity with the common people. Also at the end of the eighteenth century, the Opera House in Porto Alegre contracted the "representative comic", Maria Benedita de Queiroz Montenegro, for a year, with regular appearances that included the presentation of two new operas and two interludes (short acted and sung farces) each month. In these cases it was always emphasised that the actresses were ladies. Everything suggested that, although generally relegated to the confinement of the home, women in the colonial period could enjoy immediate notoriety by exposing themselves to public curiosity from the height of a stage. It is therefore not surprising that up to the beginning of the twentieth century public health authorities demanded medical certificates from actresses to prove that they were not carrying any diseases. In any case, stories of scandal surrounded the French actresses who arrived in Brazil from 1860 on to perform operettas in the theatres of large towns – especially the famous Alcazar Lyrique in Rio de Janeiro, a theatre so large that it occupied three buildings. Many of these actresses were said to have destroyed homes and fortunes in conquering the hearts of Brazilian politicians and wealthy men. The most famous of all, known as Mademoiselle Aimée, left Brazil with a considerable fortune in jewels given to her by lovers and admirers. It is said that passing the beach of Botafogo in Rio, the ship taking her back to Europe was fêted with fireworks and rockets from families happy to see her go.[3]

One of the greatest proofs of notoriety and, often, of the poor quality of the colonial theatre was the fact that the regular theatrical companies were – according to foreign travellers from the eighteenth century on – made up of blacks and mulattos. As whites, particularly in the ruling classes, despised the theatre and actors, nothing was more natural than that the profession should end up the province of blacks and mulattos (slaves or freemen), whose degraded social status meshed perfectly with the outcast thespian art. These contemporary pariahs had nothing to lose in terms of social prestige. Thus the oldest theatrical company known in Brazil was composed of mulattos led by Fr Ventura, connected to the Rio de Janeiro Opera House, in 1748. In 1767 the French navigator Bougainville reported attending a performance of the works of Metastásio given by a cast of mulattos in the Opera House. Still in Rio, in 1780, there is information about another permanent company whose members were probably all negroes or blacks performing as singers, dancers and comics, also in the Opera House. In the town of Cuiabá in 1790 there was notice of the performance of the comedy *Tamberlaine in Persia,* with a cast exclusively of negroes who "performed very elegantly and the ladies" – transvestites – "in complete clothing", according to a chronicler of the time – as well as singing "many recitations, arias and duets which they had learnt with much work".[4] In Bahia in 1818 the German traveller von Martius reported the existence of an almost exclusively black cast in the Theatre São João, where whites performed "only occasionally, in the roles of foreigners".[5] In São Paulo von Martius saw the French opera *Le Déserteur,* performed in Portuguese by an all-black cast. In the same city in 1819, the traveller Saint-Hilaire watched a theatrical performance in which the actors were almost all mulattos (who seemed like "puppets moved by a thread") and the actresses were all public women ("whose talent runs parallel with their morality"). Visiting a theatre in the then famous town of Vila Rica in Minas Gerais, Saint-Hilaire noted a very curious thing: most of the actors were mulattos who had taken care to cover their face and arms with a layer of white and red paint – "but their hands betrayed the colour which nature gave them".[6]

Although Vila Rica was famous at the time as the source of the best actors in the country, who were noted for their excellent diction and talent as declaimers, Saint-Hilaire said that the actors gesticulated as if moved by springs and their voices were not clearly audible, being only as loud as the prompter's. The poor quality of theatrical performances was confirmed by Tomás Antonio Gonzaga, a contemporary poet from Minas Gerais. In one of his poems he wrote; "Prepare too that in the theatres/ The three most beautiful dramas stumble/ Repeated from the mouths of mulattos." With the arrival of João VI from Lisbon at the beginning of the nineteenth century, black actors began to be given only secondary roles, as the principal characters were played by members of foreign song and dance companies that were quite frequently brought to the Court in Rio de Janeiro. However, the nationalist and xenophobic cultural movement which followed the abdication of Pedro I in 1831 caused foreign actors to be removed from the stage, giving way once more to Brazilian mulatto actors – as also occurred with the musicians in local orchestras. Work was then improvised more than ever and substitutions hurriedly made so that the standard of acting seems to have fallen noticeably. In 1844, for example, Carlos Humberto Lavollé attended operas put on at the São Pedro de Alcântara Theatre in Rio de Janeiro and said that the choruses were made up of mulattos who performed very badly, while Norma's sons, in Rossini's opera, were played by two fat little blacks.

There are other clear indications of the theatre's poor reputation. At the start of colonisation theatrical performances were usually held in public squares or church porches and consisted of pantomimes and lascivious dances. These were called the Madmen's Feasts, in which the people totally lost their inhibitions. This was not prevented by the episcopal warning that "a good sermon" should be given before the play began. To stop abuses, Jesuit missionaries wrote sacred plays, sometimes even in Tupi, and put them on in the churches, with the intention of converting the Indians as well. Despite these efforts, the theatre's primordial function continued to be entertaining the public, with results that were certainly contrary to the Christian enlightenment intended by the ecclesiastic hierarchy. La Barbinnais, a French traveller, wrote that in the Convent of the Wilderness (in Bahia) in 1716 he watched a performance in which the nuns themselves took part before an audience of aristocrats. Definitely shocked by similar events which confirmed the perverse aspects of the theatre, the Bishop of Olinda published a pastoral letter in 1726 prohibiting theatrical performances in the churches of his diocese. When that did not satisfy him, in 1734 he prohibited every kind of theatrical performance in any territory under his jurisdiction.

The Portuguese Crown also made efforts to impose an educational character on the theatre. Thus in 1771 the Marquis of Pombal, then a minister of Jose I, recommended that public theatres should be raised on Brazilian territory, to be "well regulated, because they are the school where the people might learn the healthy maxims of statecraft, morality, love of country and fidelity with which they should serve their sovereign".[7] It seems, however, that such proposals did not have practical results. For example, it was said that in the Opera House in Recife, built in 1772 as part of this educative effort, there was great promiscuity between the theatre-goers and prostitutes, without mentioning the fights and shouting that broke out during performances as much as in the intervals.[8] The situation does not seem to have improved with the arrival of the Portuguese royal family in Brazil in 1808. As new and more theatres were built, it became the fashion for the best families to display their sumptuous clothes at performances. While a few had gone to watch the play, the majority were there exclusively to admire the others in the audience. In 1812, in an attempt to put an end to the "scandalous negligence and the inconveniences which arise from such abuse", the authorities in Recife prohibited men from the ladies' galleries and installed "sentries" in the stalls of the Opera House as well as appointing an inspector responsible for the place.[9] Even so, in about 1824 the people of Recife were enchanted by the presence of a certain Joaninha Castiga who, accompanied by her husband, danced and sang extremely lascivious duets, with belly-dancing, hip-waggling and dubious words.

Things came to such a point that in 1830 a local newspaper complained about the immorality of the plays which the public applauded and encored: "Most fathers of honourable families do not dare take their wives and daughters to such a place. What good man could cold-bloodedly allow his family to hear the obscenities spoken there?"[10] In the same year Emperor Pedro I established nationwide censorship to "prevent the theatre degenerating from its laudable aims through the introduction of doctrines, some of which are contrary to good custom and public morality, others tending to inflame excitable passions and destroy the constitutional system by any means".[11] Yet things do not seem to have changed much, if we take into consideration the evidence of Louis Léger Vauthier, a

French engineer, who walked out of the Opera House in Recife in 1841, scandalised by the grossness of the dialogue and situations in a performance in which an old actress had lifted her skirt to the audience while the character of the Judge threatened to pull down his trousers and a girl, "with the appearance of a virago, taking large paces, gesticulating and shouting, seemed ready to kick the speaker even when resting".[12] Saint-Hilaire tells how he was invited to a puppet show in Barbacena in Minas Gerais at the beginning of the nineteenth century. The group was presenting Biblical scenes but the place was, he said, frequented by "low-life women", giving the impression of being in reality a place of tolerance.

Even when the provinciality of the theatre was under attack, promiscuity was still present. The performances attended by the Emperor at the court in Rio de Janeiro tried to imitate the European cultural ambience and impose a note of finesse on theatrical events. Yet even though the two sexes were separated in the stalls by a gilded grille, the gentlemen paid little attention to the play, prefering to visit the ladies' boxes. If on the one hand Rio de Janeiro high society considered it a veritable lack of decorum to pay attention to the stage, on the other hand foreign travellers reported that a good number of the women at performances were prostitutes – which may be some exaggeration. In any case it means that theatrical presentations did not lose their character of mundane obscenity even at Court.

In the last analysis, theatres in Brazil were notable as masculine places of such ill-fame that performances were eventually forbidden to foreigners, as at the end of the eighteenth century in Rio de Janeiro, on the orders of the Viceroy, the Marquis do Lavradio, who was concerned with the repercussions that they might have abroad. In this climate so inclined to lasciviousness, it can be imagined how the absence of women on the stage created unexpected and unusual circumstances in a country far from everywhere, where the law was only taken seriously when it was convenient. An English writer, anonymously quoted in an old book by a Portuguese author, described a performance in the important Rua dos Condes Theatre in Rio de Janeiro in 1787: "Here a cheerful shepherdess in original white garments can be seen, displaying a soft blue-dyed beard and prominent clavicules and holding a bunch of flowers in a hand that might be capable of knocking down Goliath. A row of milkmaids follow with long strides, lifting their skirts above their heads with each movement. I have never seen high kicks jumps and obscene glances like that and hope never to see them again."[13] In reports on the 1790 theatrical season in Cuiabá (an important city in the tropical interior), the lack of actresses was absolute. In the various plays put on in a month of festivities female characters were played by men who, considering the stability even of amateur casts, seem to have specialised in women's roles. In this season alone a Silvério José da Silva played six important roles, including the mythological Portuguese heroine Inês de Castro and a princess called Phoenix. Moreover, a chronicler of the time considered him as "outstanding" in the role of another woman, Branca in the comedy *Count Alarcos*.[14] Others who played the roles of princesses and queens were Joaquim de Mello Vasconcelos, Manuel de Souza Brandão and Manoel de Barros, while Xisto Paes specialised in roles of maids, gracious anonymous ladies and gypsies.

In this same season at Cuiabá (then probably Brazil's third largest city, with 30,000 inhabitants, compared to Rio de Janeiro's 100,000 and Salvador's 70,000) there was even an opera, *Ésio in Rome*, written by a tailor and with an all-mulatto cast. The principal female role, Honória, was played by Joaquim José dos Santos Nery, "a musician by profession, voice and style" – who was certainly a soprano.[15] He should not, however, be confused with the refined Italian castrati who lived in Portugal and were brought in João VI's retinue to sing in the Royal Chapel when he fled to Brazil in 1808. The most famous of these were Tomassini, Bartolozzi and Fasciotti, all of whom also acted in plays in Rio de Janeiro.

The phenomenon of transvestism in the theatre was not confined to large urban centres. In Porto Alegre around 1830 there was a Little Theatre Society which had several youths in its troupe who specialised in female roles. In the same city at about the same time, chroniclers mention a certain Pedro Nolasco Pereira da Cunha, who was "unsurpassed in female roles". Even in the distant state of Maranhão in the north of the country there were plays in the middle of the nineteenth century where men took all the women's roles – eg. Augusto Lucci, who played the part of Dorotéia, a judge's daughter, in the comic opera *The Girl Who Sold Turkeys*, performed in 1854. (It is perhaps only coincidence, but in Portuguese *peru* [turkey] also means 'cock'.) The famous were not immune from this pleasure. In Bahia around this time José Maria da Silva

The poet Roberto Piva, visceral worshipper of adolescents (p. 109)
Photo: Paulo Klein

Patrício Bisso in his television role as the "Russian sexologist" Olga del Volga (p. 128)

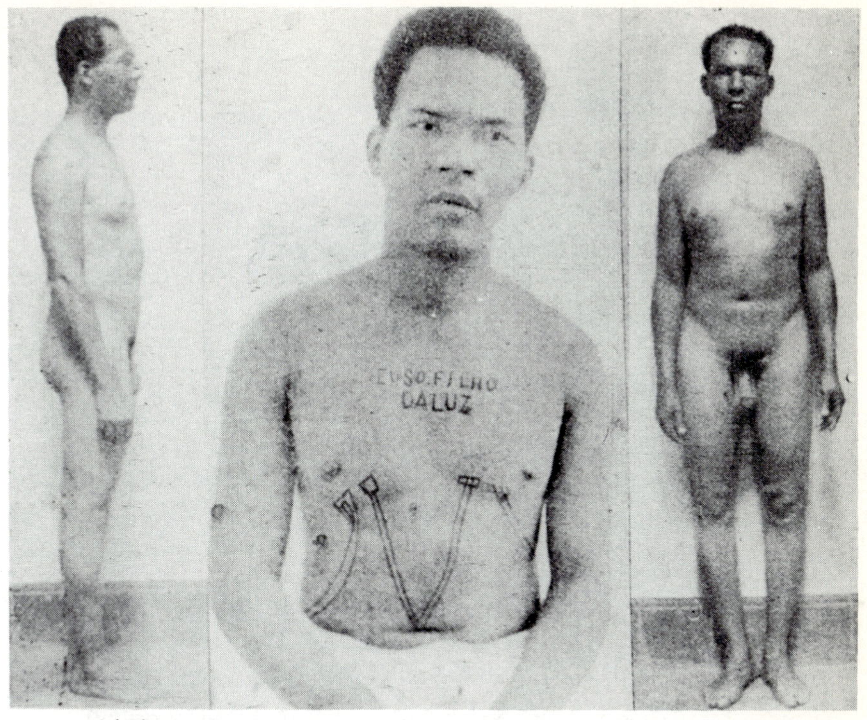

Febrônio Índio do Brasil, in police photographs from the 1930s (p. 79 ff.)
Photos: Ed. Max Limonad

A scene from *República dos assassinos*, 1979, by Miguel Faria Júnior (p. 126)

Paranhos, who became the Viscount do Rio Branco, an eminent figure in Brazilian history, "made a great impression in the roles of leading lady in the group Dramatic Regeneration, founded in 1854".[16] Although it may now appear odd to us, even the royal family kept good relations with local transvestites. Passing through Rio de Janeiro in 1846, Ida Pfeifer, a Viennese, came to the military barracks in the Rua dos Barbonos to attend the celebrations for the baptism of Princess Isabel, Emperor Pedro II's daughter. There she watched dances performed by excellent ballerinas "who were none other than the soldiers themselves".[17]

Although restricted – as far as is known – to the theatre, the practice of transvestism occurred in a context that was anything but innocent and which certainly had connotations that were not exclusively professional. It is worth remembering that homosexuality was scandalously common even at the beginning of the nineteenth century in cities such as Rio de Janeiro – especially among small shopkeepers, where immigrant Portuguese predominated, often keeping their sales clerks as lovers. In 1885 the tragic love story of Cândido, a 26-year-old Portuguese widower, became famous. Because he intended to marry a young woman with whom he had fallen in love, he was murdered with a hammer by his employee and lover Alberico, a 22-year-old Brazilian with whom he had been living. After a sensational trial, Alberico was sentenced to 30 years' imprisonment.[18] The sociologist and historian Gilberto Freyre adds that the Portuguese Consul, Baron de Moreira, was so concerned with eradicating male prostitution from the Portuguese districts of Rio de Janeiro that in 1846 he encouraged the importation of female prostitutes from the Azores, who were soon followed by Polish and French women.[19] At the beginning of the twentieth century the hygienist, Pires de Almeida, stated that "male prostitution has notably declined, for the sole reason that female prostitution has risen dramatically".[20]

It is therefore legitimate to assume that there were more or less underground connections between transvestism and homosexuality, in the almost exclusively male ambience of the theatre of the time. Yet, as customs were relaxed, homosexuality in Brazil did not come to an end with the institutionalisation of female prostitution, nor did male transvestism die out with growing presence of women on the stage. As part of the Brazilian centenary celebrations in Recife in 1922, the comedy *The Mother-in-law*, by Aloísio de Azevedo, was presented with the two female roles played by male law students.[21] Moreover, Luís da Câmara, a well-known folklorist, has shown how transvestism has travelled in time in the traditional dances of the north-east known as *bumba-meu-boi*, in which only men take part and dress up to play the roles of ladies. Cascudo attributes this to "the old prohibitory precepts of the Portuguese Crown" which, he says, excluded women from public festivals as well as the stage.[22]

It seems that this kind of theatrical transvestism has evolved into two different types in Brazil. One – merely playful – has flourished in a light-hearted vein for three days every year in Carnival, with hundreds of adult men dressing in the clothes of their wives, sisters, mothers or girlfriends. The other type has returned to a more professional objective with the rise on the stage of the transvestite-actor who earns a living from imitating women and who is often also a transvestite in everyday life. In 1921 the quality newspaper *O Estado de São Paulo* advertised a show by Darwin, a famous "imitator of the fair sex" on the stage of the São Paulo Cinema. In 1922 the actor Ramos, another "imitator of the fair sex", appeared at the Apollo Theatre; there were still reports of his success on the São Paulo stage in 1924. In 1926 the same newspaper announced *The Eye of Providence* (and what eye would it be that sees to everything?), a show performed by a transvestite, probably the actor Palmeirim, at the Boa Vista Theatre.

It is interesting to note that even the newly-born and in many ways still timid Brazilian cinema absorbed this form of organised transvestism, known as *transformism*. Luiz de Barros' *Augusto Aníbal quer casar* ("Augusto Anibal Wants To Marry") was made in Rio de Janeiro in 1923 and distributed throughout the country. Augusto Anibal, a comedian, played the part of a "young man with a burning heart" who was anxious to marry. Tired of his importuning, some women resolve to teach him a lesson. They go to the house of the actor-transvestite Darwin – who gets prepared by dressing up as a beautiful girl – and write to Anibal, asking him to turn up immediately to get married. Augusto Anibal hurries to the address given, where he meets Darwin, dressed as a girl, and a false priest, both ready for the wedding ceremony which follows. During the honeymoon, however, Darwin begins to talk and walk like an ordinary man. Anibal panics at the mistake he has made and flees in his shirt and underwear "through the streets of the town, along the quays and even by sea, in a plane in which he has taken refuge, resolved to find a bride... in the heavens".[23]

In everyday life there were certainly many people who neither panicked nor fled. One sign of this was the proliferation of transvestism, which spread from the stage to the streets and back to the stage again, where it tried to legitimise itself in transvestite shows. In Chapter Six I will refer more specifically to the survival of transvestites off-stage. For the moment it is enough to say that transvestite-actors were able to find more professional space in the musical revues which began to proliferate on the Brazilian stage in the middle of the nineteenth century. Of French origin, but duly absorbed and transformed in Brazil, this genre was Brazilianised as contemporary events, ideas and fashions were brought into the revue in comic form. It was the revues that launched Carnival music and new belles, who became ideals of national beauty. The public rushed to see the country's most beautiful stars parading in minimal clothing and dancing in magnificent sets including lit fountains – all to the sound of large orchestras. Even famous authors specialised in writing revues – among them Artur Azevedo and Gastão Tojeiro.

In time, however, the revues lost their splendour and quality and what had been comic became simply obscene. By the middle of the twentieth century the revue had evolved into the so-called *teatro de rebolado* * where pornographic jokes alternated with virulent political criticism. Thus the *teatro de rebolado* had everything necessary to absorb the transvestite – which it did. Totally in decline in recent years thanks to the competition of television and pornographic films, the *teatro de rebolado* has been followed by its natural successor, the transvestite show, which has taken its place in Brazilian theatre. The apotheosis was in 1980 when Rogéria – probably the most famous Brazilian transvestite today – won the Mambembe Trophy, awarded by INACEN, the National Institute of Scenic Arts, for Best Actress (in Rio de Janeiro), for his part in the play *O Desembestado* ("The Man of Passion") by Ariovaldo Matos.

At present, even when confronted by unemployment, the poor quality of shows and starvation-level wages, transvestites can depend on minimum work as actors. Nádia Kendall (in homage to the North American Kay Kendall), for example, is

*Literally, "theatre of the hip-wiggle," *rebolar* being the hip-shaking action of samba [Trans. note].

proud that he is registered as an actor-transvestite with the Ministry of Employment as well as the Actors' Union. Furthermore, Nádia (who was 50 in 1984) has been working in transvestite shows for more than twenty years, starting with the famous *Les Girls*, which ran for a year in the 1960s in Rio de Janeiro. As well as the shows often put on in small theatres, there are regular groups of transvestites in certain gay nightclubs in the cities. Of the six revues advertised in Rio de Janeiro in 1980, four were transvestite shows. It is true that apart from improvisation, each show's structure is almost the same as all its predecessors', constrained by a lack of resources which has the transvestite double as comic, dancer and singer. It is perhaps this flexibility, which keeps the costs of production down, that allows the existence and persistence of someone like Brigitte Blair – a female impresario who specialises in transvestite shows and maintains an average of thirty employees in the two theatres in Rio de Janeiro which she owns. Some shows have been very successful, eg. *Mimosas até certo ponto* ("Mimosas, Up To a Point"), which ran for three years. The public who frequent such shows are generally poor and range from single men to middle-aged couples who take great pleasure in laughing at the four-letter words and laboured jokes.

The more sumptuous shows are generally put on in Rio de Janeiro, where some impresarios try out recipes for success, presenting transvestites as fundamentally consumer objects. *Gay Fantasy*, *Rio Gay*, *Transvestites Ltd* are shows with a specially written script, polished soundtrack, meticulous choreography and truly dazzling costumes. They employ respected professionals such as Biba Ferreira, a director, and Joãozinho Trinta, scenographer, who has been responsible for the success of more than one samba group in Rio de Janeiro. The scripts, however, do not generally surpass the frivolity of the stereotyped transvestite, always trying to create exotic situations from the curious lifestyle rooted in androgynous ambiguity which has fascinated people since the remote past. Thus, for example, the show *Transvestites Ltd* took advantage of the film *Victor, Victoria*, inverting the ambiguity and dressing the transvestites in tails and bow ties as proof of their now exposed "masculinity". These shows might not be very imaginative – their life comes from the most conventional glamour – but the formula seems to be successful. *Gay Fantasy*, the first in the series, ran for more than a year and toured the whole country. Perhaps a result of the recent notoriety some enjoy, transvestite-actors here and there have gone into more intellectual productions. Andrea de Maio – a millionaire transvestite who proudly claims to have had thousands of dollars of silicon injected into his 110 cm hips – played the role of a transvestite in *A ópera do malandro*, a much-acclaimed musical based on *The Threepenny Opera* by Chico Buarque, a famous and radical composer. In its new setting Jenny, the whore in the original, is the transvestite Geni (an oxytonic Brazilian name very popular among ordinary people). In the Rio production, the transvestite was played by an ordinary actor, but in São Paulo Andrea de Maio took the role. This seems at least to have increased his notoriety. Today he boasts of receiving love-letters from many men. He has three cars and an apartment with a swimming-pool as well as being part-owner of a night-club. Swearing that he never shows any lover his penis ("the only defect in my authenticity"), Andrea nonetheless displays a certain critical sense in observing that: "The people who point at me in the street during the day, sleep in my bed at night."[24]

These Stories of a Damned Love

The first known references to homosexuality in Brazilian literature come from the great erotic-satirical poet Gregório de Matos, who lived in the seventeenth century in Bahia and was known as the "Mouth of Hell" because of his virulence. Famous for molesting nuns and black women, Gregório de Matos became the enemy of the then Governor-General of Brazil and dedicated some verses of incomparable baroque irony to him. After calling him a sodomite, molly, "shit of the nobles" and "eternal cow", Gregório accused him of having an arsehole "scourged by abomination". Observing weals there, he refers to a presumed lover and asks: "Would these be love-bites/which Ferreira the sorcerer/has given him?" Then in magnificently expressed sarcasm, dripping with double meaning, he calls him "goat of the mattresses* stabbing him in the loins/ you harpoon tapeworms/ in the lagoons of the eye" – "eye" referring to anus, as "tapeworm" means "penis" and "stabbing the loins" is a reference to anal penetration.

The case of the romantic poet Álvares de Azevedo is quite

**Cabra dos colchões* is a Brazilian idiom referring to the farm she-goat that all the men reputedly have sex with [Trans. note].

different. His work is at the same time full of revelry plagiarised from Byron and modest circumlocutions very much in the style of Brazilian romanticism. Manuel Antonio Álvares de Azevedo, who was born in 1831 and died before his twenty-first birthday, lived in what Mário de Andrade euphemistically called "fear of the sexual realisation of inverted love". Probably less from voyeurism than a personal interest in the topic, de Andrade (whom I will shortly discuss) said that when analysed in detail Álvares de Azevedo's work can "lead us to psychopathological suppositions"[25] – by that he is certainly referring to the young poet's implicit homosexuality. There were indeed curious aspects to Álvares' life. He displayed an excessive love for his mother and, on a lesser scale, for his sister. Each time love for women is mentioned in his works, it is always in terms of filial love – even when referring to the women lovers which, it is supposed, he never had. These are generally treated with an almost comic respect; in letters to friends his mother is referred to as a saint whom others adore "but do not love". Yet the theme of libertinism with women is central to his work, which, according to de Andrade, becomes "theatrical falsification" since his references are obviously superfluous and superficial. In a sonnet to his lover, it is curious that he, not she, faints from love; he trembles and sweats and his lips go dry like a young virgin's.

If Mário de Andrade had gone a little further in his analysis, he might have concluded that the sexual disregard Álvares had for women – allied with the feminine taste which in him was the presentiment of a delightful queen – was superbly complemented by some quasi-mythical facts about the life of this young romantic poet raised and educated by the women of his family. His love for and identification with his elder sister, Maria Luiza, which was perhaps a jealousy of complicated origin, once led him to appear at a Carnival dance at the age of nineteen dressed in her clothes. He was presented to the French consul, Maria Luiza's fiancé, who is said to have been interested in the masked "girl" and to have invited her to dine alone, at which point Manuel Antonio identified himself. Rubem Fonseca, a contemporary Brazilian writer, has written a brilliant story based on this incident, with Álvares just returned from the ball, taking off his women's clothes, necklace, jewels and wig at the mirror while telling his sister about his adventure. To save him from "injurious inferences", his biographers have attributed the episode to the young poet's satirical humour. That was certainly not the case, Mário de Andrade believed, associating the incident with Álvares' contempt for the girls he knew. He might call them asses and crones, clumsy and venomous, but in his letters he would give detailed descriptions of their ball costumes, even noting the cloth with which they had been made.

As well as extensive correspondence with his mother, Álvares wrote to Luís Antonio da Silva Nunes, a friend who had been a fellow-student before moving to Rio Grande do Sul. The tone of these letters is of ardent love: "The three months which have yet to pass until this yearning falls silent are very long," he wrote to Luís. "The thought of having a friend, although absent, is very sweet but agonisingly sad."[26] Then he confessed to being impatient: "So you won't come to São Paulo with me. Living there with you would have consoled me." He added, hurt: "Luís, there is something in my heart, I do not know what, which tells me that perhaps everything is ending between us. (...) Perhaps my friendship, Luís, will have to live on my nostalgia once again." In an icy presentiment of his coming death, he added: "If I die young, in a fever of ambitious hopes, in some of my letters to you there is a complete story of the last two years, a legend, sad but true, an autopsy of suffering." "Luis, it is my fate to love greatly and be loved by no one," he complained, and added in a very literary fashion commenting on the love of women: "They are dreams – dreams (...) Luís." His farewell was: "As much as I love you, love me. In the prairies of Rio Grande do not forget (...) your friend."[27]. He died two years later, almost unexpectedly; on his study wall he had written, in advance, the date of his death, the cause of which has never been clear – perhaps tuberculosis, perhaps cancer. Many say that he let himself die of sorrow – in his mother's bed. Despite claiming that Álvares never had an emotional relationship with a woman, Brito Broca, a writer on literature, has tried to dilute his relationship with Luís, referring to the great "spiritual friendships" common among the romantics and citing the cases of Goethe and Schiller, Byron and Hogg.[28] However, I recall that certain authors, when writing about Álvares de Azevedo, believed that he wished for and achieved his own death from pure disenchantment. Would this not be the real result of carnal love poorly disguised as spiritual friendship?

The grand myth of homosexuality in Brazilian literature however, and the first time a black appears as the protagonist, is Adolfo Caminha's novel *Bom-Crioulo,* which was published in

1895. In a period when medicine was codifying those on the fringe of society, the first characters clearly identified in a homosexual relationship appeared in naturalist literature (so obedient to scientific dictates). According to Winston Leyland, the publisher of *Bom-Crioulo* in the United States, it is the first novel throughout the world to tackle homosexual love with courage and boldness. Edward Lacey, the American translator, claims: "Like Mary Shelley's *Frankenstein* and Goethe's *Die Wahlverwandtschaften* (*Elective Affinities*), it is one of the supremely idiosyncratic works of nineteenth-century fiction."[29] Caminha was a midshipman who travelled to the Antilles and United States. On returning to Brazil, he was at the centre of a serious scandal when he became the lover of an army officer's wife. *Bom-Crioulo* was published a year before he died of unexpected tuberculosis. A great admirer of Emile Zola's naturalism, Caminha's story is that of the love between a white adolescent cabin-boy, Aleixo, and the black sailor Amaro, also known as Bom-Crioulo ("Good Nigger"). Rigorously structured and elegantly written, the book goes to the heart in its dissection of this passion and includes detailed descriptions of sexual acts between the two young men. The atmosphere of the passionate relationship is well captured, from the moment when the black receives 150 strokes for defending his lover in a fight to the violent ending in which, abandoned by Aleixo, Bom-Crioulo goes mad with jealousy and kills him.

The result is almost a mirror-image Carmen with all the melodramatic outbursts, which is perhaps why it has remained not only readable but enchantingly modern after almost a century. Brazilian literature has rarely produced a work so courageously direct on forbidden love. In a provincial country which had only recently become a republic, Caminha treated homosexuality as a specific and irrefutable fact, even showing a legitimate tenderness between two ordinary men. It is true that his comments are often stereotyped and reflect the scientific prejudices of the time, especially in calling the two lovers "sickly beings". Thus the black subjugates the blond as he would a woman ("he only lacked breasts") and without doubt Bom-Crioulo's homosexuality is seen as a savage component of his blackness – "Black is the devil's race, it does not know how to forgive, does not know how to forget."[30] Yet where fiction is given free rein, Caminha is miles ahead of his time. He was, moreover, violently criticised as immoral. In his defence he said that art was not immoral and that everything he had written were events that he had witnessed while at sea. He also cited earlier Brazilian and Portuguese books which had dealt with the same theme – eg. the unknown *Um homem gasto* ("A Wasted Man") by Ferreira Leal, also a Brazilian.[31] His book was banned from school and public libraries for several decades. It is said that during the dictatorship of Getúlio Vargas and his fascistic New State (1937) the navy asked for the novel to be banned. After becoming rare, *Bom-Crioulo* has only recently reappeared. That it is still surprisingly relevant can be seen in the fact that it has again been rejected by the mainstream. When it was republished in 1983, Leo Gilson Ribeiro, a famous literary critic on the *Jornal da Tarde* (a São Paulo newspaper), had his review rejected by the editors on the pretext that the paper's owners did not like its theme.

The same curse lies on the work of João do Rio from Rio de Janeiro, who, together with Mário de Andrade and Olavo Bilac, formed the triad of renowned early twentieth-century writers known to be homosexual. Olavo Bilac, whose works are venerated in schools and read by all Brazilian children, is the most academic and official of Brazilian poets and wrote the words of the national anthem. Others said, spitefully and with little secrecy, that he was "the greatest pederast in the country".[32] Mário de Andrade, one of the fathers of modern Brazilian literature, wrote some beautiful poems gently praising soldiers and adolescents, as well as several stories with homoerotic content. A very beautiful diary of his from 1931 begins with the words: "It is because of my shoeshine boy that I am now completely desolate. My shoeshine boy has left me." The object of recent reappraisal in the press when more explicit references to his homosexual life came to the surface, Mário (who died in 1945) was called "Our Miss São Paulo translated into the masculine" by Oswald de Andrade,[33] his old companion in the literary vanguard. There are insistent rumours as to his private writings, which have not been published – and, as a condition of his will, will not be until 1995. Asked about music by a friend, Mário is said to have replied: "For me there is no more beautiful music than the sound of a marine's belt hitting the chair of a hotel room in the Praça Mauá".[34] Very discreet about his private life, this confirmed bachelor complained in a letter to a friend a few years before he died: "What's wrong with my drinking to forget? I don't know. I don't know what I have or what I don't have. It is a great rambling pain, a great dark disgust..."[35] Might this syndrome be the same as Álvares de Azevedo's?

João do Rio was a most interesting (and forgotten) writer who died in 1921 at the age of forty. A famous journalist, member of the Brazilian Academy of Letters and founder of the Brazilian Society of Playwrights, João do Rio was the cause of many scandals. He was called "the tropical Oscar Wilde" for his worship of decadent aestheticism and social life – as well as for his well-known homosexuality (see the analysis by Dr Neves-Manta in the previous chapter). His stories and novels, long out of print, cultivate the ambiguous and paradoxical. A tropical dandy, he was nostalgic for the paradise of Europe, behaving, as had Álvares de Azevedo, like an exile in his own country – something very obvious in his "unfocussed" style. This feeling of being out of place was emphasised by his homosexual experiences. He particularly liked to visit the slums and shanty-towns of Rio de Janeiro, where he was fascinated by the "rabble's unnameable vices". That nourished another kind of nostalgia – of primitive purity, where sin is entertainment.

From that João do Rio created a world populated by debauched and cruel revellers, eccentric counts and barons, actresses in cynical pursuit of success, together with ambiguous mincing men, hysterical whores, anarchists, corrupt gypsies, Chinese opium-smokers and promiscuous thieves. With João do Rio, however, most important was the question of style. He captured reality in a sinuous, distorted, displaced language turned into a fictional labyrinth; the result is a literature of dissonance, en route to deviation. The sinuosity of his style can be seen in the abundance of neologisms, in the affected constructions of his phrases, and in expressions which are Carnivalesque or cross-dressed in their opposite meaning. João do Rio's extreme decadence is the opposite of complacence, just as his apparent futility is provocative and inventive. All this is very close to the contemporary mannerism of camp, which is as much on the boundaries of homosexuality as experience of transvestism and make-up. Unfortunatly, João do Rio has never been examined from this perspective. In the film *Tabu* (1982), Júlio Bressane – a follower of Pasolini's *cinema de poesia* – linked him with Oswald de Andrade, the magus of Anthropophagy,* and Lamartine Babo, the magus of irreverence, in a delighful homage to the perversion of language.

It is interesting that the cinema has also sought to rescue another writer's work from oblivion, one who was in his own

*See page 117 below [Trans. note].

way a mannerist – the mysterious Lúcio Cardoso, whose characters preferred to live in theatrical shadows. While Cardoso (who died in 1968) swung between mysticism and paganism, his characters were surrounded by an atmosphere of poorly explained, diffuse and incomplete malevolence. His loose style was perfectly suited to the melodramatic metaphysics and decadent spiritualism which runs through his writing. Here too the result is a kind of modern mannerism, or camp, where subterfuge and disguise are taken seriously. His works have occasionally been adapted by the Brazilian cinema, but these attempts have almost never succeeded in creating images from the indefinable essence of Cardoso, a homosexual tormented by the fascination and fear of the forbidden. Without doubt, the director Paulo Cesar Saraceni is the one who has come closest. One of the handsomest stars of the old Cinema Novo ("New Cinema") and to a certain extent its covert sex symbol, Saraceni had direct contact with Cardoso, even spreading the legend that the writer had discovered him as a typical beach-bum in Rio de Janeiro. Together they made one of the most provocative, extraordinary and forgotten films of the Cinema Novo: *Porto das Caixas* (1963, script by Lúcio Cardoso, directed by Saraceni). In it a woman decides to kill her aging husband and looks for lovers who will do it for her. In the end she discovers she is stronger than all of them and ends up killing him herself with an axe, then goes away happy, scot-free, liberated. The whole film is syrupy, an example of rare tropical expressionism.

Saraceni also filmed the most admirable, twisted and accomplished of Lucio's novels, *Cronica da casa assassinada* ("Chronicle of the Murdered House"). In the film, made in 1971, Timóteo, a screaming queen, is growing old, locked away in the room where his aristocratic but impoverished family of landowners tries to hide its black sheep. Timóteo dresses up in his dead mother's clothes and senses the thrill of liberation when his new sister-in-law, Nina, arrives – played most subtly by Norma Benguell, the most electrifying actress in the Brazilian cinema. At the end, after Nina has inexplicably died, Timóteo enters the room where the body is laid out, bearing himself like a prince and dressed like a prima donna of the Belle Epoque. Before the appalled eyes of the stern landowners present, he throws himself on the coffin and declares his love for Nina's son. A melodrama which goes from the sordid and corrupt to the most absolutely lost faith, *Cronica da casa assassinada* is also about the unity of holiness and sin, demon and angel, love and death. In the film, moreover, inadequacy and deviance are incorporated in a deliberately sluggish aesthetic approach.

There are numerous scattered references to homosexuals by many writers in contemporary Brazilian literature. Jorge Amado, for example, likes to put ordinary gays into his novels – for example *Capitães da areia* ("Captains of the Sand"), where there are various homosexual relationships in a gang of juvenile delinquents. It was from these scattered references that Gasparino Damata edited a curious anthology in 1967 of homoerotic literary texts by important Brazilian writers, including Machado de Assis (a rigid aesthete from the end of the nineteenth century) and the modernist Graciliano Ramos (about whom it was said that he washed his hands after greeting any gay man).[36] Gasparino Damata edited another important anthology in 1969, this time of Brazilian poems inspired by or connected with homosexual love, including such important poets as Carlos Drummond de Andrade and Jorge de Lima.[37]

In the mid-1970s a new generation of writers emerged who were much less inhibited in turning into fiction their experiences, affections and concerns as homosexuals. Aguinaldo Silva can be taken as the precursor, with the publication of his beautiful and unusual novel *Primeira carta aos andróginos* ("First Letter to the Androgynes", 1975), which was followed – as part of an irregular work – by such delightful narratives as those of a timid queen who goes into the Íris cinema, a paradise of popular cruising in Rio. In the depths of its stinking toilet he discovers, written in enormous black letters between erect cocks, the phrase "THE ÍRIS IS ALSO BRAZIL" – a story memorable, in my opinion, for its style and implications. Another book which should not be forgotten is *Passagem para o próximo sonho* ("Passage to the Next Dream"), an autobiography marked by an approach of beauty, sincerity and great poetry. In it Herbert Daniel tells of his participation in the Brazilian guerrilla war and his problems as a homosexual who, after fleeing Brazil during the recent period of dictatorship, ended up as doorman in a large gay sauna in Paris.

Even more significant is the emergence today of poets of both sexes who are directly involved with homosexual erotica – an unheard-of situation in Brazil, where poets have only dared to tackle the theme very metaphorically and vaguely. Among these new poets the truly exceptional are Roberto Piva and

Glauco Mattoso. Piva has been stubbornly writing his solitary and very personal poetry since the 1960s. Descended from the metaphysical poets (Blake), the drug-takers (Baudelaire), the beatniks (Ginsberg) and surrealists in general, there are almost no boundaries between his life and his poetry. For these reasons (and for his cosmopolitanism) he is a poet unusual in Brazil. His verses, besides being as dense and explosive as grenades ("I am the jet-set of damned love"), are surprising in that they do not seem to have precursors: "Sweet shock at the gate of his innards/ sweat is his friend and concubine". The conjoining of opposing images in delirious metaphors gives birth to such verses as: "Before the moon comes/ bite my heart at the street corner/ and do not forget me". Or: "Dove-boy at the snack-bar counter/ waiting for the mosquito of Death." In Piva love is eternally renewed, as is his inspiration – "This is how I want you: a burning angel in the embrace of the landscape". A worshipper of adolescents, Piva dedicates to them visceral poems:

> I am going to grind your brain.
> I am going to shred your white and hairless thighs.
> I am going to lavishly spend the richness of your adolescence . . . I am going to burn your
> eyes with a red-hot brand.
> I am going to incinerate your heart of flesh and
> from your ashes I am going to make the
> maddened substance of
> love letters.

Glauco Mattoso's approach is anarchic and dadaist, frequently tinged with semiotic suggestions whose nuances of magisterial ambivalence come from the insertion of an obscene element by which the attempts at academic intellectualisation so typical of semiologists are seen to be destroyed. Thus the foul-mouthed Glauco speaks: "I want poetry to be much more lascivious,/with athlete's foot on the tongue, sweat in the saliva,/cum in the phlegm, piss on the gums,/prick in neutral, cunt in raw flesh." With a destructive sarcasm that places him in the tradition of Gregório de Matos, he often adopts various pseudonyms such as Pedro o Podre ("Peter the Putrid") who adores scat-games – "If a poem seems to me to be shit, I eat it. This is being a coprophagic poet." Glauco is also brutally irreverent and virulent in his creation of apochryphal texts by such personalities as Pol Pot, Edith Piaf, Tennessee Williams, Shakespeare, John Paul II, etc. Thus he sarcastically places this phrase in Khomeini's mouth: "If sodomy is committed with an ox, ram or camel, the animal's urine and excrement becomes impure." But perversion and deviance, which he uses to explosive effect, are the medium as well as the message, for Glauco adopts the marginality of his poetic work and simply prints subversive pamphlets which he sends through the post to his chosen readers. His work seems to me to have that breath of radicality rare and necessary to poetry, which thereby loses its limits and inhibitions and contaminates everything: "Oh shit with your sea of urine/ with your fetid sky/ you are my continent fertile land where germinates/ my independence my indiscipline."

The Bolivian Thief Usurps the Nuptial Bed

The homosexual experience has intruded just as viscerally on playscripts as on the pages of Brazilian literature. It could be said that this eloquence had its initial impulse in Rio Grande do Sul in 1866 with José Joaquim de Campos Leão – the famous Qorpo Santo – who intended to revolutionise Portuguese orthography and wrote, in only four months, almost twenty plays of the most authentic Theatre of the Absurd before its time. Indeed, in the play *A Separação dos dois esposos* ("The Separating Couple") Qorpo Santo introduces, as suddenly as is his style, two male characters called Tatu and Tamanduá (the names of exotic Brazilian animals, the second of which is almost extinct), whose employers – a married couple – end up killing themselves so that they can stay together. The two employees talk about their own relationship, calling each other "sweetheart". Tamanduá, not content to love his friend platonically, assaults Tatu and promises to do everything to satisfy his carnal desires. Tatu pushes him off, protesting that it is "the most harmful vice that man can practise". Unlike the tragic straight couple, they end up wrestling each other farcically, tearing each other's clothes off while the radical Tamanduá ironically demands that they divorce "carnally and spiritually" since for him it is a case of all or nothing. It should be remembered that these plays were written during a bout of insanity and that the author spent a good part of his life in mental asylums.

In the twentieth century the modernist Oswald de Andrade sprinkled his theatrical and literary works with homosexual situations and characters, endowing them with a sensibility which caused them to be associated with decadence. In his play *O rei da vela* ("The King of the Candle", 1933), he satirises the unhappy Brazilian capitalist whose fortune depends on the "generosity" of the British and the Americans – at the cost of the country's foreign debt. The play includes a character called Heloísa de Lesbos, the daughter of a decadent coffee baron, and her brother Totó Custard-Apple, a suffering but dangerously seductive queen who robs women of their lovers. Totó, who has broken with his lover Godofredo and spends his time eating sweets, comes on stage saying "I am a shattered woman" – a phrase still used self-mockingly in the gay ghetto today. With farcical obscenity and sarcasm, Totó sets about seducing an American magnate whose fortune is the object of dispute between the local bourgeoisie and aristocracy. Someone, commenting that the American likes masculine women, concludes: "Mr Jones is a lesbian!", to which one Joana, who is also known as John of the Divans, retorts that he is not; what the American really likes is lorry-drivers! At the end of the play Abelardo I is dying, under threat of substitution by Abelardo II, another nouveau riche bourgeois, whom the former calls "a man exhausted by Brazil, a product of the climate, the slave economy and the inhuman morality which creates millions of desperate masturbators and pederasts..." Before breathing his last, he suddenly calls Abelardo II "Febrônio disguised in the streets of Brazil!"[38]

A man of contradictions and paradoxes, Oswald de Andrade was a chauvinist who celebrated matriarchy, a child of bourgeois culture who wanted to destroy the bourgeoisie. It is therefore not surprising that homosexuals are the subject of such mocking prejudice in this play, while effeminacy is wielded as a weapon to provoke the strict morality of his time. His virulent and innovative novels should also be remembered. In them the author's aesthetic (or anti-aesthetic) intentions are to be found in a context of extraordinary humour and devastating irony against the Brazilian bourgeoisie and the colonised intellectuals. Thus Oswald himself, whose credentials are fundamentally rooted in Paris, is swept up in the whirlwind of his own mockery, which spares no one – very much in the style of the dadaists, where he imbibed his iconoclasm. In the novel *Chão* ("Floor") from his still immature period, he complacently introduces homosexual characters (Quindim and his lover Cláudio Manoel, and the little girls Pichorra and Xodó) in an attempt to explain them through ill-digested psychoanalytic theories. In the novels of his more virulent period, Oswald presents us with delightful situations where pederasty functions in a climate of corrosive amorality and depravity. In *Serafim Ponte Grande* (1929), the character Serafim is aroused by his friend Pinto Calçudo (literally "young cock" – a name which also gives the idea of the devouring penis) and he also wants to have sex with a strapping young man ("an Apollo") who has become his neighbour. Another time Serafim dreams that he has changed sex and become Pinto Calçudo's bride. As stubborn as a tropical Casanova (or Cascanova – "new shell" – as he calls himself), Serafim finally sodomises his submissive wife, Dona Lalá. In New York he meets a painter who admires the Germans for their "polysexual talents"; they talk about uranism until Serafim offers him his "urinary tracts" – allowing Oswald to make a caustic pun on the words "uranism" and "urinary".

Coelho Neto, a successful academic writer at the beginning of the century and the author of the play *O patinho torto ou Os mistérios do sexo* ("The Ugly Duckling or The Mysteries of Sex", 1931) was very different. With his irretrievable literary conventionalism, Coelho Neto wasted the corrosive possibilities of a delightful story. A young girl who is engaged but who loves ball games and smoking, unexpectedly discovers that she is a man. To avoid scandal, her family tries to arrange his engagement with his ex-fiancé's sister, which gives rise to some hilarious situations. In a near-farcical atmosphere the play on ambiguity never becomes inflammatory or explosive, for the author was afraid of breaking the conventions of his time and only superficially touched on the questions of alternating sex roles and the emancipation of women, topics repugnant to him.

Apart from the bold and isolated modernists, Brazil – even in the 1930s – was a province swathed in the most virginal modesty, something well manipulated by the ruling classes. It should be added that this was the period when "integralism" (Brazilian-style fascism) flourished, producing a theatre of militant nationalism that defended traditions, the family and religion. Thus in the play *Morrer pela Pátria* ("To Die for the Fatherland", 1936), Carlos Cavaco attacked in one blow homosexuality and moves towards female emancipation. (It should be remembered here that the struggle for women's votes in Brazil had been going on with some intensity since the beginning of the century.) Revolted by modern customs, Cavaco's hero attacks the vice of smoking among women, whose hands "were made for the delicate and subtle touch of petals and furs" and not for "this unaesthetic and smelly object, a cigarette". Protesting that a woman's beauty lies precisely in the basic difference between her and man, he gives a perfect example of confusing physiological sex roles in commenting: "If the effeminate man is contemptible for appearing ridiculous each time he imitates or displays feminine mannerisms, imagine the arrogant masculinised woman competing with men in taking on responsibilities and adopting vices!"[39]

Rejection of the "womanlike" or "effeminate" man did not come only from the integralists or in the 1930s. The Teatro de Arena in the 1960s, one of the most important Brazilian nuclei of socialist experimental theatre, did not allow openly homosexual actors to join the group. Even more recently, in the 1970s, Luís Sérgio Person, a director-producer, is known to have prohibited homosexual actors from being offered a part in the cast of *Lição de anatomia* ("Anatomy Lesson"), which had a resounding success and ran for years. The justification was that, since all the actors appeared nude on stage, homosexuals could create problems... I do not know what kind of test was used to detect this aspect of the actor's personality, but the method certainly failed, since I heard of it from one of the actors in the play who was also active in the gay movement in São Paulo. It is interesting to note that both Arena and Person belonged to the sectors of Brazilian society which claim to be the most progressive. It is enough to add that the famous "Theatre of the Oppressed", founded in Brazil and now based in Paris, is the direct descendant of Arena, Augusto Boal having been the director of Arena and also the Parisian group's intellectual mentor.

In literature, I have personally experienced the moralism of the Brazilian left. When trying to have my book of short stories published in 1976, I met a socialist editor who offered to publish only the stories he considered political; the others he saw as "decadent" for having homosexual experiences as their theme. Even more recently my first novel was rejected by the most progressive publisher in São Paulo, who considered it "a masterpiece, a possible best-seller, but too homosexual" (sic). That was the first time I realised that there was a chart which measured degrees of homosexuality in the same way as a thermometer measures the temperature. That was in 1982.

Homosexual themes are present, in an especially creative and innovative manner, in the theatrical work of Nelson Rodrigues, certainly the most original of modern Brazilian playwrights and one who has been most persecuted by police censorship. Presenting plays of great impact from the 1940s, Rodrigues (who died in 1980) is reminiscent in many ways of Oswald de Andrade's stance towards homosexuality. Ranging between "the perverted and highly moralistic" (in the words of one newspaper), he defined himself as a reactionary – but provoked protests from the most conservative sectors. It is said that at the first night of his play *Viúva porém honesta* ("The Unmerry Widow") in the 1950s, a parliamentary deputy pulled out a gun in the middle of the stalls and threatened to shoot if the performance continued. Rodrigues was also generally mauled by the critics before he became a national hero.

In Rodrigues' work it is unusual to find a character who is "normal and honest". They are all as deviant and neurotic as in Tennessee Williams, except that in Rodrigues' plays there is more mockery and, as a result, self-irony – a component which transfigures it and makes it a kind of poetry. In fact, Nelson Rodrigues' theatre boasts a devastating gallery of bandits, hysterical and unfaithful women, cuckolded husbands, sleazy or martyred queens, thieves, old pedophiles, incestuous and guilty fathers, false virgins of fifteen, etc. In his world one can find a faithful portrait of the imaginary city-dweller of Rio de Janeiro where the country's most cosmopolitan petite bourgeoisie live.

The dubious anti-homosexual paranoia which Nelson introduces into his work is also part of this same middle-class world. Thus in *The Anti-Nelson Rodrigues*, one of his last plays, young Osvaldinho is cruelly accused by his mother of having various vices, including being gay. The youth reacts: he might be anything, but not that. "I am not queer," he says with exaggerated indignation. "I have such a horror of male nudity that I don't like to look at my own naked body." It is not difficult to see that this hatred is simply a defence against an irresistible fascination for the forbidden side of masculine love, which often emerges from the simply factual to determine the actual structure of Nelson's works. Thus in plays like *O Beijo no asfalto* ("Kiss on the Asphalt"), *Viúva porém honesta* and deviant characters and/or situations clarify the general contradictions.

In *O Beijo no asfalto* (1960, prohibited by the censor in some states), Arandir is a young man who publicly kisses the mouth of a man about to die. The gesture, which he does not explain, makes his life hell. He loses his job, his wife leaves him, his neighbours ridicule him, the newspapers play up the event and a corrupt policeman wants to make a career out of his "immoral attitude". All this takes place, of course, against a background of tropical expressionism where the darker aspects meld in with mockery until the explosive finale. Then Arandir's father-in-law, apparently his worst enemy, kills him out of jealousy, admitting that he is passionately in love with him. In *Viúva porem honesta* (1957), Dorothy Dalton, a transvestite and dangerous villain, becomes a newspaper theatre critic – Rodrigues' malice against reviewers. Unexpectedly, the fifteen-year-old daughter of the owner of the paper becomes pregnant and has to be married off immediately. To everyone's surprise, she chooses Dorothy as her husband, despite being surrounded by ambitious suitors. The situations created are extremely sarcastic.

But it is in *Toda nudez será castigada* ("All Nudity Will be Punished") (1966, banned by the censor more than once) that "homosexual perversion" acquires tones of apocalyptic redemption in such a delightful manner that the script becomes pure poetry. In terms of drama, it is one of Rodrigues' most perfect plays, with a structure of small cinematographic scenes. These give it a very lively rhythm and sharp dialogue with absurd morbidity (it is enough to remember the prostitute tormented by the suspicion of having breast cancer). Very beautifully filmed by Arnaldo Jabor in the 1970s, *Toda nudez* was subtitled "An obsession in three acts" by Rodrigues himself, who presented in the film his double-edged view of the deviant aspect of homosexuality. Herculano, a widower, is going to marry Geni, a prostitute, having taken a vow of chastity out of respect for his dead wife. His son, Serginho, a puritanical adolescent who will not undress in front of anyone, even his doctor, is revolted by his father's attitude and leaves home. Arrested for drunkenness, Serginho is raped in prison by a Bolivian thief and taken to hospital with anal hemorrhaging (like a virgin's blood on first penetration). His family are as traumatised as the youth, whose grandfather used to say that if he were Hitler, he would have had all pederasts killed. As far as the family are concerned the rape has actually made Serginho an incurable pederast, and little by little the spectre of the handsome Bolivian thief gnaws at the fear of each of them. To avenge his mother's memory, Serginho becomes his stepmother's lover with the aim of punishing his father with this incestuous treachery. He is also transformed, now not only undressing before the doctor but revealing himself to be very virile. However, tormented by paranoid fantasies of the Bolivian thief, he disappears. In the end the family discovers that he has indeed gone to meet the handsome thief and has flown away with him to "continue the honeymoon".

Here, therefore, homosexual desire, rising above aberration, scandal and domination thanks to its radical innocence, becomes a focus of subversion against the puritan world, which is basically sado-masochistic and guilt-ridden. From rapist, the Bolivian thief becomes lover. Serginho, in fact, only becomes virile after being taken – made female in cultural terms. And the throne of poetry is conquered by execrable pederasty. Let us agree that this constitutes a rare blow in Brazilian artistic production, even today. In the theatre of the macho, Nelson Rodrigues' homosexuality-as-a-deviant-experience functions as a whip to punish an irrecoverably rotting society. If he believes that deviance is always next to madness,[40] the only possibility of redeeming this society is to plunge it into deviance/delirium. Or, as Nelson Rodrigues – a nihilist, reluctant atheist and enemy of psychoanalysis – himself said, our option as human beings "is between anguish and gangrene". Which is why, in his opinion, "only neurotics will see God".[41]

The 1970s: Laid-back Gays . . .

The 1970s in Brazil were a period of cruel dictatorship which only relaxed in the last years of the decade. The need to modernise against a background opposed to the practice of democratic politics perhaps favoured the rise among young people of liberation movements that were almost always free from precise ideologies (see the following chapter). One of the key words of the period was "arseless". An individual "lost his/her arse" the moment s/he rejected – often apparently irresponsibly – compromises with the militarised right or left of the time in order to discover a personal liberation, based on non-party-political solidarity and almost always associated with drugs and with homosexuality (then discreetly called "androgyny"). The beginning of this phenomenon could perhaps be detected in three inflammatory nuclei in the theatre and popular music. I am referring to Caetano Veloso, a composer-singer, Dzi Croquetes, a theatrical group, and Ney Matogrosso, a singer.

Caetano Veloso has been the enfant terrible of Brazilian music since 1969. After a short flirtation with the orthodox left, he proclaimed his independence from committed music. At the same time he broke with the idea of "pure" Brazilian popular music to use electric guitars and present a view of the world somewhere between irate and erudite and less linked to the left's proletarian-nationalist limitations. Caetano preferred to speak of a modern Brazil which was entering the world with great difficulty, emerging from the womb of electronics, television and the media in general. Possessing an extraordinary musical talent, the audacity of his ideas made him a contradiction perfectly expressed in his personal appearance and his shows. Normally seen in shocking plastic clothes, he would suddenly appear stripped of all ornament, singing only to an ordinary guitar.

Coming from Bahia – with its own deep-rooted culture which the so-called Marvellous South (São Paulo and Rio de Janeiro) did not understand – Caetano held a deep respect for the religion of *candomblé* (his African saint is Oxossi) at a time when every progressive under the dictatorship had to be a materialistic atheist. Criticised by the orthodox left as an "alienated petit bourgeois", he – with his partner Gilberto Gil – was nevertheless arrested by the military for supposed offences against patriotic values. It is said that his hair was cut (the dictatorship did not like long hair) and burnt in front of a complete battalion and the hoisted flag. He and Gil were then expelled from Brazil and he lived in London for two and a half years, where he made a beautiful hybrid record in 1970 with some songs that he had composed in English.

The ambiguity which disturbed both the military and the left was also reponsible for the image of a Caetano unorthodox in his habits. His friendship with Gilberto Gil, from whom he was inseparable although both were married, always gave rise to intentionally malicious speculations. Although he said explicitly on many occasions that he did not have sex with men, Caetano caused uproar when, on his return from London, he appeared on stage wearing lipstick and a bra and mincing camply like Carmen Miranda.

At the time, moreover, Caetano actively participated in a movement called Tropicalism with various other artistes, singers and composers of popular music. In the spirit of the vanguard of Anthropophagy created by Oswald de Andrade at the beginning of the century, the movement proclaimed the need to fearlessly absorb foreign influences in order to create a modern and vibrant Brazil. As a fan of the Rolling Stones, Beatles and Bob Dylan, Caetano did not hesitate to incorporate electric guitars in his music – which was profoundly connected to his Bahian roots – because, he said, the electric guitar had long been used by the *trio elétrico,* a kind of band that plays in the streets of Salvador at Carnival.

Furthermore, one of the movement's intellectual mentors was Hélio Oiticica, an artist who in the mid-1960s had proposed an "ugly art" concerned less with the eyes and more with the body as a whole, an art to be worn or penetrated – and which would then no longer be strictly art (something transcendental and erudite) but simply *creation*. An adherent of the Rimbaudian "systematic disorder of all the senses", Oiticica (who had spent years in London and New York) praised the dangerous bandits of the slums of Rio de Janeiro, objects of both his desire and his anti-art. To kill the conformism with which so-called "art" complied, he wanted a creation that was not only marginal but for marginals; he was pleased that his *"parangolés"* (items of clothing that he invented) were worn by the blacks of Mangueira samba school, which he venerated as much as rock music of the Stones and Jimi Hendrix. In one of his last public appearances (before dying of an overdose in 1980), Hélio Oiticica took part in a demonstration against the commercialisation of the arts. He appeared in the street in the briefest swimming-trunks and Carmen Miranda shoes – camp, as ever.

Tropicalism soon died, but Caetano Veloso followed his own path, confirmed as the great youth idol of the 1980s. In a recent interview he referred to homosexuals as "my brothers". He had earlier referred explicitly to his wish to be *multiple,* and confessed to having had a strong and conscious feminine identification since childhood. Even more provocative in his current shows – true festivals of campness – Caetano usually kisses each of his musicians (and some of them are very attractive!) insistently, for a long time and on the mouth, in front of an audience that roars in delight. His songs, which see the world with great sensitivity and poetry, reveal an undisguisable erotic fascination for masculinity. Thus, in a song in homage to the typical athletic and handsome youth of Rio de Janeiro who lives on the beaches of Ipanema with his surfboard, Caetano sings: "Lazy boy/ dragon tattooed on your arm/ shorts body free in the air/ when I see you I desire your desire/ Rio boy/ heat which makes me tremble/ take this song as a kiss." His companion Gilberto Gil also likes to touch on the theme of love for men, referring to it in one of his songs about a kiss between men – an obsessive topic: "I spent much time/ learning to kiss/ other men as I kiss my father./ When I kiss a friend/ I am sure of being someone/ like him [father]." Or in *Super-Homem* (*A canção*) – "Superman (The Song)", an ironic reference to *Superman* (*The Movie*) – Gil says "The womanly part of me/ which until then had kept quiet,/ is the better part/ which I now carry within me,/ and is what makes me live."

Along with these gestures rejecting the left and right, the beginning of the 1970s saw the rise of Dzi Croquetes, a unique theatrical group who tried to eliminate the role models of masculinity and femininity from their performances. In the same anthropophagic parody of absorbing to make one's own, the group were naturally inspired by The Cockettes of San Francisco. The caustic "cockette", however, became the mocking "croquete" – a kind of meatball very common in Brazilian snackbars, usually made from the left-overs of other meat. Even in its name, therefore, there was an ironic reference to its parody of the American group. Also influenced by the "gender-fuckers" in the United States at the time, Dzi Croquetes brought to the Brazilian stage an ambiguity unheard of in its virulence. Moustachioed and bearded men appeared in women's clothes and false eyelashes, wearing football stockings with high-heeled shoes and brassières over hairy chests. Neither men nor women – or rather exaggerated men *and* women – they danced and told double-edged jokes in an attempt to break through the noose of repression which censorship and the police drew round the slightest deviation from what was permissible in the period of the dictatorship. Dzi Croquetes were a great success among the more dissatisfied young people of the time, being both on and off stage a very important focus for questions of sexual morality and experimentation with drugs as a means of self-knowledge. Being so radical ("Live dangerously to the end"), the appearance of Dzi Croquetes initiated the discussion of both sexual roles and of gay ambiguity vis-à-vis gay normality (see more references in the next chapter). It was they who brought to Brazil the most recent and searching questions of the international gay movement, particularly the US movement with its sorely missed "gender-fuckers" as seen in the streets of San Francisco before the detestable and conformist fashion of Gay Macho.

The mythical figure of Ney Matogrosso, another pop music and show-biz phenomenon, must not be forgotten. Having come to the public's attention in 1973 as the vocalist in the group Secos Molhados, he soon stood out from the others and became an overwhelming national success. Sometimes fully made-up, bare-chested and in long skirts, sometimes covered in feathers with enormous horns on his head and wearing a miniscule loincloth, Ney waggled his hips like one possessed and sang with a contralto's voice. His nationwide success with every age and class confused the media. Man? Woman? Queer? His voice – in reality a rare contratenor register with no falsetto – contrasted with his masculine body and hairy chest. In him Dzi Croquetes' ambiguity became a veritable paroxysm. As if that was not enough, *Vira* ("Become"), one of the songs on his first record, was a dubious and scandalous invitation played on the radio day and night: "Become, become, become a man/ become a wolfman." The wolfman might easily be an ironic reference to those nocturnal city cruisers in search of a partner. In gay nightclubs this meaning was obvious and the song became something of a gay hymn.

Shortly afterwards the group fell apart and Ney Matogrosso remained gloriously alone. Brazil had probably not seen the rise of such a fascinating and exotic pop music idol since Carmen Miranda. Bolder than anyone had dared to be before him, Ney had to confront much aggression and many insults wherever he went, but the love which men and women, old people and children everywhere have given him has been incomparably more surprising and comforting. His importance in changing habits in Brazil can only be compared with the power of television in imposing fashions. Now a millionaire, revered as one of the best interpreters of Brazilian pop music, he continues to provoke – because "for me it is a mission to put an end to the idea that homosexuality is something sad and suffering, something which has to stay hidden".[42] Ironically the son of a soldier, Ney admits to having so-called "feminine" qualities and says: "I am a person who has emotions and sensitivity and I am proud of never having to hide them. I display them. Now, if that's within the bounds of femininity, so what?"[43] And – a sign of the times! – he dares to say openly things which, even today, are quite rare for Brazilian performers when dealing with their homosexuality. For example, he admits that women are mad for him "when they find out I'm homosexual", but "when I'm in bed with a man, I'm not a woman, I'm a man" because "whether you like it or not, I'm male and wouldn't change my cock for anything in the world."[44]

As if echoing the myth of the kiss between men inaugurated by Nelson Rodrigues and promoted by Caetano Veloso, Ney let himself be photographed kissing Caetano himself on the mouth. When asked why he had kissed another man on the mouth, he answered, "I adore Caetano. I would kiss Caetano anywhere, not just on the mouth."[45] Ney is even more contentious: "I want to have the pleasure of a son. I would love my son very much. I never kissed my father when I was a child and I really wanted to. I would kiss my son a lot. Even on the mouth, because the mouth is part of the face and isn't taboo. I only kissed my father after I grew up, in the street in São Paulo. He was really shocked because the whole street saw a man kissing him and no one knew it was his son."[46]

He confesses, moreover, that his saint in *candomblé* (his favourite religion) is Oxumaré, a being that is a woman for six months and a man for six months (see Appendix). Very aware of his significance on a cultural level, Ney's songs have become more and more dubious and malicious. The result, obviously, is the fundamental and healthy confusion which his image continues to stir up in many people's minds. He recently recorded a song translated freely from the international success "Tell Me Once Again" (which was composed in English by Brazilians). In his version the first verses are an audible parody of the original – *Telma eu nao sou guei* – "Thelma, I'm not gay", The song is about a gay man who wants to marry a girl (Thelma) and who tries to convince her that, despite his past, he has become indisputably straight. The evidence he offers, however, becomes more and more compromising – "these boys are just my friends" and "this nightgown isn't mine". There is nothing more paradoxical or hilarious than hearing children or my neighbour's maid bellowing out this song, which became a great nationwide success. I can also confirm that adolescents understand its ambiguity, for they maliciously sing it each time I pass.

Ney had earlier recorded a *machista*-style song from the north-east. The result is, to say the least, shocking when he sings in his contralto voice such verses as: "I am a man with an M/ and with an M I am much a man./ If you doubt it/ look at my name./ Now I'm dating/ dating and going to marry./ Ah! Maria say that I am/ I am a Man with an M." Or Leo Jaime's priceless adaptation of Chuck Berry's "Johnny B Goode", which Ney sings as *Johnny pirou* ("Johnny Flipped") in a recording of 1982. Prohibited by the censor from being played over the radio, the Brazilian version tells of the burning passion of an American executive called Johnny for a big black from Rio de Janeiro during a football game between Flamengo and Fulminense in Maracanã stadium. Johnny's life literally changes at the moment when Flamengo scores a goal and the black, full of joy, grabs him by the waist and kisses him on the mouth, while the ball shamelessly runs between the legs of the "impassioned goalkeeper" (notice that kiss on the mouth). From then on Johnny has flipped...

Despite accusations that he has conformed, Ney still sings the length and breadth of Brazil, swathed in jewellery, near-nude, limp-wristed and mincing. In his words: "Insofar as it's possible, that's what I want people to see in me: freedom."[47] Whenever I feel depressed by the fact that I live in a province, not a country, I think, "Well, at least we have Ney Matogrosso." And I sigh with relief.

...in the Limelight

In 1973 Darcy Penteado, a well-known painter and portraitist – who later was to become a member of *Lampião*'s editorial team – held an exhibition where, for the first time in Brazilian painting, male nudes were not only the basic theme but were also integral to the style, allowing brushstroke and medium to display an unequalled eroticism. In the same period Maria Betânia and Gal Costa, both famous singers of popular music, let themselves be photographed at the end of a show giving each other a tender kiss on the mouth – which, to a certain extent, broke the ice between women. Their gesture was symbolically continued by such other female singers as Ângela Ro-Ro, Leci Brandão, Simone and Marina Lima, who in one way or another all let their love preference for women be known. In the 1980s Marina has preferred to appear as a saucy youth with short hair and in a suit and tie, singing in her very personal style: "You need a man to call your own/ even if that man is me."

But not even the festival of "forbidden" kisses at the beginning of the 1970s provoked such frenzy as the play *Greta Garbo, quem diria, acabou no Irajá* ("Who knows if Greta Garbo ended up in Irajá?"), which portrayed onstage the intimate lives of gay men and became one of the greatest all-time successes in the Brazilian theatre. It was also put on abroad and its New York production was highly praised. Fernando Melo, its young author, has often been a victim of government censorship, each time because of homosexual themes. Perhaps because it was the first to make this "exotic world" familiar, *Greta Garbo* ran for three years and has been regularly revived in new productions. Its story tells of an old queen who picks up a naive youth recently arrived in the big city from the interior. One of the queen's various pecularities is the fact that he likes to be called Greta Garbo during intercourse. The play humorously shows the evolution of a relationship which comes to an end when a woman arrives on the scene. As can be seen, the theme is not new (and has been exhaustively explored since then), but the play shows good commercial judgement, has a lively rhythm and sharp dialogue, as well as the caustic humour of the stereotyped screaming queen who makes a feast of his bitterness.

These characteristics might be said to have made *Greta Garbo* the first typical example of one style of "gay theatre" in Brazil. Strongly influenced by Plínio Marcos (a dramatist who always writes about the underworld where ruffians, prostitutes and queens mix), *Greta Garbo* also relies on melodramatic scenic effects and a keen ear for a queen's everyday language. The situations and characters are expressed by means of a love triangle designed to bring about predicted consequences, where the old queen's only advantage is his savoir-vivre and his caustic tongue. The (young and easy) woman's fundamental function is as his counterpoint and confederate while the (good-looking and naive) youth is the object to be conquered. As the first in this series of "theatrical revenge" (many were to follow), the older man wins the confrontation – certainly art's revenge on life. His victory, however, is provisional, because no one really wins anything: the resulting bitterness is less a component of ambiguity than a confession of impotence. *Greta Garbo* also suffers from a common trait of the "gay theatre" which followed it: the (naturalist) characters never stop talking in brilliant oratorical arguments where the author seems more concerned in displaying his own subtlety and gay humour – creating something like a theatrical exorcism, the result of which is, at the very least, complacent.

In the mid-1970s the theme of gay love began to break through the barrier of censorship and extreme reaction and even reached the covers of national magazines – such as *Istoé*, which had two men tenderly holding hands on its cover two years before *Time*. Commercial advertising has not lagged behind. An advertisement for Rastro perfumes covering three complete pages of various weekly magazines used very attractive photographs of three couples – a man and a woman, two women and two men – with the phrase "for irresistible encounters of the first, second and third kind". Another advertisement at the time created a very significant situation by claiming that a certain cream was *really* fresh. In Portuguese the word "fresh" (*fresco*) is also slang for effeminate, allowing the 15-second commercial to play on this linguistic uncertainty. As a very camp and aristocratic butler shook a carton of the cream, a group of girls in the background could be heard shouting "fresh, fresh". Instead of being offended by the comment, the butler drew himself up proudly until he realised that the cream was being praised, not him. At which point, indignant and quite enraged, he walked off. Conservatives protested, accusing the advertisement of making a "pernicious campaign" in favour of homosexuality and demanding that it be taken off the air. They were unsuccessful because there was a surprising increase in sales of the cream; research into the success discovered that 84% of television viewers had loved the advertisement, which not only stayed on the air but set a marketing precedent. In Brazil homosexuality could now facilitate consumption. It was an important advance for the Gay Boom.

In this propitious climate the theatre underwent a veritable volte-face. Of the 25 plays running in São Paulo in the first half of 1978, 11 dealt directly or indirectly with homosexuality – including some by foreign authors and the indefatigable *Greta Garbo*. Most, of course, subscribed to the recent trend of "gay theatre", always keeping a careful eye on the box-office. Government censorship had been permanently alert to what it called the "exploitation and praise of homosexuality" since 1968 when Plínio Marcos' play *Barrela* (where a man in prison was raped) had been banned – as was the Brazilian production of *The Boys in the Band*. Unlike earlier plays on homosexuality, a good many in the 1970s were written by gay writers who, in one way or another, put their personal experiences on the stage. "The homosexual" in the theatre was no longer either Nelson Rodrigues' distant and mythologised being or Plínio Marcos' disgraced pariah. His whole life was now opened up to audiences who became familiar with a multitude of gay characters that, no matter how shocking or exotic they might be, all had a certain *normality* in common. The stage was invaded by boys who had become prostitutes at a young age, by old queens who advertised in lonely hearts columns, by couples (male and female) that fell apart through external interference or because of a third person, by the lives and passions of transvestites, by the problems of dressmakers arguing with their lovers, by tragedies of gay men who marry women for convenience, by brothers incestuously in love, by decadent queens and ingenuous youths who fall in love unthinkingly (only the audience realises), by communities of queens who fight over a Real Man, even by a life of Carmen Miranda (played by a transvestite) and a gay version of Dracula in love with a traveller whose blood he sucks. Not to mention the international triumphs which were successfully produced in Brazil such as *Bent, Chorus Line, Boy Meets Boy, Village, Zoo Story, The Kiss of the Spider Woman* (in a theatrical adaption by the author of the novel, Manuel Puig), etc.

The mediocre or merely conventional level of most of these plays caused one annoyed critic to complain about this obsession with contemplating one's own navel. He claimed that "the poorly verbalised revolt of homosexuals is as conservative and uninteresting" as plays about chauvinists, because "when someone appears on the stage underlining again and again and again the fact that homosexuals are *people*, we are at the limits of redundancy".[48] The criticism makes sense. Gay plays have suffered from a complacency that sometimes touches on exhibitionism. His air of martyrdom included, the gay man going through a process of self-assertion – as was (and is) common on the Brazilian stage – has been made safe and normalised (as a consumer product) in language if not in theme; in other words he has conformed. Even when the individuals and situations are scandalous, the stage space legitimises those on the fringes of society who expose themselves to generally bourgeois and conservative middle-class audiences. Furthermore, this crucial preoccupation with affirming one's identity makes the gay character the object of some holy cause in an attempt at exorcism which ends up in fashionable clichés, As well as domesticising, banners and clichés are usually very far from poetry. So this heroisation is less a gesture of subversion through art than an attempt at integration in the market; the gay boom becomes something new for the system to consume.

This attitude of consumerist integration has not been retricted to the theatre. The Brazilian cinema has specialised in presenting homosexual characters as objects of ridicule since the 1970s, particularly in *pornochanchadas* – very commercial, mediocre and moralistic films which still infest the Brazilian cinema and are almost always very successful with the public. Generally caricatures, gay men serve as nothing more than a pretext to provoke mocking laughter from the macho spectator. On the other hand love between women has always been treated with the debatable complacency of a voyeur – proving that the purpose of such films is basically to satisfy the most sexist masculine public. There too mediocrity and moralising are the general rule. Cassandra Rios, a writer who specialises in best-sellers on lesbian love, has recently been in vogue with several little more than sufferable film adaptions of her works. Even the less commercial branch of cinema, directed towards a more educated public, has often borrowed the theme of homosexual love, repaying with some scenes of indisputable beauty, some photographically innovative outlines and even some disturbing characters – eg. the transvestite Eloína, perfectly and with the greatest individuality played by a straight actor, in *República dos assassinos* ("Republic of the Murderers"); the attractive backsides of the two incestuous brothers in *A intrusa* ("The Intruder" – based on a story by Jorge Luís Borges); and the dense malice of *Toda nudez será castigada* mentioned above.

Among short films, which less easily gain general release, there have been some very disturbing works (documentaries and others), even if the results have not always been satisfactory from the point of view of poetic creation. *Daniele, Carnaval e cinzas* ("Daniele, Carnival and Ashes", 1979, made in Super-8) documented the day-to-day routine of a transvestite, including life with his lover. *Profissão: travesti* ("Profession: Transvestite", 1982) and *Ritos e passagems* ("Rites and Passages", 1983) were also concerned with the daily life of transvestites, although from different angles. Unlike the light-hearted ambience of the latter, the suffocating and distressing mood of *Profissão: travesti* showed horror at the transvestites' fate. It did, however, present one wonderful scene: before going out on the streets a transvestite changed clothes on a wasteland at night; under his everyday women's clothes were other – dazzling – women's clothes giving the effect of a mask under a mask. There was also Sandra Werneck's recent documentary *Pena prisão* ("Punishment Prison"), about a women's jail where 80% of the inmates are black and mulatta. Its daily life and preoccupations are portrayed (reasonably successfully) by the prisoners, who speak about themselves with great dignity and bear witness to the struggle they have to go through to be able to live their loves in prison.

And Now With You: The Electronic Gay

Brazilian television, which is almost totally dependent on private capital, is under the particularly close eye of political censorship and obeys a strict moral code that prohibits the broadcasting of obscenities or forms of sexual perversion, only "allowing suggestions of sexual relations within the scheme of normality" (sic). Despite this and protests from conservative groups, television has also exploited homosexuality – and not always with half-measures. Even the delightful Chacrinha, who since the 1960s has been presenting the campest and most anarchic amateur talent show, has followed the trend. Dressed as Nero or a bride or a clown, old Chacrinha interrupts his "happenings" to ask the public such rogue questions as "Who likes to suck lollipops more, men or women?" (*Pirulito* – "lollipop" – also means "cock" in children's language.) And as he throws dried cod or bananas at the audience the refrain of a song begins which they take up: "Maria Big-Shoe is Maria by day and Joseph by night." (*Sapatão* – "big shoe" – is also used for masculine lesbians.) Or he repeats the chorus of an old Carnival song: "Look at Zezé's hair-do, is he perhaps. . ." which the audience completes in unison, "gay, gay!"

There have recently been obvious and explicit gay relationships in various very popular soap operas and series. At least one of the latter tackled the problem directly – the very well-known *Malu mulher* ("Malu – a Woman"), in which a kind of stereotyped feminist is the protagonist of stories which vary from episode to episode. The one entitled "Something that didn't work out" told of the conflicts of one of Malu's young friends when he discovered he was in love with another man – as Albinoni's *Adagio* played in the background. The funniest aspect was that the series was bought by Cuban television, where the actress who played Malu, Regina Duarte, became a national idol and was even received by Fidel Castro himself on her visit to the country in 1983. While on the subject of soap operas, it is worth remembering a curious fact: police censored the story of (suggested) love between two female cousins in the recent soap opera *Homem proibido* ("Forbidden Man"), based on Nelson Rodrigues' stories. Are Brazilian homes more susceptible to lesbianism?

Gay references and characters also proliferate in television comedies. One of the very popular *Os Trapalhões* ("The Bunglers"), who generally love appearing on television camping in women's clothes, has all the characteristics of voice, gesture and posture of a very fragile doll; his tics alone cause the audience to laugh. *Chico City*, with Chico Anísio, an equally popular comic, has the delightful character Painho, a gay priest in *candomblé* who dresses and speaks affectedly, tends to faint when confronted by handsome men, displays open sexual indifference for women and is continually arguing with his rival, another gay priest. In comedy, however, the boldest character is Captain Gay, played by Jô Soares, a very fat and individual actor, who also takes the roles of a gallery of humorous feminine types, from the air hostess who is afraid of flying to an enormous protest singer delicately called Little Norma. One of a pair of gay Supermen – his assistant is a tall mulatto with lilting voice and exaggerated gestures who wears a blue Afro wig and answers to the androgynous name of Carlos Suely – Captain Gay was at one time a veritable nationwide craze. It is particularly amusing and ironic to come across in the neighbourhood, as I did, groups of small boys playing and warbling "Captain Gay's Rock". Attacked by moralists (who accuse the programme of defending homosexuality), and by those gay militants who hate to see the nation laughing at queens, Captain Gay pokes fun at both the right and left, defining himself as a "defender of minorities against tyrannies". His feathers and pink clothes are a parody of Superman's uniform and, also in parody, he appears whenever someone needs his help. He also carries with him a magic wand with which he creates a lot of confusion, but always manages to find surprising solutions in the end.

Patrício Bisso, an Argentinian transvestite-actor, plays another very successful comic character on television at a more intellectual level. Satirising the fashion of sexual advice given on women's programmes, Bisso created Olga del Volga, a "Russian sexologist of the Soviet liberal line", who answers (generally fictitious) letters from her distressed viewers on such subjects as sadomasochism, orgasm, homosexuality, mastur-

Mário Miranda/Maria Aparecida, *candomblé* priest, at his temple in the slums of Recife (p. 175 ff.)

Covers of *Lampião* magazine from 1980 – "The Church and Homosexuality" and "The Orphans of the Sierra Maestra". Fidel Castro is singing, "I don't believe in fairies, but they exist, they exist . . ." (p. 136 ff.)

Carnival in Rio, 1985

LAMPIÃO
da esquina

DENÚNCIA

PEGA PRA CAPAR!

Nas impressionantes fotos de Juca Martins/Agência F4, cenas da caça aos travestis, um esporte a que a polícia paulista vem se entregando com todo o empenho de que dispõe. Noticiário completo sobre os desmandos do delegado Richetti e os protestos contra a sua atuação arbitrária, nesta edição.

Police repression against transvestite prostitutes in São Paulo, as documented by *Lampião* magazine (p. 163 ff.)

bation etc. Olga's mission is to "raise the Brazilian per capita orgasm index". When a viewer wrote in that she had finally achieved orgasm the previous night, "but I don't know if it was a real orgasm," Olga replied: "Don't worry. Orgasms are like buses. If you miss one there's another one along soon." In another fictitious letter someone asked her which clothes were best recommended for the sexual act, and a fausse-naive wanted to know how to perform oral sex. Olga's answer was: "It can be done by telephone, shouting out of the window or even gargling beside the loved one."

The widespread success of all these characters would be shocking if they were not already routine on Brazilian television. The various debates on AIDS broadcast nationwide are one proof of homosexuality's guaranteed audience. Another is the resounding success on women's programmes of Clodovil Hernandez, one of the country's most famous fashion designers. He first appeared giving advice in an acidly effeminate tongue, and after achieving national fame was given his own weekly variety programme. For the launch, broadcast live at peak viewing time, there was a cocktail party in São Paulo's most luxurious hotel. Clodovil appeared against the "chicest" of backgrounds, his name shining in blue neon. Duly advised by a team of dancers and technicians, he sings, dances, recites poetry, presents fashion shows, interviews personalities and makes ironic remarks. Surrounded by 35 genuine brides-to-be, Clodovil gave advice on matrimony – with the most delicate and feline affectation of Brazil's newest star. The wave of success has also put him on stage. In a specially written play he has travelled the length and breadth of Brazil with the story of a dressmaker arguing with a rich client over a handsome and poor youth. Where have we read this story before?

The discovery of homosexuality has also affected transvestites, who, until recently, were strictly forbidden from appearing on screen. On Saturday nights (the time when the holy Brazilian family is always relaxed and ready to consume entertainment) an endless stream of wretched transvestites compete in a contest of impersonation in *Hora do Bolinha* ("Cake Time"). Obviously there is a large audience for this parade of little talent and overblown exoticism. Trickery, however, also extends to selling. A recent television commercial had a very beautiful and very sensual dark-haired woman in a low-cut dress presenting a new type of wardrobe and insisting that people should not let themselves be taken in by appearances.

However, through a careful campaign complementing the commercial, the public were surprised to discover that they had let themselves "be taken in by appearances" – the fascinating dark-haired woman was in fact Roberta Close, a transvestite who was famous from then on, even making the cover of Argentinian magazines. She was held to be an "example of the beauty and sensuality of Brazilian women"...

Our Rubbish, Our Art

Once the period of integration initiated by the gay boom had passed, what remained was a kind of great defensive shell, on the cultural level, against homosexuality. Some parts of society began to show the indifference of someone who "knows the subject inside-out". It was like peeling an exotic fruit and discovering it had a very ordinary taste. So the husk was left and the means of oppression became more sophisticated. Not long ago the *Folha de São Paulo* – now the country's most liberal paper – reported that the launches of two gay books were being held on the same day and at the same time. With veiled irony, but without noticing that it was committing the same sin, the article said that one had to turn up at both places "so as not to appear prejudiced". In other words, only appearances count and this caricature of liberation reinforces defences. Why? Because in this era of artificial flavouring, permissiveness is a magic spell by which liberation is put on display so that in reality nothing changes. And how much responsibility do the (sometimes complacent and self-pitying) pro-gay arts bear in bringing us here? It is not a question of pointing out the guilty parties, but we cannot ignore the suspicion that the arts (gay or not) have been amazingly naive in raising the veil from the world of gay men and lesbians and judging that to be in itself a gesture of liberation. Above all, this art has generally been far from poetic and, insofar as cultural creativity is concerned, it has been a resounding failure. This has probably been the highest tribute demanded by the ideology of consumerism – even when the intentions have been the best possible.

Of the real remnants, use was made of the only element left: rubbish. And with rubbish a fascinating experiment was created – Vivencial Diversiones,* a theatre company which

*Lit. "Living Entertainments" [Trans. note].

existed in Recife between 1979 and 1981. In a squalid theatre at the edge of a shanty-town, an ex-Benedictine monk – who liked to have sex with delinquent youths and make pregnant the women who fell into his bed – brought together a group which basically consisted of shanty-town dwellers and talentless transvestites who walked the streets of the neighbourhood, almost all adolescent, illiterate and very much on the fringes of delinquency. Under his direction, the group began to vomit its deliria onto the stage, sometimes pirating texts, sometimes inventing with their love of obscenity. In fact it was continuing the tradition of the *teatro de rebolado* and, perhaps inadvertently, the experimentation of Dzi Croquetes – but now with a component of radical outlawry which came from life onto the stage, where it was both topic and style. In other words, with Vivencial Diversiones being gay was an inflammatory element of subversive invention.

There were kilos of significant rubbish in the wings of the theatre: pieces of clothing, cardboard boxes to create improvised backgrounds, old lumber for many unexpected uses. In the pit – which had small tables as in a café-theatre, but on a floor of trampled earth – transvestite chorus-girls sold pornographic books and chocolates, as well as little carved dolls with the pompous pseudonyms of gay artistes: Grace Flórida, Luciana Luciene, Lee Marjories, Andrea Coccineli, Celi Bee, Lara. On the stage famous women singers were impersonated with delightful sarcasm. There were biting dramatic sketches, narratives and poems and a parody of Genet's *The Maids* in the purest trash-style. The actors were almost never convincing. The real show, however, was in the asides, and its originality was more important than its beauty, because rubbish was truly transformed. The secret was precisely in the ambiguity. The men answered to feminine names or feminised their virility in some way. Beto Hollywood, a handsome hairy youth with fair hair, brought his long curls to one side to fasten an old crepe flower; he wore a rumba dancer's costume and did variations on ambiguity. Marquesa, a "cockerel" (*frango* – Recife slang for a gay man) who had children and everything, wore stockings over hairy legs and came on in women's clothing, mixing with the audience and slandering the country's politicians – "the opposition is part of the situation". A cynic and a pessimist, Petronius was the group's punk surrealist: he came on stage with an enormous black eye, playing the part of a gay man who had cruised a tough guy who had ended up by greedily grasping the gay's cock – variations on ambiguity. Celi Bee, with a little boy's hard face and the bony body of someone starving, impersonated a drugged Janis Joplin, ending with the words: "The prick" – of a needle – "kills! The prick is really great!" Petronius returned to the stage, now in a wig of purple and pink straw turning faster and faster in his impersonation of a famous lesbian singer. Then someone did a complete striptease; to the public's surprise it was Juraci, the only woman in the group. She returned to the stage shortly afterwards, this time with Andrea, a blond transvestite with an aristocratic air. They stripped together. Finally, when both were quite naked, they turned back to back, took each other's hands and turned slowly to the sound of music. The public could see that Juraci had a cunt and Andrea a prick; or perhaps it was the other way round and Juraci had a prick and Andrea a cunt. Eloquent silence. On stage was the relativisation provoked by this difficult art of ambiguity.

Accused by the left of being a band of irresponsible queens and branded as communists by conservatives, Vivencial Diversiones suddenly became the greatest theatrical success in Recife and the height of fashion. Its walls, which were not really walls but curtains, were pulled down and real walls were built. At weekends the predominantly heterosexual public fought over seats in the small auditorium – even entire families came. Many people could not get in, despite the fact that the price of tickets was high in a generally poor city and each production ran for months at a time. One day Vivencial came to an end. It had run out of ambiguity and originality. I do not know how far success was responsible. I would risk saying that Vivencial Diversiones could not survive because it came too close to the centres of power and thus abandoned the difficult art of tightrope-walking which came from being on the fringe. It dried up. In absorbing it, the system perhaps robbed it of its poetry.

CHAPTER FIVE

Gay Politics and The Manipulation of Homosexuality

"I go out in secret,
I look for you
but they find me.
Dad hits me.
The headmaster punishes me.
The left tries to kill me."

Glauco Mattoso (1982)

One of the most serious problems in countries rigidly controlled by a dominant elite is that history passes them by like water over an impermeable riverbed. At least that is the impression in Brazil, where history twists along a course that seems to return to the same spot until explosively exhausting a cycle and leaping violently onto the next stage. Partly because it lives on the periphery of the West and partly because few of its inhabitants are consumers of culture, Brazil appears to have great difficulty in absorbing contemporary themes, preferring to modernise itself only when confronted by faits accomplis. Accustomed to grand spectacles, its cultural elite copies the latest fashions from Paris or New York, but is seldom inclined towards real change. As a result, modernity in Brazil is easily reduced to a phenomenon that simply follows the latest fashion. Gay liberation has developed along the same lines. If it arrived in Brazil at least a decade late and then entered a cul-de-sac, this is largely due to the basic conservatism, insensitivity and self-indulgence of a cultural elite which feeds on fashions in order to recycle itself. Thus the present profusion of homosexual characters on Brazilian radio, television and cinema is a source of excitement for this modernised elite which prides itself on being able to accept queers and dykes – "Except in my family, of course!..." Let's be up-to-date, yes, but there's no need to go too far.

A Delayed Start

Living on the periphery, we Brazilians feel distanced from the rest of the world. It could be said that the emerging gay movement is part of the same vain attempt to open up, seek a dialogue with our contemporaries and modernise ourselves. Since 1975, the relaxation of the most recent in the cycle of Brazilian dictatorships has been accompanied by the outline of a new movement towards cosmopolitanism. It was hardly a secret that the 1964 military coup was marked by an element of nationalism and xenophobia which the left shared – despite the serious differences between the two ideological poles. Paradoxically, by causing the exile of a large number of intellectuals and placing them in brutal contact with the outside world, the military caused a compulsory modernisation, culturally speaking, in this period of Brazilian life. Years later, when the amnesty allowed them to return, they brought back experiences which they had absorbed in the time they had been forced to stay away from home. Eurocommunism came to us in this way, as did ecological concerns, feminism, and anti-racism, which at that time were all flourishing in advanced capitalist countries. At the very least this is an aspect of the "Anthropophagy" very common in Brazilian life – the phenomenom of absorbing the foreign in order to secure a perilous identity. Modernisation, therefore, can also be seen as a Brazilian means of survival.

I too went into exile (for three years, voluntarily) and, on coming back to Brazil in 1976, brought back novelties from the outside world. Being totally involved in the facts narrated below, I have absolutely no intention of being scientific in writing about them. On the contrary, I intend to make a kind of statement as the protagonist I often was. The truth is that, returning from a fruitful stay in the United States, Mexico and various other Latin American countries, I felt I had become a very hybrid being whose characteristics could not be restricted to one cultural identity. Outside Brazil I had had innumerable experiences, from which I had retained the aspects that seemed to me most important and most pleasant. Having lived with militant American gays, foreign feminists and exiled Brazilian revolutionaries, I felt doubly alone when I returned "home". I could not exchange ideas with my old comrades, I was shocked by the lack of punctuality and the irresponsibility of drivers, and I was irritated by the consumer mentality of the enlarged gay ghetto which I found in Brazil at the end of the seventies.

This feeling of inadequacy led me to try to bring together some gay university students in São Paulo in 1976, to form a discussion group on homosexuality. There were never more than a dozen at the meetings, all young men. Some came with vague liberal and assertive propositions, while the thoughts and feelings of others were hampered by the ideology of the old left. We tried to study some texts. However, the participants, who were very reticent about the experiment, were paralysed by feelings of guilt – even when they had been humiliated by their party comrades for being homosexual. The big question they asked themselves, frequently heard in gay groups in the movement's first phase, was: Is it politically valid for us to meet to discuss sexuality, something generally considered secondary given the serious situation in Brazil? All movements ran up against this question, without reaching a clear answer. As if that was not enough, 70% of the group frankly admitted that they considered themselves abnormal because of their homosexuality. In such circumstances it is not suprising that the project fell apart after a few painful meetings.

Two years later the political scene had appreciably evolved. There was a certain insolence in the air, as much towards the official left as towards the police state. In 1978 groups of women – who were still very stifled by the party line – began to explore, timidly and from an increasingly feminist perspective, such sacrilegious topics as sexuality and abortion. They also tried to impose a principle of autonomy on their discussions, which broadened as newspapers were founded and women returned home from exile. Blacks too began their first attempts at discussing racism, culture and organisation outside the iron circle of the old left's parties and centralism. At the same time several serious ecological disasters – poisoned rivers, excess pollution that caused the birth of acephalous children, oppressive devastation of the Amazon forest and the babylonian nuclear programme secretly begun by the military dictatorship – had led to the setting up of various ecological action groups. All this presented new problems for the orthodox left. While the topics of sexuality and racism were discussed outside the parameters of the class struggle (or "greater struggle" in their jargon), abortion created disagreeable friction with the left's ally, the progressive wing of the Catholic church. Furthermore, the question of nuclear technology emerged as fundamental to the continental geopolitical situation insofar as nuclear development in Brazil and Argentina signified a crack in American imperialist hegemony, by making possible the proliferation of atomic weapons which the United States so feared.

It was in this context of agitation that some gay intellectuals and artists from São Paulo and Rio de Janeiro met at the end of 1977 to discuss an anthology of gay Latin American literature to be edited by Winston Leyland of Gay Sunshine Press. From there came the idea of forming a collective to found a newspaper for homosexuals which would discuss a wide range of matters and be sold monthly at newsstands throughout the country. The group (of which I was one) met frequently and the project flourished, although with an uncertain financial infrastructure. Number 0 of *Lampião* appeared in April 1978 – an almost scandalous event for the prurient left and right, who were accustomed, above all, to reticence. For good or bad *Lampião* signified a break: eleven mature men, some well-known and intellectually respected, were involved in a project where the topics dealt with were those considered "secondary" – sexuality, racial discrimination, the arts, ecology, machismo – and all this in the generally camp and insolent language of the homosexual ghetto. As well as publishing guides to gay cruising in towns all over the country, it used words forbidden in respectable vocabulary (such as *viado* and *bicha* [both = "queer"]), allowing its articles to enjoy a healthy independence and a difficult equidistance from the various groups of the institutionalised left. It was in many ways a disobedient paper.

At the same time as *Lampião* was born in Rio de Janeiro, in São Paulo a group of homosexuals interested in organising discussions and liberationist activity began to meet; I was very happy to join it. Predominantly made up of young actors, members of the liberal professions and students, the group was small and remained so for almost a year, going on to serve as a model for those which came afterwards. From then on the gay movement in Brazil had a backbone of groups which brought activists together rather in the manner of private clubs for gay men and lesbians. Of course each group tried to have its minimum rules and its individual style, accentuating differences in order to find its identity – principles which might be considered as defence systems against a hostile environment.

Something similar seems to have occurred in the early days of the American and European gay liberation movements, with the Mattachine Society in the United States and Arcadie in France.

From our very first gatherings, styles and concerns emerged which were rare in the meetings of young leftists of the time. We tried to focus topics on the individuals present and their daily experiences, doubts, problems and plans, the aim being to act on reality, starting not with *another* but with ourselves. Up to a point the model was the American gay consciousness-raising group, through which we sought a social identity. In any case this attitude came from a firm decision to take responsibility for ourselves, to become aware of our own bodies and sexuality and to reactivate forgotten aspects of our personalities in the group relationship. The experience or contact which many of us had had with political parties of the left also preoccupied us with disaligning ourselves, in the sense that we wanted to undertake political actions whose roots were deep within our lives and far from any central committee. We deliberately intended to put aside the hysterical and sterile political discussions which organised the revolution of *others*. From the beginning we were concerned with bringing our public and private lives together to allow our individual consciousness to levels, and to transform society. We knew that many militants of the left plunged blindly into political activism as the result of a subtle sexual repression. In an article collectively signed by the group, we considered the sexual act as a political act because political activity should "be full of the tenderness which we have learned both in the bedroom and elsewhere."[1] We began, at first timidly, to consider pleasure as every citizen's legitimate right. We wanted to believe that joy was not ruled out by poverty, particularly in such a poor country as Brazil. We encouraged demonstrations of tenderness and fraternity amongst ourselves and opposed parliamentary-style representation and all forms of leadership. In addition, the topics that were emerging centred on the tearing down of sex roles, the breaking of the heterosexist model of relationships, and polygamy as a proposal for potential transformation. In short, we saw the time offered by weekly meetings as a fundamental opportunity for solidarity and transformation where frequent cruising and sexual activity also took place – and were considered legitimate components of these meetings.

Meanwhile, one problem that we were constantly aware of in this initial period was that the number of women was small and fluctuating. Those who happened to come – generally brought by gay male friends – did so once and did not return. The situation was considered serious by those members of the group who were interested in a feminist analysis of sexual repression and in an alliance with the groups of liberationist women then emerging. It was not, however, only the number of women that fluctuated. Many men came to look and did not come back, disappointed by our "lack of objectivity and organisation" and by the fact that, compared to political groups of the time, we had no "ideological consistency". Before leaving, many asked us to tell them when the group was ready to take a definite line. People who still had links with the student movement found it difficult to understand that the group was formless and restless precisely because its aim was to ferment new ideas of political practice. There was therefore a growing concern with opposing activism as a form of seeking and exercising power. Even if it was at random, our small group wanted to challenge the very question of power, aware that our sexuality (our no-man's-land) suffered under the social control inherent in any form of disputed and conquered power. It was a very bold suggestion at a time when the echoes of Guevara-style revolution were still heard and obeyed, for it also challenged the legitimacy of self-appointed vanguards of the left taking power "in the name of the people".

New Ideas to the Fore

In February 1979 the group found itself at an impasse when it made its public debut in debate at the Social Sciences Faculty of the University of São Paulo, one of the centres of official Brazilian progressivism. The auditorium was full. On stage were the group's representatives (myself included), who had stuffed themselves with tranquillisers and were suffering from diarrhea. Positions hardened. On one side students and teachers of the university left proclaimed their faith in the dogma of class struggle and in the divine grace of the proletariat. On the other side we stood by the originality of our argument and the independence of our analysis, which was not neccessarily part of the class struggle but was no less concerned with social change. The first position represented the "greater struggle", according to which there were revolutionary priorities – the greatest priority of course being the struggle of the proletariat, which would ignite and lead the revolution, in the widest meaning of the term, while anything else, in terms of social revolution, was irrelevant and even divisive. In comparison, we were the "lesser struggle" for the very reason that we questioned the sanctification of the working class. Blacks, who had begun to organise against racial discrimination and to assert their culture, had already been accused of initiating worthless "existential discussion" of their problems.

Nevertheless, since those of us on the platform that night knew that the auditorium was full of gay men and lesbians, we had agreed to throw questions back to the public whenever possible. They could then take over the debate and there would be no need for spokespeople. When, at the end of heated discussion, a member of the orthodox left commented that the homosexual struggle greatly devalued the issue of class struggle, I could not contain my anger. I stood on a chair and asked people in the audience to give concrete evidence about how *we* homosexuals were devalued in the very name of class struggle. The reaction was devastating. Men and women, emotionally moved and unafraid to appear in public as gay, stood to describe how they had personally experienced discrimination by progressives for being homosexual. One example given was that of a teacher of that same university who had asked students for an essay analysing the reasons for the absence of homosexuals among the working class.[2] That was, furthermore, the same opinion held by Lula, a messianic union leader who at that time considered feminism "something for those who have nothing to do".[3] Insults were exchanged between representatives of the student movement and homosexuals – a sign that we were no longer apologising for our actions.

At the end, our sweat-soaked shirts gave the impression that the Brazilian gay movement had just taken its rightful place in society. We were thrilled and kissed each other in public, no longer shy. We did not know that this first public confrontation with the student left would be neither the last nor the most violent. Later we learnt that in the same faculty where the debate had taken place a gay activist (who provocatively liked to introduce himself as Taís – a woman's name – and to walk through the streets of São Paulo at night in drag) had been pulled into some bushes in the neighbourhood and given a beating which cost him a broken tooth. As they hit him, the four militant leftists (whom he knew) accused him of trying to divide the proletarian struggle and advised him to stop "this impudence of a homosexual movement".

The most concrete result of the debate was a surprising increase in the number of participants in the group, which from then on called itself *Somos* ("We Are") – a name that was "expressive, assertive, palindromic, rich in meaning and with no negative connotations", as stated in a document we published at the time.[4] From just ten we soon became an average of a hundred people. Since various smaller groups had formed to talk and exchange ideas, such affluence forced us to reorganise our structure into a more systematic form. Meetings were held in rotation in the houses of different members; we had nowhere like a headquarters and, to avoid being centralised and bureaucratic, did not want one. We also wanted to maintain an air of semi-secrecy, then still necessary in Brazil, and because there were signs that the police were watching us. After a time no new member joined *Somos* without first attending informal meetings where people talked and exchanged experiences in what came to be called the "admission or identification" group, the molecular base of our activism in its initial phase.

Most surprising of all was the fact that the number of women suddenly grew until it almost equalled the number of men. Gradually the majority of them felt they had to meet in an exclusively women's group, the arguments for which were related to the discriminatory and chauvinist way in which gay men in general treated them. It was true that men could often be heard referring to the women in pejorative terms. The situation was a hot potato for all of us. When the men tried to be unprejudiced the result was almost fatally paternalistic. It was then that we began general discussions on chauvinism and feminism, but these did not always end well, the women becoming very impatient and the men stubborn. In any case the lesbians' intention to form an autonomous and exclusively feminine sub-group started a heated debate which lasted several weeks and made it very clear that being a homosexual man did not automatically mean a closeness to women – sometimes even the opposite.

In Rio de Janeiro, meanwhile, things were not going well for *Lampião*. Since August 1978 we had been the subject of a police inquiry in both Rio and São Paulo, accused of offending public morality. The letter from the federal police requesting the inquiry referred to the editors as "individuals suffering from serious behavioural problems", so much so, they claimed, that we were cases on the boundary of pathological medicine. The letter asked that we be tried and sentenced under the so-called Press Law, under which we could receive up to a year in prison. Even before any trial began we were threatened and interrogated by the police, photographed and identified as criminals; in short they had prejudged and found us guilty. One of the first questions put to various of the editors under interrogation was to confirm that they were homosexual. Luckily, the Journalists' Union in Rio and São Paulo offered the free services of a lawyer and gave *Lampião* every help. I remember that I was photographed with a kind of yoke around my neck. On it, coincidentally or not, was the number 0240. In Brazil the number 24 is pejorative, being equivalent to "queer".

Soon afterwards, in a subtle change of tactics, the police demanded the paper's account books in the hope of finding irregularities and closing it for tax reasons. In the second half of 1979 bombs exploded at kiosks in various parts of the country while anonymous leaflets demanded that they stop selling alternative papers (almost always left-wing) or periodicals they considered pornographic (*Lampião* appeared on one of the lists). The government vaguely blamed the bombs on para-military groups. However, no enquiry was set up to find out where the members of such groups – New Fatherland Phalange, Moral Brigades and Anti-Communist Commandos – came from or who they were. This dark cloud hovered over *Lampião* until the middle of 1979, when the police inquiry was shelved for lack of evidence. In any case, it was amusing to discover that the primary accusation against us was the cover story of issue 0 on Celso Curi, a journalist who had been on trial since 1977 for the same crime of offending public morality. This had allegedly been by a gay column in a São Paulo daily in which, according to the Public Prosecutor, he had encouraged "meetings between abnormals".[5] Luckily Celso Curi was acquitted shortly afterwards, the judge stating that he did not consider it a crime for homosexuals to try "to place themselves as a structured segment within society".

By that time there were other gay activist groups in São Paulo, Rio de Janeiro, Niterói, Belo Horizonte, Salvador, Brasília, Recife, João Pessoa and the interior of the state of São Paulo. *Somos*, meanwhile, had matured and the group tried to tackle more complex issues. As it grew, so did its bureaucracy, although it still tried to keep to the principles of autonomy. From each work-group – which ranged from research to writing letters of protest, organising public debates, parties and contact with other countries – a coordinator was elected to sit on the general coordination committee for one or two months. In this way we tried to be better organised without being less flexible, since the large turnover of people within the group very often brought work in progress to a halt. As part of our intention to claim our place, we tried to undertake actions in coordination with two other gay groups in São Paulo. A Committee for the Defence of Homosexual Rights was set up, but it was not really effective and did not last long. One of the few joint activities was participation in public debates, seminars and university symposia. However, this was not the only diet for liberationist gay men and lesbians. Much attention was paid to leisure – after all, one of the demands we all agreed on was the right to pleasure. Parties were often held in private houses or gay clubs and members went on excursions to the country. These were also ways of trying to increase the possibilities of meeting others outside the consumerist limitations of the ghetto.

I believe that in that golden era of *Somos* there was a series of interesting attempts at different styles of political experience on the day-to-day level. One of the key ideas, present since the group's beginnings, was that homosexuality should be determined by homosexuals themselves. We viewed with antipathy the assaults of psychiatrists, judges and priests and their theories and dogmas on the subject. We did not like being objects of research. I remember the violent discussion which exploded when one of the group, an anthropology student who had decided to write his thesis on *Somos* and gay activism in Brazil, started taking exhaustive notes at meetings. He was only allowed to continue under a series of conditions, the most important being that he write a paper about himself.

Another topic frequently discussed was the rejection of leadership in order to avoid once again becoming the victims of spokespeople and interpreters. I do not know how viable this might be. In any case informal proposals of self-propagation and direct action developed gradually and unanimously in *Somos*, perhaps a result of the disagreeable experiences which many of us had had with the centralism of the orthodox left. The preoccupation with challenging the messianism of leaders, however, came from the concern that each of us should control our own destiny. That was also the source of our principle of independence, autonomy and non-alignment with party politics – *Somos'* most consistent political attitude until the confrontation with Trotskyists who shortly afterwards took over the group and imposed their own party line. What we wanted, in short, was that organised homosexuals should discover their own way of taking action, which would be an indication of their originality as a new movement in Brazilian life. We wanted to offer our own contribution to restructuring society and demanded our own place within it where we might grow. I fear that this has been denied us by the institutionalised opposition as much as by the system itself. We will soon see how.

Other important themes – either discussion topics or permanent aspects of the group's activities – centred on change at the day-to-day level. It was thought that the revolution should start at home and concern itself with major taboos – such as monogamy and possessiveness in love. Group sexual activity was therefore not uncommon. There was also the common practice of changing partners, which sometimes led to more stable relationships. We often discussed our relationship with our own bodies, thinking of a more gentle and less genitalised sexuality. In this respect I had a singular experience in *Somos'* studies sub-group. We no longer knew what to study, since, ill-at-ease as zoological specimens, we could not take any over-theoretical debate on homosexuality seriously. So we said: If we are to study ourselves, why don't we begin by looking at our own bodies, the first and most confusing evidence that we are different from each other? We decided to meet with the sole aim of undressing in order to touch each other indiscriminately and so reveal the flesh which our campaigning activities insisted on camouflaging. The intention was perhaps very naive, but it made sense at the time, for we were eager to throw daily life into the whirlwind of change that we dreamed about.

The truth is that it was more difficult than we expected. Some members of the sub-group opposed the idea from the beginning and withdrew horrified. Almost two months went by as we discussed whether or not to meet in the dark, with or without music, what type of music, where, etc., etc. Prolonging the discussion to such an extent was proof of the panic which undressing (unmasking) provoked. At last, one night one of the queens dressed up as a harem woman and danced for us, then the collective striptease took place. Our glances became adolescent and we measured each other up in astonishment as if we had just got to know each other properly. So that was what his chest looked like? and his backside? and his cock? I didn't know he had spots on his back and so many hairs on his thighs! Everyone was fascinated. We resolved to repeat the dose another time. On that occasion we touched each other in the dark, indiscriminately, for more than an hour. I remember the fascination of feeling with one hand the swollen texture of an Afro haircut and with the other the swelling of a generous prick, both giving themselves to my caress. We were so enchanted by the experience that we thought sarcastically of proposing general nudity at left-wing party meetings in order to subvert discussions on the different paths to revolution. That was at the end of 1979 and seems to have been the swan song of our attempts at political activity and autonomy.

Cooption, Institutionalisation, Dilution

At that time intensive preparations began for the first Brazilian Congress of Organised Homosexual Groups, which finally took place in São Paulo in April 1980, bringing together (in the middle of Holy Week) more than 200 men and women representing the nine organised groups which were then in existence throughout Brazil. For three days various topics were stubbornly debated in an atmosphere of unpleasant competitiveness and hostility, at a meeting which had been intended for solidarity and an exchange of experiences. A general and lamentable homosexual conceit was also evident – an ill-resolved ancient chauvinism which continued to divide the world into good guys and bad guys – except that the good guys were now gay men and lesbians. It was like a student congress where each political line fought to have its representatives on the committee. In fact there was not even a committee to be elected, although the Trotskyist wing, anxious to form another cell, demanded that we create a structure centralising the gay movement on the national level – forgetting that our representative status was very debatable.

Apart from xenophobic and provincial disputes between groups from different cities and regions, two opposing political tendencies began to emerge (not always subtly) on the question of the autonomy of liberation movements vis-à-vis political parties. The word "fascist" flew like a dart in every direction. Trotskyists appeared with an unexpected contingent of representatives, arousing the suspicion – later confirmed – that they were not gay activists but party militants in drag as queers. Despite being few in number, their members were very experienced in political debate and it was not difficult for them to use manoeuvrist tactics and conspiracies to impose their positions and prevent their opponents winning. Of course one of the innocent gay movement's favourite topics of the previous two years disappeared: challenging the idea of power. At the congress (or miscongress), those who did not want to were forced to come out fighting for power. And what power was that? Gay Power, which was in the process of being born, which capitalist consumerism was nurturing to the point of deceiving us with empty promises. Thus the Brazilian gay movement's search for its own space began to falter as it seemed to run the risk of seeing its demands diluted in party political proposals.

Moreover, the organised left had made it clear more than once that it intended to place (and dominate) homosexuals, like women and blacks, in separate sections in their parties. In order to oppose Stalinists who had strayed into the gay movement, the Trotskyists had set the example of founding a Gay Section of their organisation, which was doubtless the best way of exercising control over homosexuals, making them an extension of and motor for the party. Gay power would then be delegated by the centralised power of the central committee. It was of course another ingenious form of modernisation, changing absolutely nothing.

The most crucial moment and the one which best revealed the divergences in this first national congress was the vote on a motion which would oblige the whole gay movement to participate in First of May celebrations in a football stadium in the industrial town of São Bernardo, near São Paulo. The group swollen and inspired by Trotskyists proposed an obligatory and unrestricted attendance. The opposing group wondered whether such a small number of homosexuals had the right to represent the movement and, consequently, the gay community. As an alternative it proposed that there should be no obligation on groups but rather a decision on the private or individual level. I was one of those who opposed compulsory attendance, horrified by the pocket leftists there. Furthermore, I knew that so-called "proletarian leadership" often hides every kind of demand and manipulation under its appeal for unity, and the only unity it accepts is that dictated by its central committee. I was also aware that behind the scenes the Trotskyists wanted to draw obvious benefits from the presence of homosexuals under their wing on May Day. In order to achieve this, they had been offering us for some time duplicating facilities and rooms in their headquarters where *Somos* activists could make banners and meet. It was clear that the very idea of the autonomy of liberation movements was at stake. We did not want to be the vanguard of a doubtful gay movement, much less to obey orders from a political party.

This was indisputable proof that the gay movement had begun to interest the electoral left, who now sent emissaries to watch and control us. On the last day of the congress, an "authentic worker", brought by the Trotskyists, appeared in the midst of the lesbians, gay men and transvestites. At the microphone he told us how police torture had made him deaf and, having duly presented his credentials, gave us his message and warning: "If we are able to meet here, it is thanks to the efforts of the working class in their struggle against the dictatorship." The working class, naturally, meant that vanguard under his party's protection. Here was further proof as to how self-defined "proletarians" tried to coopt homosexuals by pointing out the debt we owed to the greater struggle. Abdias do Nascimento, an influential activist in the Brazilian black movement, had already baptised this leftist opportunism with the delightful and eloquent name of Machoist-Leninism.

Starting with the congress, certain underground manoeuvres came to light, some in retrospect. The seed of "proletarian vanguardism" had already been seen months earlier in an important discussion on the restructuring of *Somos*. It was not coincidental that the leader of the Trotskyist wing had proposed that the group be restricted to a small and select number whose objective would be to *orientate* (sic) new activist groups to be formed by *Somos*, at least in São Paulo. Equally subtly, the small but active number of Trotskyists became more powerful in the internal information sub-group, which had very few members and whose aim was to encourage activities and theoretical discussions within *Somos*. Thus the courses and talks proposed by the sub-groups came to be "graciously" offered by the Trotskyists themselves itself at their headquarters. There was a course on Reich, then considered by fashionable progressives as the great Marxist theoretician on sexuality – his name was certainly chosen to lure us with its nod to modernity. The offer, which was very appealing, was so successful that an ideologically cohesive, closed and inseparable little group was set up in *Somos* and began to inspect the positions of others in order to impose their own. Only months later was it discovered that, again not coincidentally, this little group was made up of individuals taking a secret course in Marxism given by the Trotskyists at their headquarters – a course generally given only to future party members. The clearly proselytising implications of this episode frightened us, particularly because the participants had been secretly hand-picked, since the course was not open to all. Meanwhile those who protested against this entryist manoeuvring were cynically accused of being paranoid – they were imagining things, that was all!

The Trotskyists began to unmask themselves soon afterwards. They publicly and unequivocally admitted the need for a party that would "orientate the gay movement" and give it a proletarian orientation. Indeed they worked with this end in view. Having seen their proposal defeated at the congress, they put forward the idea of a Homosexual Committee for Labour Day and organised a gay contingent to march in the mass of workers. It was under their banners that a group of gay men and lesbians took part in the May Day celebrations in the Vila Euclides stadium in São Bernardo. They proudly paraded in front of thousands of left-wing unionists, students and intellectuals without realising that they were there to present their good-conduct certificate and to ask for their superiors' blessing. Naturally they were approved in the form of applause. To me, however, this represented the beginning of the taming of the newly born gay movement, whose originality, if still crude, was being cut back before it had even flowered.

In opposition, a group of gay men pejoratively called "anarchists", "surrealists" and "reactionaries" preferred to rebel in authentic limp-wristed style. We filled our little baskets with snacks (yes, I was there) and went to picnic in a park, where we came across thousands of resting workers. On Labour Day we workers and gay men celebrated our right to laziness and disobedience. This gesture of ours, however, exploded like a bomb among the masses of the aligned left in *Somos* – we had betrayed the proletarian struggle! From then on animosity grew, positions hardened and territorial disputes became more bitter in episodes that would have sounded hilarious if they had not been steeped in ill-feeling. Political opponents, for example, had sex with the exclusive aim of "collecting information" on their adversaries' activities. Planned seductions took place with the exclusive aim of proselytisation. It was what we sarcastically called the "politics of the bed" as distinct from the politics of the body; the bedroom had become so political that it had become an extension of the party.

Very cohesive compared to the cautious positions of the rest, the small Trotskyist group continued firm in its intention to take charge of *Somos*. Scandal erupted with the discovery of a confidential document from the Trotskyist organisation, a complete manual with specific recommendations on how to take power in the gay movement. It saw *Somos* as the springboard for the proletariat in the Brazilian gay movement. The Trotskyists naturally elected themselves the only vanguard capable of giving the movement proper revolutionary direction. The document even foresaw the slogans to be used on International Gay Pride Day! There were also recommendations for controlling unions considered to have a large number of homosexuals (sic), such as the Artists', Teachers' and Bank Employees'. It even suggested the eventual need to coopt non-gay militants to make up a National Gay Coordinating Committee – an important Trotskyist banner in the gay movement.[6] Considering the atmosphere of party-politicking unbreathable, the group of opposing activists decided to leave and formed a new group which then tried, in vain, to make the proposals of autonomy consistent. The lesbians, wavering, but inclined to accept the Trotskyist case up to a point, took advantage of the occasion to leave *Somos* and set up a separate group. They then returned to the feminists, with whom they had a brief love affair that ended in disenchantment. The most cautious wing of Brazilian feminism was forcing a discreet divorce from lesbianism, an uncomfortable impediment to their alliance with sectors of the political left, to which they were still linked by an umbilical cord.

Some months after this double dissent, another contingent withdrew from *Somos*, fleeing the Trotskyist hegemony, which was becoming more and more uncomfortable. Thus all the strength of the country's first and best structured group of gay activists died through fragmentation. From then on energies were divided and the gay movement's ability to mobilise as a whole diminished alarmingly, especially in São Paulo. The last concerted action with other gay, feminist and black liberation groups was a demonstration against the beatings and arbitrary imprisonment ordered by a police commissioner in areas in São

Paulo frequented by homosexuals, prostitutes and transvestites. On that occasion the proposal was not to march but to hold the centre of the city captive in a festival with samba dancers and bands. As well as distinguishing our action from the orthodox student movement, we intended a less serious protest, one which fitted our right to exist and cruise in public. We were accused by the cohesive group of Trotskyists of trying to traditionalise and dilute the political gravity of the march. It is curious that two years later, during the 1982 state elections, the Workers' Party (PT) – at the centre of which these same Trotskyist groups were now concentrated – used samba dancers in excess to publicise their candidates at festive rallies in the centre of São Paulo. Of course tradition was no longer feared.

Somos changed from that time on, losing its innovative character and becoming institutionalised. It opened an office, which it shared temporarily with a municipal directorate of the PT. The ideas of an autonomous gay movement were drastically forgotten or laundered. Even the language used by its members changed, as old leftist jargon replaced the hesitant autonomist terms. At meetings gay men now had to call each other "comrade" – the sacred word of the political left. It was another sign of conformity. Effeminate queens came to hold lesser or less noble roles in the group's actions. The strangest aspect, however, was that the Trotskyists relaxed their control from the moment when *Somos'* numbers fell. As soon as their hegemony appeared to be consolidated, the most active group of Trotskyists dispersed and left *Somos*, as if their aim had been more tactical than strategic, intending to destroy any possible opposition rather than properly construct a movement of gay struggle. Furthermore, their direct contact with heterosexist members of the party had unforgettably disenchanted those gay men aligned with the Trotskyists. There was the case, well-known at the time, of a few gay men from *Somos* who went to the opening of a new Trotskyist office in the industrial town of São Bernardo. Ecstatic with the illusion of being in on things, they began kissing at the party. One of the leaders came up to the group and, finger pointing in warning, stated that men kissing was "contrary to proletarian morals". Of course these gay men understood at once that at the very least they had been deceived. Several months later one of them struck a blow at the party; he robbed its safe of all the money and fled to Australia with his lover, where it seems they still live.

At the same time part of *Lampião*'s editorial team, shocked by the arrogant cooption of large parts of the gay movement in various towns in Brazil, began to dissassociate themselves from any moral obligation to organised groups, proposing complete autonomy and showing frank hostility to the bureaucratisation that was beginning to mould gay activism. It was true that, amongst other things, gay activists gave the impression of living in an atmosphere of total victory – their actions often seemed more like a political hobby which turns out disastrous in the medium term because of their basic compromise and underlying opportunism. Many tended to adopt a vindicatory attitude towards society and the state, which was obvious in their anxiety to raise gay people to the category of "normal citizens", depriving them of any ability to question – more or less as black Americans had seen their potential to resist neutralised when the goverment began to absorb them into the system, thereby imposing on them the white majority pattern.

In an article I wrote for *Lampião* at the time, I touched on precisely this serious point: that we were using homosexuality as a religion which begged a doctrine and a faith – two doors through which "institutionalisation can enter the gay movement, and strategic objectives, proselytising tactics and centralisation can then be expressed in the best power-struggle style", characteristics of party politics which the gay movement claimed to avoid. The truth is that in this society, where the centres of power are shared by "specialists", the activist becomes "the specialist in political planning or in decreeing this new form of transcendence, called *revolution*."[7] The activist therefore became, by default, a new mediator between society and homosexuals, reintroducing the politics of the spokesperson and representative so dear to the mechanisms of social control. Furthermore, I remember that in the last months in which I was a member of *Somos*, a number of us were very surprised to discover that there was no longer enough time for sex or personal pleasure. All our time was taken up by meetings and other "sexual liberation" activities – which seemed to us an unpleasant paradox.

All this and much more appeared in the pages of *Lampião*, whose divergence from the general direction of the gay movement became more and more pronounced. The greatest split was with the groups in Rio de Janeiro, who forged fragile and hasty alliances with other groups in the country in an attempt to isolate the paper. In reaction *Lampião* childishly radicalised its repudiation of gay activism. Certain members of the editorial team sought refuge in a vague populism, praising the transvestite as opposed to the macho gay, which gave the paper almost as sensationalist an appearance as the heterosexist gutter press. It lost even more of its character and there was a noticeable reduction in circulation. Unable to get advertisements, *Lampião* had always depended on sales, making it financially very weak. This weakness made it impossible to fulfil the growing journalistic demands imposed by political changes in the country. Its initially original and innovative stance had been imitated in diluted form in the pages of the more progressive and more professional daily papers, where articles on feminism, blacks, ecology and homosexuals had frequently appeared in recent years. In addition, *Lampião*'s timid infrastructure led to a centralisation of power, as a result of which decisions ended up in the hands of one or two editors, who vetoed or cut as they pleased, making broader discussions on new directions for the paper more difficult or impossible.

The end result was that *Lampião* pleased neither one side nor the other. This became obvious in one of the most important issues, where a number of wide-ranging and serious articles on the question of homosexuality in Cuba was published. To the editors' amazement, it was the worst selling issue in all the history of the paper. Symptomatically, the following number – which carried scandalous Carnival photographs – was one of the best sellers. As differences within the editorial team became more bitter, it was decided to close the paper in July 1981, after three years of life and 37 monthly issues.

A Melancholy Outcome

In the end, what had always been a shaky movement was reduced to what it had never ceased being – no more than a rise in the homosexual profile. Gay consumerism continued to grow as clubs, saunas and bars proliferated and made themselves more exclusive. Television stations absorbed the wave in their own way, seeking to increase their audience, very often at the price of sensationalism as we have already seen. Contrary to the naive dreams of certain activists (myself among them), subversion is not latent in gay lifestyles as the Greeks lurked in the Trojan Horse. Nor does sexuality in itself have the gift of guaranteeing solidarity among the oppressed – desire obeys neither principles nor ideologies, no matter how excellent they might be. If it is true that the gay experience implies the potential for change, it also seems to be true that very little can be expected from the remnants of the gay movement in Brazil – confused activists in scarcely representative liberationist groups, exhausted and incapable of debate or mobilisation.

Not even the arrival in Brazil in 1982 of Félix Guattari, a French psychoanalyst and philosopher, mythologically singing the praises of liberation movements (which he baptised as "molecular"), succeeded in changing this desolate landscape. Precisely because in anticipation of Guattari's proposal – he said he himself was collaborating with the French Socialist Party – many members of the old Brazilian gay movement had, like prodigal sons, already joined parties on the left. Athough there was no cooption en bloc, it could be said that there was a general realignment of groups towards progressive parties, especially the PT (Workers' Party). The PT, previously reticent, had resolved to include the gay issue in its manifesto some months before the state elections. According to João Antonio Mascarenhas, a Brazilian writer for the North American *Paz y Liberación*, there were 51 candidates in the 1982 local elections who expressed explicit support for homosexuals: of these only 16 were elected.[8] The most significant case was that of the deputy Liszt Vieira (PT), who presented one of the most coherent programmes of all the candidates, combining an eminently populist vision with a keen concern for the questions of women, blacks, ecology, daily life and gay liberation. Liszt Vieira won a seat in the state assembly of Rio de Janeiro; it would not be exaggerating to say that this was due above all to the firm and intelligent assistance of Herbert Daniel, an ex-guerrilla who, since his return from long exile, has become fully involved in gay activism as much as party politics.

Most recently few liberationist groups have been outstanding in more than apathy and conventional letters of protest, petitions, participation in public demonstrations and marching with banners and generally redundant slogans. The Gay Group of Bahia, for example, is conducting an uncertain campaign for the withdrawal of homosexuality from the INAMPS (Brazilian Department of Health and Social Security) code of mental illnesses. In 1981, claiming the need for an opportunity to discuss anti-black racism, the *Adé Dudu* ("Black Gay" in the Nago language) group was founded in Bahia. It sems to have been the only successful effort to bring together black gay liberationists. The group published a curious research document on discrimination against blacks in the gay ghetto. Unfortunately little is heard of *Adé Dudu* today. Among the others, the most stimulating and original group was perhaps *Nós Também* ("We Too") in the small and conservative north-eastern state of Paraiba. Organised in a quiet provincial capital, the group's members were men and women connected with the university, teachers as well as students. Its pugnacity and originality consisted of a militancy that was less conventional and more cultural. Its members disrupted both the urban landscape with provocative street theatre and the local cultural life, showing films, holding debates and distributing very intelligent leaflets. In addition, they produced mail art, Super-8 films and comic strips which emphasised the gay element and sought an analysis through feminist references. They also made the only known film on the Inquisition in Brazil (*Baltazar da Lomba*), which relates one of the innumerable cases of homosexuals interrogated by the Tribunal in the sixteenth century. Nós Também is now inactive.

Paradoxically, the most relevant remnants of the Brazilian gay movement today are academic papers and sexual anthropologists. Some of the latter are more critical and take as their base more sophisticated theoretical precepts. Others essentially want to integrate homosexuals into the system, making them tame enough to be acceptable to society. Whatever the hypothesis, an adequate analysis of the ins and outs of homosexuality as a "question" in Brazil seems to me impossible without taking into account the anthropologists who specialise in sexuality and who have emerged as the latest means of recycling the knowledgeable elite in control of sexuality. Those anthropologists whose position is more critical seem most worthy of attention. They start from the presupposition that gay liberation stimulates the formation of a "gay identity" and thus continues the normative function of doctors and psychiatrists by surrounding sexuality with definitions and categories. Despite the reasonable criticisms which can be made of the conformist road which the gay movement in Brazil has taken, this does not justify the contempt these sexual anthropologists have often shown towards gay liberation as a whole, perhaps resenting a certain anti-intellectual tendency quite common amongst gay activists. The truth is that such professors, isolated in their ivory towers, are ignorant of the subtleties and rich contradictions of real gay activism and tend to leave to one side important discussions which have been earnestly debated in many of their areas – eg. the question of autonomy and its political repercussions in the sphere of human relations.

Moreover, I fear that the hesitant gay movement in Brazil has followed the easier road precisely because it lacks those many gay intellectuals who prefer to protect their academic careers by not getting their hands dirty. Thus very promising proposals are left to die and never become effective. If any of these intellectuals have flirted and even become intimate with the gay movement, it is very strange that in criticising what they have experienced they place themselves above criticism. Furthermore, retreating from the thorny question of a "gay identity" as the devil flees the cross, such sexual anthropologists, I fear, run the risk of leaving in its place an apparent vacuum very similar to old-fashioned academic modesty, and ending up back at the starting-point – the closet before the gay movement.

In the last analysis, the painful impression remains that the most innovative ambitions of the brief gay liberation experience in Brazil have been frustrated. Having emerged from the consulting-room, homosexuality has been imprisoned as a topic to be dissected in the lecture halls of social science courses. Put another way, after passing through media consumerism it seems to have arrived at academic consumerism. No longer remembered as the fruition of desire and a factor of possible change (an idea dear to the country's first activists), the gay question continues to be passed from hand to hand, embedded in theses as if in formaldehyde and manipulated by new, now more civilised, interpreters – which is no consolation, since the most sophisticated knowledge can also formulate the most subtle repressions. It is perhaps useful to remember that, like doctors and psychiatrists, anthropologists also "participate actively in the history of homosexuality".[9] It would be healthily subversive if many of them, as homosexuals, lived this history from within, resolutely making themselves subjects and not the camouflaged (ie. pretending to be neutral) objects of their own academic research.

CHAPTER SIX

Paradise Lost, Paradise Regained

> "You will eliminate sickness and barium.
> The pleasure of men will remain
> because you were the androgyne."
>
> *Oswald de Andrade* (1946)

The Mask and the Parody

In the garden of the Capulets, Romeo declares his love for Juliet, who answers him from the balcony immediately above. Hilariously honey-tongued, with black tresses that fall to the ground, trembling African lips and enormous false eyelashes, Juliet is played by Grande Otelo, a great Brazilian black actor, while the nervous and grimacing Romeo who improvises fatuous phrases of love is none other than Oscarito, a well-known comedian. The scene is from *Carnaval no fogo* ("Carnival Ablaze"), a Brazilian film of the 1950s and a typical *chanchada* – a kind of comedy then very much in vogue. Not only were characters in drag common in *chanchadas*, but the genre itself was based on "anthropophagic" parody and on transvestism as a mask indicating uncertain identities. Hollywood films, classical characters and famous actors were all parodied. Played by Oscarito, Elvis Presley became an exquisite comic creation in this process of assimilation whereby a new identity seeks to emerge from the very act of imitation.

In a country like Brazil, as distant from the centres of political decision-making as it is dependent on them, "world" events arrive distorted, to the same extent that international phenomena or fashions appear there quite out of place. Styles imported from highly developed countries, such as rock'n'roll and punk, put down eccentric roots in Brazilian soil and, imposed on a Third World reality, flourish with the unaccustomed characteristics of mimic and disguise. What happens then? Their initial significance is lost and replaced by various connotations with new and metaphorical meanings so that their ultimate meaning no longer exists. The result is a fundamentally inconclusive work which can be interpreted in many ways. In short, it is a case of the baroque proliferation found again and again in Brazilian life, already thick with disguise situations that result in farce or in many false appearances. Thus some European customs, when transplanted in Brazil, display curious phenomena of inversion, creating a context of gratuitousness as a result of their bastardy. European Carnival, the festival which presaged spring, strayed on Brazilian soil and became, as a result of the change of hemisphere, the last profane festival before autumn. Carnival gaiety then acquired connotations of fatality because it was the final carnal delirium before the penitence of Lent, a Christian interruption of the pagan festival. Carnival is now the dance before death, the gaiety which announces the end. Death and celebration intermingle to the point where one can no longer be distinguished from the other – which almost literally happens during the Carnival follies.

According to the famous statesman, Baron do Rio Branco, in Brazil "only two things are organised: disorder and Carnival". He was referring, ironically, to the same phenomenon of ambivalence. This Brazilian festival, with its explosion of laughter and its generous exposure of the body, favours broad communication to bring together diversities, cultivates various degrees of parody in its disguises, makes a virtue of transgression and proclaims the rule of ambiguity. As the realisation of a fantasy, Carnival demonstrates the triumph of imagination over routine by inverting norms so that masculinity and femininity are confused (many men wear women's clothes) and the poor become rich (by wearing luxurious fancy-dress or appearing as aristocrats). It is therefore no exaggeration to say that Carnival and deviation go hand in hand, which can be verified by a simple glance in the street or dance-halls in the midst of the festivities.

Once, during Carnival in Florianópolis (the quasi-provincial capital of the state of Santa Catarina) I saw a whole parade of dozens of men dancing the samba dressed as brides – grotesque brides, splendid brides, even pregnant brides. In Carnival in São Paulo there is a football match where the stars of various teams play side by side with amateurs – all dressed as women; the players commonly exchange the most intimate caresses and touches camouflaged as mocking gestures. Lace panties can even be seen when a goal is scored and the players raise their skirts in celebration. In Olinda, in the state of Pernambuco, there is the curious group of "Virgins" with 200 to 300 men – registered beforehand – who parade dressed as women. Their costumes are very fastidious and chic, with wigs and high-heeled shoes. The participants usually imitate actresses and famous singers. At the end of the parade there is a competition to choose the "most beautiful and most sensual virgin" and present him with a trophy offered by the local authority and local industries. The strangest feature of this Carnival club, organised by soldiers, is that its rules prevent well-known homosexuals from joining and forbid over-feminine gestures. In other words a mask should be worn over the mask – again an affirmation of the baroque.

If Carnival and deviation go hand in hand, the phenomenon of inversion is not restricted to those few days set aside for festivity. It could be said that an everyday carnival exists in Brazil, for the very reason that deviation is at the heart of Brazilian life, itself built on bastardy. Was the country not born of a deviation in the route of Pedrálvares Cabral, so becoming a parody of India? Compare also the insidious and widespread worship of Afro-Amerindian gods in what is nonetheless the largest Catholic country in the world. Or the ritualised and manic devotion to football, the national passion. This picture of Carnival and deviation has even been present in Brazilian political life – from its mimicry of European monarchy, the near-fiasco of the inaugration of the republic, to the repeated frustrated attempts to install democratic government.

Ecstasy and Agony

Like Carmen Miranda's dancing, it can be said that homosexuality in Brazil has this same baroque love of excess, fantasy, colours, disguise, festivity, spontaneity, parody and deviation. Its deviant character is certainly one of the reasons why homosexuality in Brazil is at once so diffuse and so camouflaged. In its most spontaneous and popular form, however, homosexuality carries a non-pragmatic, free, playful and infantile component; thus certain sectors of the population see homosexuality as "something childish". Rooted in the impetuosity of desire, free of institutions and ideologies, homosexuality as generally practised in Brazil is related to generosity. This is a result of the cultural phenomenon of baroque exaggeration with marriage/family at one extreme and transgression at the other – a horseshoe of which the ends are simultaneously opposite and near. Moreover, the natural paradox of the Brazilian homosexual experience lies in the proximity of these extremes, where delight and horror, passion and fear, fascination and repulsion mingle in equal quantities.

Another aspect to be stressed is that homosexuality in Brazil is also part of the Carnival experience, since it benefits from deviations in the structure of Catholicism itself. Unlike Protestantism, where the believer lives the terrible experience of judging and forgiving himself, in Catholicism forgiveness comes from outside, through ritual gesture. This allows for deviation, since "something can be worked out" with God. The sin of sodomy has always been unconditionally condemned, but at the same time there has always been the possibility of forgiveness obtainable at confession. Confession may therefore become exorcism and even the condition for being able to sin again. In a wider sense, there is also the possibility of all-embracing and final forgiveness through the extreme unction administered by the priest before death – guaranteeing the old sinner a happy eternal life. One can therefore sin in greater tranquility without demanding a great ideological reckoning with one's conscience.

I remember that when I was in the United States I was intrigued to read in an informal report that homosexual activity between men there generally starts relatively late. That was perhaps why I seldom met openly gay adolescents there, unlike in Brazil, where they proliferate both within and outside of the ghetto. In Anglo-Saxon culture one probably has to go a long way in order to rationally work out one's desire, while in Brazilian culture the tendency to give in to desire exists without the need for elaborate rationalisation. Of course one cannot generalise in either case – it is enough to witness the anti-gay terror often instilled in its children by the Brazilian middle class. It is also true, however, that the practise of "tit-for-tat" between childhood friends is very common ("you put it in me and I'll put it in you") as well as adolescent sessions of collective masturbation.

There are also *machista* implications. I mentioned earlier that machismo is the other face of homosexual desire. As will be seen, anti-gay violence is simply one of the subterfuges used to punish one's own desire. There are others. I have, for example, heard from female prostitutes that many men who frequent them achieve orgasm when the prostitutes put a finger in their rectum – evidence, according to one, that "the number of queers is growing" among her clients. What is certain is that in homosexual as much as heterosexual experience, the *machista* elements in the Brazilian melting-pot favour a rigid division of sexual roles, so that it is very easy to find limp-wristed *bichas* (the object of social scorn) at one extreme and those *machos* who fuck *bichas* (without having their social virility diminished) at the other. Yet even here it is not possible to generalise, since this division is often simply to hide the stigma. In bed the masks fall and desire eagerly emerges. Often in a male couple where the "queen" can be easily identified, what is important in this scheme of polarisation is more the guarantee of a visible virility than the actual fulfilment of the roles themselves. It can be imagined how much conflict is caused by these internal contradictions, which often come to a violent end.

In the police archives a large number of cases of murdered gay men lie still unsolved – because of the police negligence, because the victim's family prefers to keep the matter quiet, or because the victim always led a double life, keeping his relationships secret. However, the greatest hindrance to solving such cases is the apparent "lack of motive" for crimes committed in surprisingly similar circumstances. In a good number armed robbery was not the primary objective, for the murderers often left behind valuable objects or even jewels. Another element common to most cases is violence, so exaggerated that it seems gratuitous. There was a case in which the body was placed with its head in the lavatory bowl. When Décio Escobar, a well-known artist, was murdered, the three rent-boys wrote on the walls in mustard (imitating excrement): "He was a queer and a cocksucker."[1] The complexity of motives can also lead to refined sarcasm, as in the case of the killer who left "Who's the Next?" (in English) playing on the record-player. Gil Brandão, a famous dress-designer, was killed by three youths who used various knives with such violence that one of them broke. Then there was the horrifying case of Fred Feldman, a pianist from Rio de Janeiro, where the murderer's *machista* complusion was obvious – he was a rent-boy who went to have sex with his girl-friend soon after committing the crime. Furthermore, to make things quite clear, he quite calmly turned up at the reconstruction of the crime, after which he went up to the photographers and told them: "I'm a normal man. I've always had a girl-friend. Dying's too good for queers." In protest, the newsletter of the Gay Group of Bahia has published lists of gay men murdered throughout the country and demanded that steps be taken by the authorities.

Most ironically, however, the violence has also struck at those who fought against it. In 1982 Cláudio Rodrigues, a spokesman for Libertus, a gay liberation group in greater São Paulo, was stabbed to death in his own home with a kitchen knife and no trace of the killer has ever been found. The popular press, of course, do not miss the opportunity to increase sales with scandalous headlines, which, not by chance, emphasise situations where the gay man is in one way or another the aggressor: "Homosexuals kidnap two brothers", "I escaped from gay hell", "Police hunt gay kidnapper", "Two gay weddings revolt public", etc, etc.

Who's Afraid of the Big Bad Wolf?

It is rash to refer to a "gay community" in Brazil as one can in the United States. Indeed the relative cultural ease and less harsh legal punishment permit Brazilians to practise homosexuality without having to adjust to ideological models or classificatory designations. It is enough to remember the insistent testimony of transvestite prostitutes that a good number of their clients like to be anally penetrated – which does not mean that they consider themselves even for an instant outside the heterosexual family structure. Such facts are proof that in Brazil there is a clear distinction between those men and women who openly frequent the ghetto, and those who have intercourse with members of the same sex but have contempt for queers and loathing for dykes. I remember relatively well-known homosexuals who, for similar reasons, were truly revolted by the appearance of *Lampião*. Indeed the small crowds seen in the gay ghettos of large Brazilian cities mean very little when compared to the vast crowd of secret or nameless homosexual acts.

In the gay ghetto itself there are gradations of practice among neighbours that are not always peaceful. Thus there are distinct boundaries between places where poorer or more effeminate gay men from the suburbs go and places frequented by more refined people, who like to be called "*guei*" (the Brazilian version of "gay") or "*entendido*" (lit. "understood") and whose most cultivated virtue is without doubt discretion allied to good dress sense. But, as in other countries, the Brazilian gay ghetto is situated at the crossroads of a number of contradictory circumstances. On one hand, it is the only alternative for people who practise homosexuality to remain at ease. On the other hand, it is clearly defined to isolate deviants and bring together the more institutionalised homosexuality. The periodic raids which the police carry out in the ghetto, arresting many people, are like warnings that tolerance of the ghetto depends fundamentally on keeping its boundaries clear. It is certainly true that the police authorities have shown themselves to be to a certain extent receptive to the ideology of permissiveness. Commissioner Richetti, famous for his violent assaults on the gay ghetto in São Paulo at the beginning of the 1980s, later came to make a curious distinction by admitting that his quarrel was only with transvestites, since in his opinion, "homosexuals don't create problems; they are discreet, sensible and modest".[2] Recently the Secretary for Public Security in São Paulo also made it clear to a group of progressive parliamentarians and representatives of the gay movement that his quarrel was not with well-behaved (sic) homosexuals but with transvestites; as proof he declared himself favourable to the idea of gay policemen. This "relaxation" proves that the organs of security are now beginning to be more interested in controlling than in truly repressing.

If gay consumerism has benefitted enormously from this liberalisation, the so-called "tip" which gay bars and clubs have to pay to the police apparently continues to be enforced. It is also true that the increase in so-called gay business has created a great expansion of the gay ghettos in the larger cities of Brazil, where gay people have many specialised saunas, bars, clubs, hotels and massage parlours at their disposal. Gay information is often commonly found in straight leisure guides and erotic magazines. Massage parlours publish advertisements in the classified columns of the country's largest papers, offering work to "unprejudiced" young surfers or athletes. In São Paulo particularly there are very luxurious saunas with gay pornographic films, orgy rooms and other erotic sophistications typical of large centres of gay consumerism. In other saunas the attraction lies in the clientele's specialisations: transvestites in one, lorry-drivers in another, conscripts in a third, even adolescents, who are freely admitted to a certain sauna on the outskirts of São Paulo, where actors and famous personalities can be seen among its customers. São Paulo has the largest number of clubs as well as the most diverse, including some which are very luxurious – boasting sophisticated light and sound systems as well as backrooms, drag shows and restaurant service. Of course proliferation has brought competition. Aiming to attract the public with the greatest disposable income, the Medieval, one of São Paulo's oldest and most fashionable nightclubs, raffled flights to the United States. It should be said, however, that gay clubs have become more and more miserly in human contact in direct proportion to their growth; there is a growing rate of sexual anxiety where the only concern is to achieve a quick orgasm. In such places sex and affection have become more and more separate.

There is much flirting – and cruising – in any public place in the large towns in Brazil. The truth is that, as well as naturally touching each other in daily life, Brazilians like to look at each other, including eye-to-eye contact with strangers – which certainly implies the establishment of relations, if not necessarily an erotic invitation. When I was in the United States, this was one of the factors which made me most unhappy: the lack of shining and generous eyes in the midst of crowds. It was only in that country that I discovered how Brazilians communicate very much by looking. At the same time there are parks, public toilets and areas traditionally favourable to gay cruising – such as the Galeria Alaska, Cinelândia, "Maisa's hole" (on the Avenida Presidente Vargas) and the Aterro in Rio de Janeiro – the last being a park where one can have sex by moonlight, running the risk of assault by thieves or the police. Cinemas, traditional cruising grounds in large towns, have also seen the number of gay men rise as the general public have preferred to stay at home watching television. Although no cinema in the country specialises in gay pornographic films, it is possible to see (and take part in) the most diverse extra-cinematic homoerotic activities in some cinemas and their toilets.

There are also rent-boys, if only in the large urban centres. Moreover, with the country in serious financial crisis, they can be found in saunas and even in ordinary taxis parked in cruising areas, waiting for passengers to whom the drivers can offer a double service in return for double fare. There are also a few male brothels in some towns. One was reported in Rio de Janeiro as long as 1894, run by Traviate, a very famous gay man of the time. The most famous in recent times was in Porto Alegre; it closed after its owner, whose feminine nickname was Luiza Felpuda, was killed by a rent-boy who castrated him and set fire to the house. One brothel – probably still functioning – exists on the outskirts of Rio de Janeiro. I once went there and was called a lesbian by the woman who owned it, simply because I asked for a young man who would be gentle and not restricted to rigid sexual roles. The "prostitutes" were local youths supplementing their income, while the brothel itself was a house indistinguishable from the other humble residences in an unpaved street. Full of ideological scruples, I went there on the pretext that I was doing research for a book; nevertheless I was struck by a revelation that shocked me politically. Faced with my partner's beautiful orgasm, I discovered that the money I had paid him had acquired distinctly erotic connotations, as the means through which he had effectively been able to express his desire outside the sexual role which his cultural level had imposed on him.

Transvestites for Export

In almost every Brazilian city with more than half a million inhabitants, active transvestite prostitution can be found side by side with female prostitution. In 1976 Commissioner Guido Fonseca, who was responsible for the repression of transvestites in São Paulo, calculated that there were about 2,000 of them working as prostitutes. In one precinct alone he counted 243 on the files.[3] The question of transvestism is obviously not simple, since prostitution is an almost inherent factor in professional transvestism. Generally from the poorest classes, these youths are allowed few options by their families and society to live as homosexuals. Despite the tradition of such annual competitions for transvestites as Miss Brazil Gay, it is indisputable that they have to prostitute themselves as the price paid for having to live on the fringes of society. A snowball effect is therefore created in terms of violence – the clients run the risk of assault and the transvestites are in danger of being queer-bashed. There are also various cases of transvestites being beaten up by groups of machos or simply killed suddenly in the middle of the street.

The police, as well as charging "protection tax", practise more direct extortion, such as raids in which transvestites are arrested and gratuitously beaten up. Moreover, it is common in some places for the police to pull in transvestites simply to have them as free labour to clean the police stations and cells. In an attempt to guarantee their right to be on the public thoroughfare without being charged with vagrancy (the crime of prostitution does not exist in Brazil), many transvestites sought and were granted writs of habeas corpus, which they carried in their handbags. The police, in a gesture characteristic of their impunity, would take these documents and tear them up provocatively in front of reporters. The transvestites often responded equally violently, attacking the police and smashing up police stations or prisons. Their classic form of revenge, however, is self-mutilation. In cells or police stations, sometimes even collectively, they cut their own wrists, arms, necks and even genital organs with pieces of razor-blade hidden under their tongues. They then have to be transferred to hospital, from where they can leave more easily. These facts were the object of a interesting work in which Luís Mott, an anthropologist, analysed how Brazilian transvestites, relegated to the position of pariahs, created an unusual system of coercion and defence through recourse to self-destruction.[4]

The grounds adduced by the police to imprison transvestites are still the subject of discussion among lawyers. In addition to the notorious charge of "vagrancy", "immoral soliciting" is also used. Thus a decree issued in 1976 in São Paulo by the police commissioner ordered immediate imprisonment for transvestites picked up on the public thoroughfare. He also ordered that they be photographed in their women's clothes so that "their honours the judges may evaluate their perniciousness".[5] Such arguments make the situation even more confusing, especially when the same commissioner accepts that, unlike male prostitution, female prostitution is an evil necessity to "preserve the morality of the household".[6] Insofar as the law is concerned, therefore, the question of homosexuality determines a distinct difference in treatment. It is in fact a moral, not legal, judgment that considers transvestites vagrants. Evidence of this is that the above-mentioned commissioner refers to them as "perverts". Judging from the information available, such confusion of concepts is not new. Since the last century the police have been putting people's names on file with impunity and sometimes initiating trials on charges of "passive pederasty".[7]

Obviously this stubborn repression hasn't resolved a single problem. The transvestites whom the police expelled from the centre of São Paulo have recently taken up residence in the most select middle-class districts. Exposing themselves semi-naked or even entirely naked under their dresses, they naturally arouse the fury of the residents, accustomed to modesty in the home. Denouncing the practice of sexual acts in cars or even in the open air, these citizens have responded with leaflets and petitions calling for police action. More recently they have begun to collate a list with the license numbers of the cars of clients who frequent local transvestites, threatening to publish it as an advertisement in the newspapers in order to stop clients attending these amorous rendezvous.

As proof that this is a very grave social problem, the transvestites' situation may be complicated by unusual factors. In 1983 the city of São Paulo was shaken by the news that a large number of transvestites were threatened by a painful death, if not in fact already dying, from the insertion – in the breasts, hips and face – of industrial silicon fraudulently sold as filtered silicon. Not even doctors knew how to prevent the rise in number of deaths, still unknown today. Trapped in a dead-end street, transvestites began to see Europe as the great dream of living a peaceful and financially easier life. Since the end of the 1970s a large number of them have arrived in Paris, considered the paradise of transvestite prostitution. There, it is said, they have managed to make small fortunes on the street or, more rarely, in cabaret shows, At the peak of this unexpected migration there were even special charter flights for transvestites from Brazil to Paris. Of the 700 transvestite prostitutes working in France, 500 are reckoned to be Brazilian – and very successful.

It is true that they are treated better by the French police than by the Brazilian. Lora, a transvestite, claims: "Here they call me *madame*, while in Brazil we are treated like animals."[8] In France, however, only the backdrop has changed, for Brazilian transvestites basically continue to live on the fringes of society and to be subject to other types of extortion, in the same spiral of violence which has even led to murder. Working in Paris, they have to pay a fortune for their "stands" in the street, as well as protection money to the police, extremely high rents and small fortunes for false documentation. In the end, they are no more than exotic consumer objects – just like the first Indians brought to Europe after the discovery of Brazil. The Association for the Defence of French Prostitutes has organised demonstrations, letters to the Brazilian Embassy, interviews in newspapers and on television, accusing Brazilian transvestites of dishonest competition as illegal foreigners who do not pay taxes. It is suspected that this episode caused the French government to demand obligatory entrance visas for all Latin Americans arriving in France. In addition to threatening the local trade, Brazilian transvestites were accused of causing the rising crime rate in France.

The Body Peripatetic

In the lit street, a gay man in costume as a fat queen gives birth to a mock baby on a car bonnet, surrounded by other gay men shouting obscenities. Nearby, there is a procession made up of a Lady of the Camellias, a Madame Mao, a Bird of Paradise, two broken-down Maids and a Punk Fairy Godmother with a green wig; all are men. In the parade there are also transvestites – displaying their silicon breasts, lamé clothes and coloured wigs – and a Cinderella in reverse, carrying a knapsack full of tennis shoes of various sizes to try on Stud Charming. The music, shouting and car-horns make a characteristic noise. It is a scene from the Brazilian Carnival, the gay festival par excellence, particularly in Rio de Janeiro, where ghetto queens have appeared in disguise at the drag ball since 1949 – even in times of great repression by the dictatorship. Today, as an official event in the Rio Carnival, there is even a fantasy parade (known as the Gay Parade) for gay men in drag. The prizes offered to winners are tickets for one of the largest balls in Rio, the Grand Gay Gala, the 1983 poster for which featured a muscular but limp-wristed Superman wearing Carmen Miranda's turban and fruit. In tune with gay consumerism, these specialised balls have spread to other cities and multiplied in Rio de Janeiro itself, where almost all the large clubs now hold balls especially for homosexuals. Exchanging insults through the press, the most important show-business impresarios compete for the gay clientele, offering astonishing novelties at their Carnival balls. One paid homage to the camp actor Cauby Peixoto, another presented a muscle show with forty young men, another held competitions with prizes of a trip to Paris for the best transvestite and a trip to New York for the man with the most beautiful muscles.

This is obviously in response to market demand, considering that gay men from all over the world now come to the Brazilian Carnival. In 1984 a travel firm flew in 370 tourists from the United States. One Brazilian newspaper manifested discreet panic at the presence of the Americans – a surprising fact given that *gringos* always enjoy great prestige among the local gay men. By chance or not, one of the most splendid gay balls had an ominous-sounding English name: The Gay After. There was indeed a subtle connection between the two facts: it was the first Carnival after the arrival of AIDS in Brazil, so the reference to nuclear holocaust had a touch of black humour.

In June 1983 newspapers splashed headlines announcing the death of Markito, one of the top names in Brazilian dress-designing. Age: 31. Cause of death: AIDS. Since then this illness, seen as coming from the US and the rich, has been the subject of sensationalism in both the media and the daily lives of Brazilian gay men. Newspapers speculated on the "gay plague". Some of Markito's customers were said to have refused to wear clothes he made for fear of contracting the disease. There was panic in the ghetto. A male couple in São Paulo were reported to have committed suicide from fear of AIDS. After being interviewed by the press, Dr Valéria Petri, a dermatologist, received a daily average of 200 local and long-distance calls from people seeking information on the disease. The saunas emptied. It became the favourite topic of conversation in the ghetto. Many, swearing that it was another heterosexist conspiracy against gay people, behaved like escapists. Shortly afterwards two more cases of AIDS appeared in São Paulo, where Markito had lived. A month later there were eight cases in the whole state, three of whom had already died. It was revealed that the disease had in fact been claiming victims in Brazil since 1982 without the deaths attracting public attention. Most of the patients (all gay men) had been to New York. Under pressure from members of the gay community, the health secretary of São Paulo – until then the only state in the country to have AIDS cases – called the ministry in Brasília. The reply was evasive; no one knew anything.

With terror on its side, AIDS fulfilled in a few months the subtle and important role that the gay movement had attempted for years in vain – it demonstrated to the nation as a whole that homosexuals did not live in another country but in every corner of Brazil. AIDS seems to have enforced this awareness for, as a stigmatised disease, it could undo carefully created camouflage and at one stroke disclose the most intimate secrets. In Brazil, a land of badly resolved guilt and abundant clandestine sex, the throwing of the first stone became a delicate matter: what if I or one of my family had AIDS? News came from

Recife that a local laboratory had discovered an anti-AIDS vaccine. In chemists the sale of drugs that reinforce the body's defence systems rose dramatically. Monogamy was put forward as the only way for gay men to survive – and with monogamy a return to the closet. The rumours multiplied. A national weekly reported that Glauber Rocha, the internationally famous film director who had died mysteriously two years before, had in fact been the first Brazilian victim of AIDS. The uncertain diagnosis of his fatal illness had indicated first tuberculosis, then cancer and finally septicemia, some doctors tending to include, given the symptoms, *pneumocystis carinii*. The most interesting fact is that Glauber had several times declared himself strongly opposed to homosexuality which, he claimed, was absent in the cinema (sic) because the cinema was uterine and not anal. Furthermore, he accused homosexuality of being the cause of decadence in classical Greece.

The remnants of the gay movement mobilised and distributed pamphlets in the ghetto, saunas and clubs. At the same time the department of health in São Paulo set out a plan of action. As well as demanding that all cases of AIDS in the state be reported to the Epidemic Vigilance Centre, it circulated information to doctors and health centres and tried to keep the gay and non-gay population informed through newspapers. A programme of diagnosis, control and treatment of the disease was set up in the Health Institute and a telephone line for public information opened. In September 1983 there were ten confirmed cases. Meanwhile the first negative public reaction appeared. *Veja*, a weekly magazine which had never hidden its resentment of homosexuals, commented ironically on the anti-AIDS programme, arguing that in Brazil the "diseases of poverty" should have priority. It concluded that a treatment centre for AIDS was "more appropriate in New York than São Paulo", where "it is as out of place as a public centre for varicose vein transplants in the dry, impoverished and starving north-east".[9]

There was also resistance within the medico-academic community, which protested in similar terms of priorities in a poor country. Even the ministry of health in Brasília commented on "this luxury" of spending time and money on a disease which – at that time – appeared to affect so few people. There were reports from Recife that many walls had been painted with such grafitti as "Queers cause cancer", "AIDS is the queers' cancer", "Watch out, queers about!", "Long live the family", etc. In

October 1983 there were thirteen cases, with nine deaths. Cases began to appear in other Brazilian states. In Rio de Janeiro alone a preliminary estimate gave 18 patients at the beginning of 1984. At that time there were 34 cases in the country, with 16 deaths. There were also reports of 12 cases in Uruguay – five of whom had regularly travelled to São Paulo before falling ill. In April 1984 a medical symposium showed concern at the accelerated rate of new cases in São Paulo where two heterosexual women and seven bisexual men also had AIDS. In the same month there were 43 cases in São Paulo (with 20 deaths) out of a total of 70 proven cases in the whole country. Cases now came from every social level from working to middle class. The health ministry asked groups at risk to abstain from giving blood.

It is true that the panic phase has passed. So far, however, it has not been possible to estimate how deep the psychological and cultural effects concerning the risk of AIDS go. It is a very new situation, particularly because anti-gay prejudice is now granted more space in the media, where it can talk of AIDS with complete freedom. The disease can also be said to have been the cause of many other strange, or at least revealing, events. The town council of Uberaba, where Markito was born (in one of the country's most moralistic states), chartered a plane to bring back his body – which had been returned to Rio de Janeiro from New York where, accompanied by his mother, he had gone for treatment. Once in Uberaba the body lay in the chapel of a college near the house where he had spent his childhood. A mass was celebrated by Bishop Alberto Guimarães, Markito's cousin, who came from Bahia especially for the ceremony. On leaving the chapel the hearse drove through the streets of the town, accompanied by about a thousand people and by the band of the 4th Police Battalion playing funeral marches. Before arriving at the cemetery, the body was taken to the Carmelo convent for another benediction. Members of the family avoided commenting on the cause of Markito's death, which was reported in full and in detail by the press throughout the country. They even published a special booklet telling the story of his life from infancy in Uberaba to the most sophisticated fashion salons in the city which the designer had moved to when very young – against his family's wishes.

What do I still find surprising in this story? Simply that the terrifying AIDS became a festival through a process of baroque recuperation. Killed by a gay man's disease, Markito became a hero in his home town and famous throughout the country; his stigma transfigured him. This nation with its baroque inclinations was more interested in the myth and its implications of celebration and festivity than in the fatality of AIDS. An old and revealing Portuguese sailors' proverb claimed that: "Sailing is necessary, life is not." In paraphrase, I would say that for these people: "Celebration is necessary, life is not," simply because celebration is more comprehensive. What counts, in all and above all, is exuberance.

Perhaps the possibility that homosexual desire will survive is to be found here – in the baroque generosity of relationships more than in the ideological insensitivity or compulsory monogamy typical of heterosexual marriage. This, in my opinion, makes sense even at this historic moment in which homosexual life has been made so much more vulnerable as a result of AIDS, an illness as serious in the weight of its social stigma as in its physical implications. Nor must it be forgotten that, as with the spectacle of life, the spectacle of desire is magnanimous in direct proportion to its fragility as an ecosystem. In other words, we must always be open to the possibility of losing it as the very condition for plunging into its magnanimity. Insofar as the fantastic universe of desire is concerned, the doors of paradise will always be open wide as long as the angels of libertinism speak the language of exuberance.

APPENDIX

Interview with a *Babalorixá*

Brazilian *candomblé,* which is similar to Cuban *santería* and Haitian voodoo, is an African cult derived from the amalgamation of various beliefs originating in the Gulf of Guinea and Angola, the regions from where Brazilian slaves came. A complex metaphysical religion, it includes elements of Islam. It is based on belief in a single and creative god, Oxalá, aided by a hundred deities (*orixás*) who inhabit the spiritual world and administer the cosmos, humanity and its passions. According to *candomblé,* the universe constitutes a harmonic whole; the material world does not exist alone but signifies only the most visible part of this universe. Popularised throughout the world in the novels of Jorge Amado, the religion of *candomblé* as such appears to have begun to form around 1830 in Bahia, in the guise of Catholic festivals celebrated by slaves. Thence its basic syncretism developed, each god corresponding to a Catholic saint – eg. St George is Ogum, Xangô is St John, Oxum is Our Lady of the Conception, the Ibejis or Erês twins correspond to St Cosme and St Damion, etc. This trait of camouflage is almost inherent in *camdomblé* – it was persecuted by the police for several decades – and corresponds perfectly to its character as an esoteric cult whose secrets can only be passed on by the priestess (*ialorixá* or "mother-of-saint" in Portuguese) or priest (*babalorixá* or "father-of-saint") to initiates ("sons/daughters-of-saint") during years of rigorous apprenticeship. Another factor underlining its esoteric character is the Nagô language, which was spoken by many of the slaves and which eventually imposed itself as the official language of *candomblé*.

As well as specific beliefs, *candomblé* also has its own liturgy. By means of dances, chants and sacrifices carried out to the beat of percussion instruments that also originated in Africa, priests, aided by their initiates, call *orixás* to the temple. The arrival of these entities in the material world is guaranteed by *cavalos* ("horses") – mediums for *orixás* – who try to re-establish the lost unity of the cosmos by reconnecting the *ayé* (visible, human world) and the *orum* (world of spirits and gods). Each god has a specific function and administers a certain part of the cosmos. Thus everything which exists has its *orixá* – a word which means "owner of the *ori*" (*ori* = head). The sea, for example, is the province of the goddess Iemanjá, as fresh waters belong to Oxum and forests to Oxóssi. In the same way each human being belongs to a god. The priest discovers each person's *orixá* and discloses the ceremonies and sacrifices which must be made to the "saint" in order to obtain protection, favours and energy. Each *orixá* or entity demands animal sacrifices and specific foods. At the festival of Oxalá, for example, goats, pigs, hens, doves and ducks are sacrificed and snails offered. Oxumáre expects goats, roosters, guinea-fowl and armadillos as well as cooked and prepared foods. Sacrifices can vary according to the request made; a woman who wants to be cured of sterility offers Oxum (the patroness of fertility) a dish of eggs or even a yellow hen (the *orixá*'s colour) to be sacrificed at the moment of offering. However, the most important bloody sacrifices take place during the initiation rites of a "son/daughter-of-saint", who makes offerings to his or her *orixá* and has the animals' spilt blood poured over the head.

In time *candomblé* absorbed elements of Catholicism and Kardecism* (this being the origin of *umbanda*) as well as indigenous rites (*catimbó*) or African rites from other nations (*macumba*). It is thus very common to find temples where *orixás* (black saints) and *caboclos* (indigenous saints) are worshipped indiscriminately – as is the case with Mário Miranda's temple, where *candomblé, macumba* and *umbanda* are fused.

There has been much speculation, based on such evidence as the large number of its gay priests, on the connection between *candomblé* and homosexuality. Yet the primordial divine essence, of undefined sex and embracing the whole cycle from active to passive without distinction, is found in the original doctrine and metaphysics of *candomblé*. The first and most important emanation of this essence is Oxalá, God the Creator, who has a feminine half and is characterised by androgyny; it is said that this *orixá* lives under a cotton plant with a young lad as his lover. There are other equally androgynous entities in the pantheon – Oxumaré, Logum-Edé, Ossanha, etc. As will be seen in the interview, Oxumaré is presented as a god/dess par excellence, with a very rich symbolism: s/he appears in the form of a rainbow

*After the French spiritualist Alain Kardec [Trans. note].

and two-headed serpent who comes out of the depths to drink the sky before returning to the depths on the other side. Ambivalent, the rainbow links sky and earth, while being all-embracing, for it brings together every colour and, as a snake, is capable of closing itself in a circle and bringing together opposites. Oxumaré is therefore the entity of cyclical situations and the bipolar force which, being constituted of essential and contradictory elements, inspires life into the Universe. Logum-Edé is another androgynous being; a child of Oxóssi (male) and Oxum (female), s/he is half man, half woman, uniting in him/herself opposing characteristics. Logum-Edé is presented as a male hunter who lives in the forest and kills wild animals to feed himself; every six months, however, he is transformed into a beautiful, vain and honey- tongued nymph who lives in rivers and feeds on fish. (It is interesting to note that Oxumaré's and Logum-Edé's colours are, perhaps coincidentally, the national colours of Brazil: in Logum-Edé the green and yellow is sometimes blue and yellow.) Another strangely oscillating being is the goddess Iansã, whose place is that of a warrior, commanding winds and storms, and who dresses like the male gods, wearing trousers under a skirt.

According to the creed, when one of these gods "falls on the head" of a human being, s/he is revealed as gay. This is the case of the *orixá* Ogum-Xoroquê, whose daughters are bearded and very quarrelsome. Founded on ambiguity and paradox, the mythology of *candomblé* also reveals many gods who marry their sisters or mothers, sometimes even through rape (as young Oranyã and his mother, Iemanjá). This obviously reveals the great distance from Western and Catholic ethics, in which incest is still a rigorous taboo.

And what about gay priests? We have to remember that *candomblé* follows a practice common in many African societies and also to be found among indigenous North Americans and Brazilians – the *shaman* (witch-doctor) is generally identified with the "feminine" as defined by these cultures and benefits in the tribe from this ambiguous state. Ruth Landes, an anthropologist, noted in 1947 that the cult of *candomblé* in Bahia was based on a matriarchal organisation, with mythical priestesses leading the religious community and jealously guarding the traditional African secrets. Yet she was surprised by the number of gay priests in the role of religious leaders. The two seemed to her connected. According to the Nagô tradition of *candomblé*, only women – because of their sex – were appropriate to deal with divinities. Thus the service of men at ceremonies came to be seen as blasphemy while the priestly function was considered unmanly and castrating. Nonetheless, following the relatively recent split which led to the worship of *caboclos* in *candomblé,* the ritual rigour weakened with more and more men being admitted into the priesthood and allowed, on a par with women, to enter frenetic trances during the ceremonies without the cult being harmed. This relaxing of tradition, however, did not undermine the fundamental principle of *candomblé,* that only femininity could serve the gods. Thus men known to be homosexual were admitted in large numbers, either for their effeminate appearance or simply for their qualities (mystical included) considered "feminine". These men in their turn aspire to remain faithful to tradition, at the centre of which is the great mother, whose reflex they consider themselves to be.

All this femininity, therefore, is ritualised in the sacerdotal trance and expressed in sensual dances which are very different from the "virile" or athletic expression of the dances in which the men take part. Indeed, the erotic is always allied to the mythic in *candomblé*: the gods themselves use the alien body to manifest themselves visibly. It is thus not surprising that physical appearance is basic in the relationship with spirits – the body plays a substantial role in rituals, being decorated, painted, robed and disrobed in its important role as the bridge to the gods. The hyper-sensibility in the *babalorixá*'s function as a medium, whose communication is above all intuitive, must also be mentioned – in our culture intuition and sensitivity are both considered equally feminine. In Rio de Janeiro I met Nívio Ramos Sales, a priest who became famous through his autobiography which was later filmed. He began his priestly function receiving a feminine being called Ciganinha Salome ("Litttle Gypsy Salome") so he dressed as a gypsy woman and danced and spoke effeminately during trances. Without concealing his homosexuality, Nívio married and had two children by an exuberant mulatta who, in an interesting transfer of fascinations, declared herself as much in love with the gypsy woman as with her husband. Furthermore, Nívio does not hesitate to assert that 80% of the priests he knows are gay, whether in the closet or out. I was also told about a Bahian priest Nezinho Boa-Bunda ("Nezinho Good- Arse"), a famous "fucker of women" whose nickname however left no doubt about his homosexual tastes. There is even the extreme case of a priestess in São Paulo who is really a man – an example of transvestism taken to its logical conclusion in *candomblé*.

The interview that follows was only made possible by the friendship of Professor Jomard Muniz de Britto and the anthropologist Roberto Motta with *babalorixá* Mário Miranda, to all of whom I am immensely grateful. In addition, Silvio Ferreira, a psychologist, and Antonio Cadengue, a theatre director, to whom I am also indebted for the meeting, were also present. Mário Miranda, who uses the feminine name of Maria Aparecida ("Mary of the Apparition") is a dark, tall and well-built mulatto. Despite his masculine body, his gestures are delicate and his manner jovial. His teeth, most of which are gold, are often revealed by his good-humoured and feral smile. Maria Aparecida appeared at the interview in a tunic of light and coloured cloth and baggy bermuda shorts; on his head he wore a delightful and sensual white turban in the style of priestesses. He also wore earrings as well many rings and innumerable bracelets on his fingers and arms. The interview took place in the temple known as the Palace of Oxum-Ceci, where Mário Miranda lives and officiates, in the heart of slum in Recife in November 1981.

*

TREVISAN. I don't fully understand the relationship between Maria Aparecida and Mário Miranda. What is it like?
M. APARECIDA. Well, the saint I adore is Our Lady of the Apparition,* my *orixum*. Her feast is on 2 February. I dedicate two Fridays in July for Oxum, who is Our Lady of Carmo, and I celebrate 2 February in homage to Our Lady of the Apparition. Everyone just calls me Maria Aparecida. And I don't find it in the least offensive. Look, I went to the government building in the Palácio das Princesas, with a letter to get a lawyer. I went in sandals, trousers and T-shirt. I got there, went in. I had an earring, see, everyone was watching me, one nudged his neighbour, said something. Shortly afterwards a man came up and said: "Oh, Dona Maria Aparecida, please!" I said: "Of course, dear, what's the problem?" It was Dr Newton calling me. I went, stayed in his office for ages and when I came out I had a lawyer. I, gay, Maria Aparecida, I go anywhere. No one's ever going to turn their back on me.
JOMARD. But it's not just that. People don't turn their back on

**Nossa Senhora Aparecida*, literally "Our Lady Appeared", a Brazilian manifestation of the Virgin Mary [Trans. note].

you because you're very brave. There's a story that one Carnival you were passing the barracks dressed as a Bahian woman and someone made a joke. You fought with the whole battalion!

M. APARECIDA. There's that, yes. Because I've never lost my courage or my good spirits. I'll give anything else away, just ask me and I'll give it, right? But I've never surrendered my courage or spirits. Never.

TREVISAN. How did you become a *babalorixá*?

M. APARECIDA. I inherited it from my parents. My mother used to go to Mr Apolinário Gomes da Mota's house. I was very young and went to watch a few ceremonies. There was food, I liked it. When I was twelve I began to receive the saint; not in the temple, only at seances. It was Oxum, who came down crying. The others thought it was a *caboclo*, but it was a saint. Then she came to the temple with me. I asked Mr Apolinário to make my first offerings, because I worked in a family, I was a cook. That was all here in Recife. Then I worked, got together some money and made my offerings. When the opportunity came to be chosen by my saint, he said that he wouldn't do it because his rhythm was Congo and my saint was from Mozambique.

TREVISAN. There's a story that you were Oxum but wanted to become Xangô. How does the story go?

M. APARECIDA. I was Oxum's child, I had Oxum in my head, then they said: "No, so that he doesn't become a sissy, get that female saint out of his head and put in Xangô, who's a male saint, a real man." But they couldn't. If you're destined, no one can...

TREVISAN. So you changed?

M. APARECIDA. No. I tried to change, but it didn't work.

ROBERTO. Who was the priestess that wanted you to change?

M. APARECIDA. Mother Rosinha, Mr Apolinário's daughter.

TREVISAN. So you changed your priestess?

M. APARECIDA. I left her house and spoke with my godmother Júlia. She told me to get ready; I got ready, meditated in my room and she made my saint. When I'd made my saint, I wanted to open my own house, but she didn't want me to. She wanted me to stay and help her, because she was very tired and I was like a son come to help her with the sacrifices. I said: "No, when you marry, you want your own house and I have my clients, my people and I want to have my own house." So I came to live here in this house, which was very small indeed. Where we are now was an enormous hole, in fact a bathroom.

So the girls and I brought mud from the Arraial road over there and I levelled it all out. I made the first living-room with coconut straw, then I got rid of the straw and put in zinc. After the zinc I put up tiles and made the living-room, first of stucco and later brickwork. At that time bricks still cost 30 mil-reis a thousand. So I made the living-room and saint's house. And here I am today, 36 years in this house. I like my house very much. I'm 53 years old and enjoying life more in old age than I did when I was young.

TREVISAN. Can you explain what these two places like chapels are?

M. APARECIDA. The first one, on the right, is the Gongá, the room where the *caboclo* people stay – the saint who is part of Mondays and Exu-Mulher ("Spirit-Woman").

TREVISAN. What is Exu-Mulher?

M. APARECIDA. Exu-Mulher is the Pomba-Gira. The one here is called Dona Leonora and is the godmother of the house. The principal *caboclos* of the Jurema Sagrada ("Sacred Acacia"), Nanã (who is the grandmother of the sect) and the spirits, the Exu-Caveira ("Spirit-Skull") for Jurema, are also part of Mondays. Their day is Mondays, which is the day of souls. And this other place is Peji's room, the *orixás'* place, where the sacrifices are done, the offerings dedicated to the *orixá* saints. It's a different room. Each day of the week is the day of an *entidade* ("entity") and belongs to the *orixá*, from the *exu* ("spirit") to Orixalá, who is the king, the superior. Monday is the *caboclo*'s day; they don't like much light, they like the weakest light or even black light. Friday is the day the *orixás* are called. At the calling, people first sing to the *exu* to please him. When the *exu* is freed, then the people call the *exus* first so that they can call the *caboclos* and *orixás* afterwards. On Friday we call from Ogum to Orixalá. Ogum comes, then Oxóssi, then Nanã, Obaluaê, Iansã, Xangô, Iemanjá, Oxum and Oxalá.

JOMARD. Who are the saints of the other days of the week?

M. APARECIDA. Monday is the day of souls and *exus*. Tuesday is Oxum. Wenesday Xangô with Iansã. Thursday Ogum and Odé-Oxossi. On Friday Oxalá. Saturday, Iemanjá. On Sunday the children, Cosme and Damion.

TREVISAN. What is the difference between *caboclos* and *orixás*?

M. APARECIDA. There is a great difference, because the *orixás* eat out of stone and the *caboclos* out of wood. The hymns are also different. And for the *orixá*, the more luxurious things are, the better. The songs are different too, the calls are different.

JOMARD. Are the *caboclos* subordinate to the divinity or are they also gods, *entidades*?
M. APARECIDA. There's no difference. Tupã is the *caboclos'* god. And Orixalá is the god of the black Africans. They're two phalanxes. And you get to just one, on top. There is only one God. Just one divided in three, you understand? God the Father, God the Son, God the Holy Spirit.
JOMARD. And which of these three are in the *orixás'* temple? Is Orixalá the most important?
M. APARECIDA. Yes. Orixalá-Lufã is the one who takes care of the night: he is God the Father. He is St Joseph, the Father. God the Son is Orixalá-Milá, who is Our Lord of Bonfim. Orixalá-Milá takes care of the day. And the Holy Spirit is an enchanted dove. You have to call to him all the time.
TREVISAN. I'm very curious to find out about Pomba-Gira!
M. APARECIDA. Pomba-Gira is a woman who likes married men very much, because she finds that married men can keep a secret and gratify women better, are more tender. A single man is different because he only has love to give and doesn't have what's better – money. A married man gives more pleasure so that she won't complain and his wife at home won't find out. [Laughs.] So she likes flowers, perfume, champagne, beer, palm oil. She eats goat-meat, chicken, guinea-fowl, apples, fruits. Any offering is good for Pomba-Gira when you want to reconcile with your lover; when you want someone you love who isn't with you, arrange something with her and it'll work out. At a crossroads put beer and a cigarette, red roses, the person's name inside the champagne or beer, because she's very helpful to those who ask her. Men as much as women. Go and speak to Pomba-Gira, talk to her and promise her a ring, a watch, a gold chain, a goat, three hens, offer her what you can. "Look, Pomba-Gira, make my love come back to me and I'll give you a wedding-ring, I'll give you a watch, I'll give you a dress" – she likes dresses...
TREVISAN. Where is the offering made, here?
M. APARECIDA. Yes, here. You have to go to her feet. This Pomba-Gira here in the house is called Dona Leonora and she has many things. I won't leave her jewels there, because many people come and go and no one knows who's honest and who isn't. But she has many things, as much as Oxum. They are thanksgivings, expensive dresses. You marry and give her a veil, a garland, a dress, you see?

TREVISAN. I've heard that Pomba-Gira is a spirit who likes or who protects or who has a lot to do with men who like men.
M. APARECIDA. Ah, she protects them because she's unisex, isn't she? I mean that a man who is transvestite or gay has a part of a woman; he has a heart, he has the right to love. So he has to come to Pomba-Gira's feet – "If you are the protector of women, protect me too because I'm unisex." And Pomba-Gira isn't going to say no because she's very greedy. [Laughs.] You arrive with the offering and she's working for you already.
TREVISAN. Do you think there's an *orixá* who protects gays?
M. APARECIDA. Ah, I'll tell you the saint who is dedicated to protecting gays: Oxumaré. Oxumaré is a very well-known saint in the south. Today everyone here is doing Oxumaré. With Oxumaré you love rainbows, nature. When this saint talks in a man's head he becomes gay: six months a woman, six months a man. So for six months he is in love with men, goes and looks for men wherever they might be. And for six months he doesn't care about men, he can even about-face, get a woman or a girlfriend. Now, when Oxumaré falls on a woman's head, she becomes a lesbian, right? She doesn't like men, starts to like women and sometimes gets money from a man to keep a woman. This Oxumaré is the protector of gays.
JOMARD. Which saint does he correspond to in the Catholic Church?
M. APARECIDA. Our Lady of the Apparition.
TREVISAN. What is the difference between Oxum and Oxumaré?
M. APARECIDA. Oxum is perfume. Oxum is sweet. Oxum is peace in the home. Oxum is money. Oxum is jewellery. Oxum is everything which is good. People love nature, right? But the Oxum I love is Oxumaré, the rainbow, who drinks water for six months and for six months is in the desert. Oxumaré is a snake as well. And that snake is called Oxumaré-Decém. So I think *candomblé* houses can't kick out a gay person because it would be kicking out Oxumaré. And that's the rainbow. He drinks water up there. And to make this saint you have to make a snake, of cotton, on the head. And come with a little snake in the hand. Oxumaré comes down whistling, jumps down on one foot only. He's a very good-looking saint. He hasn't yet come to me, but I love him and I've shaved three people.
TREVISAN. What is shaving?
M. APARECIDA. Making the saint. For love of the saint, you have to shave your head, because you're going to become a priest. You come, join, and at the first rite become an initiate. And

then you make your saint, become a *babalorixá*, you understand? To be a *babalorixá* you have to shave your head for love of the saint. Hair is something beautiful if you look after it, it's something! But to make your saint you have to shave it off. Now, it's only grass; cut it today and two or three months later it's born again. If you want, shave it again after seven years, and if you don't want, it's not a problem because you've shaved it the first time. Because the saints, the *orixás* come from Africa, which is the land of negros and negros don't have hair. But today there's no longer any distinction of colour, because many whites have turned to the saint in the sect for fear of losing their money. For the poor losing their money is nothing new – they live from hand to mouth anyway, they might eat once or twice a day. But not the rich – they have everything whenever they want. And now there are people from high society in the sect afraid of losing everything, seeking protection, security from the *orixá* saint. There are many high society people who don't come to my house so they won't be seen, so I go and consult with them in their own homes, see?

TREVISAN. I heard you suffered an accident because of love. How did it happen?

M. APARECIDA. That accident was very important. To start with, initiates are always coming here to learn about a saint or because they like a saint, and many people come to see the well-dressed Bahian women and others come to find a girlfriend. So, this boy called Luís Henrique used to come a lot. He was Iemanjá's son, about sixteen years old, a doll. He would stay and help me with the sacrifices and carry material to build the living-room. At the end of the week I'd give him pocket-money to go out, because he was young and had to enjoy himself. Now there was a blonde girl here, simply beautiful, who was very friendly. She was unlucky with her husband, so she stayed around here in my house so that Pomba-Gira would protect her and arrange someone to look after her. Then she fell in love with Luís Henrique, who'd been living in my house for two years.

TREVISAN. Were you jealous?

M. APARECIDA. Of course I was! Living with someone for two years, you get used to it. One day he came to me and said: "Mário, are you angry with me?" I said: "No, follow the voice of your heart. If it's your heart asking, follow it. A woman is something fine, she has fine things, but she doesn't have the best, which is food on time, as I give you here." He came up to me and began to caress me, and then he said: "Cida, you know what this is?" And he pulled from his belt one of his father's revolvers, loaded. I opened my wardrobe and took out my revolver and said: "You see that this here's also a gun? You see that it's fully loaded? You want a shoot-out? You've got six and I've got six; let's see who'll die first. If we both die it'll say in the paper tomorrow: Husband And Wife Died For Love." [Laughter.] Then he tried to kiss me, but I turned away. He said: "Are you refusing to kiss me because my mouth disgusts you, because of that woman?" I said: "No, it's not disgust; toothpaste and a toothbrush will get rid of any microbes. It's because I'm really not in the mood. You've lost me." Then he went away, February went by, March, April and he never came back. On 31 May I went to a "Sun Morning" (a mid-year festival) and stayed with the boys, drinking. When I left, it was with a friend of Luís Henrique's. He suggested we go down the street where Henrique lived. When I got to the corner, Henrique was sitting there in blue shorts; he looked at me and turned his back.

This was on a Sunday, right? So I went home, had a snack, took Diazepan to make me sleep and relax, on doctor's orders, and left the door open. Luís Henrique was furious and very jealous because I'd gone by with a friend of his. So he took his father's knife and came right up here to my house. He jumped over the wall, came to my room, saw that I was sleeping and stuck the knife in me. Four times, I woke up, felt the blows but didn't feel any pain. I said: "Let me sleep; who's that bothering me?" I opened my eyes but saw everything was in darkness, because he'd switched off the light and he took hold of my head and let all hell loose. I screamed that a thief was killing me. With that, he jumped over the wall and ran away, knife in hand, shirt covering the knife; he ran home and left his clothes there, covered in blood, got on a bus and went to the barracks. He spent eight days there without coming home. It was on the radio, in the newspapers, on TV, it was the most talked-about thing in the world. And no one knew who had done it. I would never have thought it was him.

So, when it was my birthday, 2 August, I put on a suit, tidied up everything, made the food. In the afternoon I sat out there on the doorstep and made a promise to Tranca-Rua and all the saints of my house: how could it be that I had a saint, loved the saint so much and the saint didn't show me who had tried to kill me? If the saint didn't show me, I was going to lose my faith and stop worshipping him. If Tranca-Rua showed me who had tried to kill me, I would give him an ox, with four goats and as many chickens as I could buy. I sat there at dawn, talked with the Estrela-Dalva [morning star], talked with the moon, because I like to talk with nature a lot. Then this boy, a friend of Luís Henrique's came over. He came up to me and said: "Look, I've something to tell you: the guy who tried to kill you was Luís Henrique. He sent me to tell you not to talk to the police or the papers or the TV any more, because it wasn't that he didn't want to kill you but because you were lucky. And if you start talking, he'll come and finish it off."

Then we had the party, I had fun, was nice to everyone, put on my dress, waltzed. On Monday afternoon I took the boy to the police station and he made a statement in front of two witnesses. So Luís Henrique was heard immediately with two lawyers, but there's going to be another hearing. He says that when he gets out of the army he's afraid to stay here. I've got nothing against him. I don't want anything from him, I know how to forgive. But I don't want to reconcile with him. I've got many children – people came from São Paulo, from Rio, my helpers were all panic-struck there at the hospital. They even asked me to be a town councillor when they saw the crowd of people who came to visit me. I didn't accept because it was an opposition party. And I couldn't be in the opposition because it was people from the governor who visited me in hospital and told the doctors that they should give me whatever I needed. And I wasn't short of doctors; there were five or six at my bedside. I was five hours in surgery. Then a group came from the town council, the mayor embraced me, a lot of good people. It was even said that I had died, so the governor said that if I had died, as King of Umbanda in Pernambuco I would have had a state funeral; but since I was fine they would do what they could for me.

I spent a fortnight in hospital recovering, everyone waiting at my house. And when I came back there was even a mass given by the bishop here in my house and there was a rite of atonement on St Anthony's day. My son made the sacrifice, all the girls helped, took the animals to each saint as his offering and, even though I was sick, I sang a lot, was very moved. Then I began to cry and they looked after me. Then I began to sing again, the saint came to me, I pulled all the bandages off my wounds. The day went by and I didn't get sick, I'm still cured today. Thanks to God I feel nothing.

JOMARD. Can you tell us something about your childhood, when the *candomblés* were persecuted by the police?

M. APARECIDA. At the time Governor Agamenon Magalhães – God grant him many years of life without us – closed many *candomblé* houses and didn't arrest the priests but confiscated all the saints' belongings. I was a small boy, still very young, and didn't have the saint at all.

ROBERTO. They said that the temples were full of Communists, didn't they?

M. APARECIDA. I don't think a Communist is going to be interested in a *candomblé* house at all. He's going to want other things. Later an officer from the Casa Amarela district was always turning up here. He was a follower of *macumba* but didn't want anyone to know and he liked rubbing people out. When we held a service that was going on till midnight, they would arrive at half-past ten and, guns in hand, order the drums to stop. Then they would arrest the priest. I would go out with that rosary round my neck and all the girls crying. I would go too because I stood up to them.

ROBERTO. What year was that, Maria Aparecida?

M. APARECIDA. Oh, my boy, I don't remember at all. I don't write down the bad things, I do everything to forget. I know that there was a feast here, dedicated to St George. My saint was eating, and the Peji was full of sacrifices. And then shortly afterwards the officer arrived with six men and called me over with a gun in his hand. Everyone ran. So I went over, spoke to the commissioner, showed my license and was ready to hit out, to fight. There were many young men in the police who were angry with me because I didn't pay protection money and most of them went to Xangô's house to eat and then take the protection money. The money I should have given them was to buy the next day's bread and pay for the saint's feasts. Afterwards, the officer was going down the hill when he fell and broke his glasses. Then they said it was a spell I had made. I hadn't made any spell; if he fell it was because he slipped. So right away I rang for St George for three days, cast spells, went into the forest, abandoned everything, said that the saint was my lawyer and waited. Three months later the officer had something for lunch, I don't know what he drank. He sat down in his rocking-chair and we're still waiting today for him to wake up. It's been almost ten years.

CADENGUE. Mário, why have you never joined the opposition? You say that you always support the government.

M. APARECIDA. Ah, even if I was starving I'd stay with the government. Because I understand nothing about politics, nothing at all. When you hear the dance, you dance what the orchestra plays. It's not just me that's suffering, it's many people.
ROBERTO. So you're not going to be a candidate?
M. APARECIDA. I don't know, my friend. It's all very vague; I don't know. I go and speak with the men from the party and they tell me to smarten up and so on. When they asked me to be a town councillor, there was a little councillor who said: "Maria Aparecida can't be a councillor, because if he was, the only people who would vote for him would be the queers." So then I said: "If all the queers wearing a suit, tie and ring voted for me, I'd have enough votes for two candidates." [Laughter.] The one who mocked me, I know nothing about his past, whether he played with dolls... [Laughter.]
TREVISAN. And you think the party would agree, simply because you're Maria Aparecida?
M. APARECIDA. I think everyone knows Maria Aparecida, the transvestite in Dantas Barreto, who goes out in a turban and earrings. Wherever you meet me – in Recife, Rio, São Paulo, Paraíba, Bahia – that's how I am; I don't change. Now, there are others who put on a suit and tie because they don't want to be recognised. Not me, my cards are on the table. And I don't criticise anybody; everyone should listen to the voice of their own heart. Today the world is full of gays and the gays are winning.
TREVISAN. As a politician, who would you consider defending?
M. APARECIDA. The people of my sect. Transvestites; I wouldn't ignore them either. Not to condemn, to protect, you understand? Principally the people of the sect, because there are more than 4,000 temples in Recife, so it isn't possible that they wouldn't vote for me.
JOMARD. And how many people do you think come here to your house often? Regularly?
M. APARECIDA. Some... some thirty people.
CADENGUE. One day we were here and a lady arrived, one of your children. She saw a photograph of you at Carnival and said: "But my father looks like a woman." So you said: "And I'm not a woman? It's just that I was born with a large clit." I don't know if you remember that. She was an old woman and was shocked. How do your flock react to the fact that you have sex with men?

M. APARECIDA. They want me as I am. So, whatever I do, they accept me. It was the reason why I left my wife. I love my daughters; everything I've got in the house was given to me by my flock. And so I could enjoy life better if I was with my wife. I left my wife for love of my daughters. They know what I'm like and love me for what I am.

ROBERTO. Have you been oppressed for being gay?

M. APARECIDA. In my parents' time, yes, because I respected them. Then I even tried to commit suicide when I was found out. Since then I've always gone on working, living my life.

TREVISAN. How old were you when you tried to commit suicide?

M. APARECIDA. Ah, I was thirteen.

ROBERTO. How did you do it, with pills?

M. APARECIDA. No, it was in the river. I ran and fell into the river, at a deep spot, you know? And where you fell you stayed, because the water began spinning and people died.

ROBERTO. So it was in your adolescence that you defined yourself as gay?

M. APARECIDA. I began playing with dolls, sewing, playing at cooking. I had a doll with me so I could say I had a baby. Then the boys said: "To have a baby you have to do this!" So I did.

ROBERTO. But it's said that you've been married more than once and have many children...

M. APARECIDA. Listen, professor, I'm going to tell you that I have only one son. I can tell you he's mine, he's registered in my name, lives in my house, Amauri. He's with a woman now, but they aren't married because I didn't know the girl, so I didn't agree to the marriage. I gave and I'm still giving him money to study, because I didn't have time to study. I lost my father very early and, so that my mother wouldn't get another man in my father's place, I had to go to a white man's house, work, cook, cut down trees, work in the garden, everything to make money so that my mother wouldn't put another man in my place. I was very jealous of my mother. God gave me this son and I'm giving him what I didn't have. He's already in the third scientific grade. I hope that he graduates. Seeing him graduate, it wouldn't matter if God called me tomorrow. He's the greatest pleasure I have in life.

JOMARD. Since you're gay, are you annoyed that your son is a man?

M. APARECIDA. He listens to the voice of his heart. I'm not going to interfere in his life, because he doesn't interfere in mine. If we're going to worship, we're going to worship. After worship,

everyone listens to the voice of their heart, don't you think? Many gays come to my house. They say that my son is good-looking. When the queens see him, they fall for him.
ROBERTO. You're not annoyed because he isn't homosexual?
M. APARECIDA. God help me, no. I have to love him as he is. He doesn't condemn gay people and he doesn't live as one.
JOMARD. But wouldn't you like it if he were gay?
M. APARECIDA. No. So as not to take my place! [Laughter.]
JOMARD. There are stories that you have other children...
M. APARECIDA. You know, professor, that I was a healthy boy and the fact that I was a transvestite has nothing to do with anything else. Women found me attractive, because I was a priest, I sang well, I could dance, I've always been friendly. So this woman called me to her room and offered me a tip to stay with her. And I, very greedy, went. I got there, she stayed all night; if she wanted satisfaction from me, she could get satisfaction... For me it was like taking a purgative of castor-oil, which I don't like at all, it was against my wishes. [Laughter.] And the other who says she has a child of mine, that Dr Mariazinha, I lived with her for eight years because she had an old husband and I was quite healthy, right? And there was a little boy but when I started going with her she already had the boy. I made his saint when he was seven and sick.
JOMARD. But there was one you married. What's her name?
M. APARECIDA. Da. Diva.
ROBERTO. And didn't she get pregnant after marrying you?
M. APARECIDA. No, she didn't have a child.
TREVISAN. How did you get married?
M. APARECIDA. I married in *umbanda*. To the world I'm single, because I don't have any documents in the registry. I married in *umbanda* because the woman had been bothering me for years. Since she was a widow, she didn't want to give herself to me and lose her name, did she? But we went out together, made love, ate out; she put money in my pocket and I paid; macho, right? But with her money.
ROBERTO. You never lived in the same house?
M. APARECIDA. No, we didn't.
TREVISAN. When was that?
M. APARECIDA. That was six years ago.
JOMARD. But she spent the night here?
M. APARECIDA. She came, pushed all clients out. My flock, when the music was over, she kicked them out. But the men, when the music was over, wanted to be with their father,

wanted to have their father's caress. So she got furious. And she said that my daughters were not daughters, they were all very friendly with me, they all wanted me. But it wasn't like that. I love my flock as if they were my own children, you know?

TREVISAN. Tell me something, Mário, do you know many gay priests?

M. APARECIDA. Most are gay. When a priest isn't gay, he has to be more macho than the rest or he isn't respected by the queens.

ROBERTO. But has something like that happened?

M. APARECIDA. No, because I don't agree with it at all. Those who have a grudge against me are jealous of seeing me happy. To go out now, I don't need Carnival. I go into my room, get my dress, put on my shoes, get my documents, put my gun in my bag and go out. [Laughter.] The police say: "Good evening, Mr Mário!" I say: "Good evening." I get to a hotel, eat bean stew, calf's trotter, whatever I want. Everyone watches me, with my earring, the way I want to be. It doesn't have to be Carnival for me to go out in a skirt. Then there are those who want to copy me but can't, they don't have the star that I was born with, so they have a grudge. One says: "Don't go to Maria Aparecida's house because he's gay." I'm gay, but no man's going to undo a spell that I've made. Not at all! Because when he comes, I'm already there! I've been with the saint for 36 years. And when I want to learn, I don't come here to Casa Amarela. I go out to talk with someone who knows more than me. After Mr Apolinário, who watched over my saint, there was no one else, so I went to Salvador to Mãe-Menininha's* house and stayed there.

TREVISAN. But why do you think there are so many gay priests?

M. APARECIDA. Because it's the times. Since I came, that's what I found. The majority. And everyone sees this close-up.

ROBERTO. Father Apolinário?

M. APARECIDA. No. Father Apolinário was a real man.

ROBERTO. Father Romão?

M. APARECIDA. Father Romão was a real man. Always with women.

ROBERTO. Father Adam?

M. APARECIDA. Always with women.

ROBERTO. So in the older generation there were no gays?

*Literally, "Mother-Little-Girl", a very famous priestess in Brazil [Trans. note].

M. APARECIDA. I'm not going to swear to that! I'm not sticking my head on the block. Someone can be very masculine, but when it comes down to it, the mask falls, you understand?
TREVISAN. In any case, why do you think that there are so many gay priests today?
M. APARECIDA. My son, it's not me who thinks that. Everyone can see!
TREVISAN. But I'd like to know your opinion: why?
M. APARECIDA. I don't know. I think because people become more attached, are in more contact with people, I don't know. I think it's the way things are, right?
CADENGUE. And your lovers, Maria? Tell us about your greatest love.
M. APARECIDA. I'm not going to talk about my greatest love because that would open a wound that's already healed. I prefer new people to increase my list of fans. Now I don't want to find any new lover at all. A boy comes, we talk, go out, have fun. No promises!
ROBERTO. With your sensuality, which seems very strong, have you ever wanted to die of pleasure in a relationship with someone?
M. APARECIDA. No, because I switch on the fan. The boy starts, "Cida, Cida." And I go "Unh, uhn!" He says, "Cida, speak!" And I go, "Uhn, unh!" And the fan has to be right on me because I'm getting old, aren't I? Full of bones and with very high chloresterol. And if the fan doesn't breathe on me, I'll die. [Laughter.]
ROBERTO. Which of your loves lasted longest? For ten years or so?
M. APARECIDA. No. Six, eight years, more or less. I get attached to people very easily. As soon as they understand me, discover my weakness, I want to hold on to them. That's why I don't want anyone to discover my weakness. All women, all gays have a weak point.
SILVIO. What attracts you most in a man?
M. APARECIDA. Tenderness, love. I also like the taste, the smell of a man, I like a man's sweat, you understand?
CADENGUE. How do men cruise you? Is it they who approach you?
M. APARECIDA. They approach me. But if I like a man's face and he doesn't approach, I do a little work and he comes crying to my house. But I have to know his name. You put his name in a bottle of beer, add a red rose, take it to a crossroads, open a

packet of cigarettes, light three, leave them smoking, call his name, ask what you want, first ask God and here in the temple Dona Leonora, the gypsy Pomba-Gira here in the Palace of Oxum. Take a pork chop, cooked very hot in palm oil and Rio flour and lettuce and put it at her feet. Then there's a *macumba.* When you see the person, before talking to him say: "I see you in front, behind I make a cross, you have to love me as much as the Virgin Mary loves Baby Jesus." When he turns his back you bless him from behind: "God rest you and your guardian angel watch over you, you're going to run after me as a donkey runs after a mare." And wait for the result.

CADENGUE. What do you have to do to keep a man?

M. APARECIDA. You have to let him sleep, stroke his head, then pull a little hair from his head, tie it to a red thread, put his name in your left shoe, you understand? On a Friday invite him over for coffee in your house. Wash your face very early. Boil that water from your face and make coffee with it for him to drink. He'll only see your face in front of him. [Laughter.]

TREVISAN. And when you want him to go away?

M. APARECIDA. Go to a cemetery on a Monday, look for a grave with a man's name, read the name that's on the tomb. Then (touching wood) call the name three times and say: "Look, I've come here for help, to get so'n'so out of my way." Then light a candle for God and another upside down for the one who is sleeping there in eternal rest. Say an Our Father, an Ave Maria, a Salve Regina, make offering to St Raimundo for that man to forget you as the dead man forgets the world. So then he'll find another queen, another woman and leave your life. But it's difficult! If you get a man and want to leave him, that man makes your life miserable!

TREVISAN. What kind of man do you like best? Young, tall, blond, black?

M. APARECIDA. He doesn't have to be young. He doesn't have to be tall or short or black or white. What I like in a man are three things. First, his teeth. I have a horror of men whose teeth are ruined at the front, I'm allergic to them. Second, I don't like men who wear boxer shorts. I get to the bedroom with a man, he pulls off his clothes and is wearing boxer shorts, I've lost my appetite. I only like men in briefs. Last: a man with a moustache. I'm crazy for them. A hairy man I worship! But I don't like men who wear perfume. What I like in a man is his natural smell. It's a fetish of mine, I don't like men who wear perfume. But if I go to a man's room, I have to perfume myself from head to foot, principally in the most hidden parts, because I don't know where he'll get to, do I? [Laughter.] So I have to be forearmed! I want to serve a man as a woman. But if we get to bed and he searches in front and wants to get hold of what he shouldn't, then I open myself up. So that what he looks for, he finds. There's a married man who comes here to serve as a woman for me. Married, with children, the lot, he comes here and wants me to satisfy him. He doesn't look for a man because people would talk, it would get to his wife's ears. So he looks for a gay. The other day I went to a dance. When it was two, I came back home. A soldier asked me for a lift in the taxi. When I got here, he got out. He came in, into the bedroom, pulled off his boots, took off his gun and put it on the dressing-table, pulled off his clothes and lay down. I switched on the fan, left him enjoying the breeze, came here into the kitchen and sprayed myself all over, because I was sweaty from dancing. Then I lay down on the bed and he started groping for what he shouldn't. A little afterwards the soldier rolled onto his front, took hold of my clit and began rubbing it against the opening. So I said: "It's mine all right. Now that you've found it, take it." Then he said: "If I meet you on the street and see you gossipping about what went on here, I'll shoot you six times in the back." I said: "Rubbish, my boy, you're not the first by a long chalk. Look, in the bedroom no one is anyone." Dawn broke. He got dressed and went away. Of course he demanded money for the taxi, didn't he? But that's okay.

TREVISAN. Men turning onto their stomachs happens often?

M. APARECIDA. Ah, it's the times we live in. And at Christmas, I'll tell you. These boys of 13 to 15, if they don't pass their exams, their fathers don't give them money for the cinema, so they run after gays to get money for cigarettes. And you can't say no.

TREVISAN. Where do you pick up men?

M. APARECIDA. I don't pick any up because I have my regular customers. This very day two came and I told them to go away because of this meeting. [Laughter.] But I haven't lost them; they're coming back tomorrow. If you like it you do it again, right? And the criminal always returns to the scene of the crime.

CADENGUE. What do men usually call you in bed?

M. APARECIDA. Cida, Dad, my black girl, my old black girl, Auntie.

CADENGUE. Do you think men have a lot of sex with men in Brazil?

M. APARECIDA. And how! And how! You walk down the street, see a good-looking youth, very chic, like a model, you get into bed and you can't tell if it's a he or a she.

TREVISAN. How do you dress at Carnival? Do you go every year?

M. APARECIDA. Every year, every year. I go as a Bahian woman, like Carmen Miranda.

JOMARD. Have you been appearing in Carnival parades for long?

M. APARECIDA. Very long. Since I started getting on with people. And in this district everyone expects her: Maria Aparecida. Sometimes I take roses to throw to the governor, the mayor, the foreign tourists. They ask: "Who's that?" It's Maria Aparecida, the transvestite! And I'm out there shaking my hips. I parade with the "Road of the Stars" group. It's good there. Real African rhythm!

ROBERTO. If you could have an operation to change your sex, would you?

M. APARECIDA. No, because I think my *odi* is very nice. It's not me who says so, it's my fans. They find it once, they want it again.

TREVISAN. What's an *odi*?

JOMARD. It's the prick.

CADENGUE. No, it's the arsehole.

ROBERTO. Do you want silicon?

M. APARECIDA. I'd like to have an operation. I was going to do it but my sugar level was very high and I didn't want to undergo it.

ROBERTO. But it was an operation to enlarge the breasts?

M. APARECIDA. To enlarge the breasts and pull in my stomach. The doctor said he would put silicon and inflate it, you know? He would make my eyes Chinese, enlarge the breast and get rid of the fat on my stomach. And so I'd be all slim, you know? Now I'm going to have a series of saunas to see if I can lose more of my abdomen. Because I'm on a diet. I'm starving so as not to get fat, but my belly won't go. My body's not so badly made. It's this stomach that stops me being elegant.

ROBERTO. Maria, how do you get on with others in the sect? Do you get on well with the priests. With Edu?*

*Another gay *babalorixá* in Recife, known as Father Edu.

M. APARECIDA. No, I get on better with the women than the men.

JOMARD. What do you think of this movement called feminism, women's liberation?

M. APARECIDA. Well, I think women follow their own hearts, you know? Everything is okay today. I don't know, women today don't like men any more, they want other women too. They're following their own hearts!

JOMARD. Do you see yourself as mulatto? Or as black? What is your colour?

M. APARECIDA. I'm dark. I talk with the mirror. My colouring is dark, a little like toast. Brown eyes. But when I do my magic, you don't see this person, you see a different one. If I think I'm getting old, wrinkled, I start putting gold in the mouth so that when I smile, men are enchanted...

Notes

Notes to Introduction

1 "Entretien avec Michel Foucault", *Masques* Spring 1982, Paris, p. 24.
2 *Brasil, terra de contrastes* by Roger Bastide, Editora Difel, São Paulo, 1975, p. 15.
3 *La separación de los amantes* by Igor Caruso, Siglo Veintiuno Editores, Mexico, 1978, p. 188.

Notes to Chapter One

1 *Casa grande e senzala* (publ. in English as *The Masters and the Slaves*) by Gilberto Freyre, Ed. Universidade de Brasília, 1973 (12th edn.), p. 177. Also *Sobrados e mucambos* (publ. in English as *The Mansions and the Shanties*) by Gilberto Freyre, Ed. José Olympio, Rio de Janeiro, 1977, p. 96 & 141.
2 In *Casa grande e senzala*, op. cit, p. 178.
3 *Retrato do Brasil* by Paulo Prado, Ed. José Olympio, Rio de Janeiro, 1972, p. 159.
4 "Jésus, les machos et les guérilléros" by Conrad Detrez, *Masques* Spring 1979, Paris.

Notes to Chapter Two

1 *A Inquisição Portuguesa e a Sociedade Colonial* by Sônia Aparecida de Siqueira, Editora Ática, São Paulo, 1978, p. 189. In the patronising language of Catholic theologians, moralists and canonists of the time, varieties of the sexual act and the genitals were referred to by sometimes curious circumlocutions. The Inquisitors, of course, used the same artifice, which did not prevent detailed descriptions of the sexual sins from being noted down – sometimes even the opposite. Anal coitus was called "sodomy", "dishonest touching", "vile

touching", "abominable sin", "abominable work" or simply "abominable". The penis was called the "virile member", "nature", and "dishonest member" when used sinfully. "Nature" was also used to refer to the vulva, as was "natural passage" for the vagina. The anus/rectum was called the "rear passage" or "posterior part". "Embrace" and "kiss" were euphemistic variants for anal penetration, as "to sleep carnally from behind" and "put their natures together in front" were variations on position. "Agent" and "patient" meant the two partners in anal coitus while the one penetrated was also the one who "performed the female duty"; "*somitigo*", "*sodomita*" or "*sodomitico*" referred to the masculine homosexual. "Dishonest touching" also applied to sinful sexual contact in general while feminine homosexual relations were called "abominable friendship" and "dishonest friendship".

2 Sonia Siqueira, op. cit, p. 237.
3 Paulo Prado, op. cit, p. 163.
4 The terms "pedophile" and "minor" are used here merely as reference for the reader who knows them as they exist today. In colonial Brazil these judicial expressions did not exist and their meaning was less rigid. Adolescents of both sexes very often married at thirteen or fourteen, especially girls, who were much sought after by elderly gentlemen. Later it will be seen how the Inquisition punished a number of adolescents, taking their age into little consideration. The truth is that the colonial patriarchial family treated children and young adults as "incompetent adults". As soon as they arrived at puberty children were expected to assume adult behaviour. The idea of the child as a different being, imposed by the growing authority of hygiene-minded doctors, only gradually asserted itself in the mid-nineteenth century. The father of the family then became considered more as a tutor while the state assumed, metaphorically, ownership of the children.
5 *Bulletin of GGB* 5, December 1982, p. 6 (xerox).

Notes to Chapter Three

1 *Livro de Bolso da Medicina Natural* by Márcio Bontempo, Ground Informação Ltda, Rio de Janeiro, 1979, p. 121.
2 *Nossos índios, nossos mortos* by Edilson Martins, Codecri, Rio de Janeiro, 1978, p. 44 & 46.
3 *Bulletin of GGB* 3, p. 8 (mimeo).
4 "Generalidades acerca da educação física dos meninos" by Joaquim Pedro de Mello, Fac. of Medicine, Rio de Janeiro, 1846, cited in *Ordem Médica e Norma Familiar* by Jurandir Freire Costa, Graal, Rio de Janeiro, 1983 (2nd edn), p. 70.
5 Jurandir Freire Costa, op. cit, p. 243–4.
6 ibid, p. 245.
7 "Homossexualismo e endocrinologia" by Leonídio Ribeiro, *Revista Brasileira* 9, Rio de Janeiro, July/August 1938, p. 155.

8 *Attentados ao pudor* by Francisco José Viveiros de Castro, Livraria Editora Freitas Bastos, Rio de Janeiro, 1932 (2nd edn), p. 220.
9 "Homosseualismo e endicronologia" by Leonídio Ribeiro, *Arquivos de Medicina Legal e Identificação* 14, Rio de Janeiro, 1937, p. 167.
10 "Etiologia e tratamento da homossexualidade" by Leonídio Ribeiro, *Arquivos de Medicina Legal e Identificação* 15, Rio de Janeiro, 1938, p. 60.
11 Viveiros de Castro, op. cit, p. 220–223.
12 ibid, p. 228–9.
13 ibid, p. 199.
14 ibid, p. 205.
15 "Considerações gerais sobre o homossexualismo" by Aldo Sinisgalli, *Arquivos de Polícia e Identificação* Vol. II no. 1, São Paulo, 1938–9, p. 298.
16 Aldo Sinisgalli, op. cit, p. 299.
17 *A arte e a neurose de João do Rio* by Inaldo de Lira Neves-Manta, Livraria Francisco Alves Ed, Rio de Janeiro, 1977 (5th ed), p. 148.
18 *As perversões sexuais em medicina legal* by Viriato Fernandes Nunes, Faculdade de Medicina, These Inaugral, São Paulo, 1928, p. 32.
19 Aldo Sinisgalli, op. cit, p. 292.
20 Leonídio Ribeiro in *Revista Brasileira,* op. cit, p. 163.
21 Aldo Sinisgalli, op. cit, p. 295.
22 ibid, p. 283.
23 Viriato Fernandes Nunes, op. cit, p. 35.
24 "Observações sobre os hábitos, costumes e condições de vida dos homossexuais (pederastas passivos) de São Paulo" by Aldo Sinisgalli, *Arquivos de Polícia e Identificação,* loc. cit, p. 304.
25 Aldo Sinisgalli, "Considerações. . .", op. cit, p. 300.
26 ibid, p. 302.
27 ibid, p. 303.
28 Leonídio Ribeiro in *Revista Brasileira,* op. cit, p. 165–6.
29 *Caminhos cruzados* by Peter Fry et al., Brasiliense, São Paulo, 1983, p. 74.
30 *O círio perfeito* by Pedro Nava, Nova Fronteira, Rio de Janeiro, 1983, p. 364–6.
31 Peter Fry, op. cit, p. 77.
32 ibid.
33 "Chrysóstomo: qual o crime?" by Aguinaldo Silva, *Revista Careta* 4 August 1981, São Paulo, p. 56.
34 *Caso Chrysóstomo: o julgamento de um preconceito* by Antônio Chrysóstomo, Codecri, Rio de Janeiro, 1983, p. 29.
35 Antônio Chrysóstomo, op. cit, p. 30.
36 *Processo Judiciário no. 21,491,* 10th Criminal District, Rio de Janeiro, 1980–82, p. 155.
37 Antônio Chrysóstomo, op. cit, p. 51–2.
38 Pedro Nava, op. cit, p. 368–9.
39 Peter Fry, op. cit, p. 80.
40 Aguinaldo Silva, op. cit, p. 58.
41 "Maus tratos", *Veja* 19 August 1981, São Paulo, p. 32.

Notes to Chapter Four

1 *O teatro no Brasil* by J. Galante de Souza, vol. I, Instituto Nacional do Livro, Rio de Janeiro, 1960, p. 118–9.
2 J. Galante de Souza, op. cit, p. 91.
3 *A personagem negra no teatro brasileiro* by Miriam Garcia Mendes, Editora Ática, São Paulo, 1982, p. 13–15.
4 *O teatro em Mato Grasso no século XVIII* by Carlos Francisco Moura, Edições Universidade Federal do Mato Grosso/SUDAM, Belém, 1976, p. 64.
5 J. Galante de Souza, op. cit, p. 115.
6 ibid, p. 116.
7 "O capoeira, um teatro do passado" by Valdemar de Oliveira, in *I Concurso Nacional de Monografias – 1976*, Serviço Nacional de Teatro, Brasília, 1977, p. 11.
8 ibid, p. 14.
9 ibid, p. 16.
10 ibid, p. 22.
11 ibid.
12 ibid, p. 16–17.
13 J. Galante de Souza, op. cit, p. 119.
14 Carlos Francisco Moura, op. cit, p. 63.
15 ibid, p. 65.
16 *História do teatro na Bahia (sec. XVI–XX)* by Affonso Ruy, Livraria Progresso Editora, Salvador, 1959, p. 63.
17 J. Galante de Souza, op. cit, p. 120.
18 *Attentados ao pudor* by Francisco Viveiros de Castro, Livraria Ed. Freitas Bastos, Rio de Janeiro, 1932 (2nd edn), p. 236.
19 *Sobrados e mucambos* by Gilberto Freyre, Livraria José Olympio Editora, Rio de Janeiro, 1977 (5th edn), p. 159.
20 *Caminhos cruzados* by Peter Fry et al., Ed. Brasiliense, São Paulo, 1982, p. 50.
21 *Livro do Nordeste*, Gilberto Freyre et al., Arquivo Público Estadual, Recife, 1979, p. 132.
22 *O teatro no Brasil sob Dom Pedro II* by Lothar Hessel and Georges Raeders, Ed. da Universidade Federal do Rio Grande do Sul, Porto Alegre, 1979, p. 307.
23 *A scena muda* 128, 13 September 1923.
24 "Andrea de Maio em busca da perfeição", *Homem* 53, December 1982, São Paulo, p. 16.
25 "Amor e medo", *Aspectos da Literatura Brasileira* by Mário de Andrade, Livraria Martins Editora, São Paulo, 1967.
26 *Românticos, Pré-Românticos, Ultra-Românticos* by Brito Broca, Livraria Ed. Polis, São Paulo, 1979, p. 86.
27 *Cartas de Álvares de Azevedo*, Academia Paulista de Letras, São Paulo, 1976, p. 146.
28 Brito Broca, op. cit, p. 86.
29 *Bom-Crioulo, The Black Man and the Cabin Boy* by Adolfo Caminha, Gay Sunshine Press, San Francisco, 1982, p. 21.

30 *Bom-Crioulo* by Adolfo Caminha, Edições de Ouro, Rio de Janeiro, 1966, p. 154.
31 "Um livro condemnado" by Adolfo Caminha, *A nova revista* vol. I, no. 2, Rio de Janeiro, February 1896, p. 40–42.
32 Interview with Paschoal Carlos Magno, *O Pasquim* 2 July 1973, Rio de Janeiro, p. 6.
33 "Revista da Antropofagia" by Oswald de Andrade, *Diário de São Paulo* 24 April 1929, p. 10.
34 "O filho de Macunaíma", *ISTOÉ* 2 December 1981, p. 58.
35 "Inojosa lembra o amigo Mário de Andrade", *O Estado de São Paulo* 9 October 1983.
36 *Histórias do amor maldito*, Gráfica Récord Editora, Rio de Janeiro, 1967.
37 *Poemas do amor maldito*, Coordenadora Editora de Brasília, Brasília, 1969.
38 *Teatro* by Oswald de Andrade, Ed. Civilização Brasileira, 1978, p. 116.
39 *Morrer pela Pátria* by Carlos Cavaco, Graphica J. do Valle, Rio de Janeiro, 1937, p. 42.
40 cf. Gilberto Velho in *Caminhos cruzados*, op. cit, p. 81.
41 *Teatro quase completo* vol. IV by Nelson Rodrigues, Ed. Tempo Brasileiro, Rio de Janeiro, 1966, p. 377.
42 Ney Matogrosso, interview in *Interview* 5, São Paulo, May 1978, p. 5.
43 ibid.
44 ibid.
45 ibid.
46 ibid.
47 Programme from the show *Seu Tipo* with Ney Matogrosso, 1980.
48 Jefferson del Rios in *Folha de São Paulo* 12 February 1981.

Notes to Chapter Five

1 "Grupo *Somos*, uma experiência", *Lampião* 12, May 1979, Rio de Janeiro.
2 "Quem tem medo das 'minorias'?" by João Silvério Trevisan, *Lampião* 10, March 1979, Rio de Janeiro.
3 "ABC de Lula", *Lampião* 14, July 1979, Rio de Janeiro.
4 "Grupo *Somos*, uma experiência", op. cit.
5 "Mas qual é o crime de Celso Cury?" by João Silvério Trevisan, *Lampião* 0, April 1978, Rio de Janeiro.
6 *Teses para a Libertação Homossexual II*, Fração Homossexual da Convergência Socialista, March 1980, São Paulo (xerox).
7 "Mendigos da normalidade" by João Silvério Trevisan, *Lampião* 31, December 1980, Rio de Janeiro.
8 *Paz y Liberación* 4, May 1980, Houston, Portuguese edition (xerox).
9 *O que e homossèxualidade?* by Peter Fry and Edward MacRae, Ed. Brasiliense, São Paulo, 1983.

Notes to Chapter Six

1 *Descansa em paz, Oscar Wilde* by Luiz Carlos Machado, Codecri, Rio de Janeiro, p. 15.

2 ''Delegade investe contra travestis'', *Folha de São Paulo* 3 January 1982.
3 ''A prostituição masculina em São Paulo'' by Guido Fonseca, *Arquivos da Polícia Civil* Vol. XXX, São Paulo, 2nd semester 1977, p. 70–71.
4 *Gilete na carne: etnografia das auto-mutilações dos travestis da Bahia* by Luís Mott, 1981 (mimeo).
5 Guido Fonseca, op. cit, p. 76.
6 ibid.
7 ibid, p. 67.
8 ''As estrelas caem'', *Visão* 23 August 1982, São Paulo, p. 46.
9 ''A doença errada'', *Veja* 14 September 1983, São Paulo.

Index

GMP is the world's leading publisher of books of gay interest. Our list includes Art and Photography, Fiction, Gay Modern Classics and a wide range of Nonfiction subjects. Here are a few of our recent publications:

Paul Binding

LORCA: THE GAY IMAGINATION

The poetry of Federico García Lorca is one of Spain's greatest gifts to modern literature. Yet just as Lorca cannot be understood in isolation from the cultural traditions of his native Andalucía, so it is also necessary to appreciate his specific perspective on the world as a gay person. This long awaited study is an original and much needed contribution to a fuller critical assessment of Lorca's poetic complexity.

"A vast improvement on the available Lorca commentaries, indispensable for all students and lovers of Lorca" (*City Limits*).

ISBN 0 907040 36 5 (pbk)
ISBN 0 907040 37 3 (hbk)

Peter Burton

PARALLEL LIVES

Among the topics covered in this crowded memoir are London's mod clubs of the 1960s; a teenage literary apprenticeship; collaborations with Robin Maugham; reminiscences of Gerald Hamilton ("Mr Norris") and Michael Davidson; touring with Rod Stewart; and the rise and fall of *Gay News*.

"As a social historian he is completely to be trusted. As a human being he is extremely sympathetic" (George Melly, *New Society*). "I am charmed by it" (*New York Native*).

ISBN 0 907040 65 9 (pbk)

Agustin Gomez-Arcos

THE CARNIVOROUS LAMB

translated by William Rodarmor

Ignacio is born into a shuttered house in post-Civil War Spain, where his father stays locked in his study and his mother refuses to acknowledge his existence. Only his brother Antonio is real – teacher, protector, and eventual lover. A story of one family's suffocation under an intolerable regime, and an incisive, savagely funny and desperate vision of Franco's Spain. (1975 winner of the Prix Hermès.)

"A carnal poem, frank, provocative, triumphant . . . and a dirge for Spain" (*Le Monde*).

ISBN 0 85449 018 3 (pbk)
ISBN 0 85449 019 1 (hbk)
This edition not for sale in North America

Michael Davidson

THE WORLD, THE FLESH AND MYSELF

Introduced by Colin Spencer

Michael Davidson was a widely respected foreign correspondent. He joined the Berlin communists against Hitler, crossed wartime Morocco in disguise, and campaigned against British oppression in Malaya and Cyprus. He was also imprisoned for his sexuality. This celebrated autobiography is now published for the first time with the author's annotations and photographs.

Described by its author as "the life story of a lover of boys", this book has also been hailed by Arthur Koestler as "the courageous and lovable story of a brilliant journalist's struggles", and by James Cameron as "one of the best evocations of the period that I know".

"More than welcome . . . narrated with the rage and wit of complete sanity" (*New Statesman*).

ISBN 0 907040 63 2 (pbk)
ISBN 0 907040 64 0 (hbk)